Big Bad Wolfe

Corey really hadn't wanted to meet any man since her divorce.

But that needed to change. She had made too big a deal of it. She really had been hiding from men by immersing herself in work and community obligations. It had been quite cowardly of her, actually.

Suddenly, it seemed very important to her to prove to herself she could be around a man without going all to pieces. Perhaps she had retreated from the world for a while after her awful marriage and divorce, but she was not afraid of men, not even a big, virile, opinionated, forceful man like Brandon Wolfe. She could meet him casually, just for the fun of it, if she wanted to. Of course, he wasn't the right kind of man for her, but that wasn't the point. She just needed to show herself she could do it. It would be therapeutic.

other. You want them to admit their feelings. This book builds to an explosive ending with emotions that will bring tears to your eyes.

—Sherry
Karen Find Out About New Books
Coffee Time Romance

Other Works From The Pen Of

Linda Wallace

Special Delivery

Scrappy Seattle bicycle courier and stuffy businessman are kidnapped to a remote island and must overcome their differences to battle criminals and the elements without losing their hearts.

Wings

Big Bad Wolfe

Linda Wallace

A Wings ePress, Inc.

Contemporary Romance Novel

Wings ePress, Inc.

Edited by: Leslie Hodges
Copy Edited by: Karen Babcock
Senior Editor: Anita York
Executive Editor: Lorraine Stephens
Cover Artist: Christine Poe
Cover photo by Linda Wallace, courtesy of Blessed Be Ranch

All rights reserved

Wings ePress Books
http://www.books-by-wings-epress.com/

ISBN 978-1-59088-543-7

Published In the United States Of America

March 2006

Wings ePress, Inc.
3000 N. Rock Road
Newton, KS 67114

Dedication

To my husband,

who provided computers and llama gloves.

And a big thank you

to Blessed Be Ranch for the llama models.

One

At the sound of children's voices and the tinkling of the nursery-character chimes that hung above the entrance to Kids' Kloset, Corey Tierney turned away from her account books and smiled as she prepared to greet new customers. Her eyes widened and her pleasant expression of welcome changed to one of amazement.

A blond giant blocked the sunlight that usually flooded her doorway. Her gaze swept up from a level of a few feet above the floor, from the shy, fresh young faces she had expected to see, almost to the ceiling. She gaped at an impressive length of worn denim encasing lean thighs, a long expanse of cotton T-shirt strained to bursting by a muscular chest and, finally, an indignant Nordic face with Old Mother Goose dangling over one dark blond eyebrow and Little Red Riding Hood perched on a crown of gleaming flaxen hair.

This golden behemoth was effectively prevented from untangling himself from the chimes by two small tow-headed boys standing on either side of him, each reaching up to cling to an oversized hand.

Mastering her initial surprise, Corey sprang forward to help. She never thought of herself as petite, measuring a shade over five foot four, but she had to stand on tiptoe to reach the small metallic figures. As she plucked Little Red Riding Hood from the Viking's fair hair, deep blue eyes, nearly dark enough to be called navy, glared down at her. She felt a jolt, almost physical in nature, as though the man had rudely given her a hard shove. *Really,* she thought with a touch of irritation, *it wasn't such a big deal. You would think he had stumbled into a bear trap from the expression on his face.*

She released the chimes, allowing them to swing free, and her bare forearm grazed a broad shoulder. Suddenly realizing how close she was standing to the man's blatantly virile body, Corey stepped back quickly. Strange—her breathing was accelerated, as though she had been pole-vaulting instead of offering a simple gesture of assistance.

Now her feeling of annoyance shifted its focus to herself. She was reacting to the man as though she had been stranded on a desert island for years, starved for male companionship. Just because very few men ever came into Kids' Kloset didn't mean she couldn't extend the usual professional courtesies, even if this particular man looked like he would be more at home in a saloon tossing back a few tall ones with his cronies than in a children's clothing store.

Brandon Wolfe frowned before he bent to gently disengage the tiny fingers immobilizing his hands. He had hoped he could find the clothes he needed for his sons here at Kids' Kloset, but instead it looked like it was just going to be another encounter with an arrogant woman who thought men didn't know how to shop for children. Those silly chimes hanging near the doorway were obviously too low for any normal-sized man to get under without ducking. The proprietor might as well have posted a sign that said, "MEN KEEP OUT!"

John and Robbie had been giggling at the sight of their daddy captured by Old Mother Goose, but now John spied a play area with an assortment of toys and books. Grabbing Robbie's arm, John dragged him over to a stuffed bear large enough to be used as a chair by little folks, plopped him down in the bear's lap and started pushing a toy locomotive along its wooden track. "Whoo, whoo," he called out, instantly absorbed in his engineering.

Brandon sighed, straightened to his full height, ran work-roughened fingers through his tousled hair and asked in a voice he knew to be hostile, "Are there any more booby traps I should watch out for?"

Corey hastened to reassure him. "I'm terribly sorry," she said and offered him what she hoped was a disarming smile. "I'm afraid you're considerably taller than most of my customers. I never thought anyone could bump into my nursery chimes." But her apology only made him look even angrier.

"I suppose you're one of those people who think only women know anything about kids' clothes," he said accusingly.

"Why no, really, not at all," she said, trying to soothe him. "Fathers, and even grandfathers, sometimes come shopping here." Of course, it had been about six months since that grandfatherly gentleman had come in, but she didn't need to tell him that. "It's just that you are larger than most of them."

Corey looked hastily away, fearful she was staring at just how delightfully large he actually was. Olive Oyl's song in that old Robin Williams-movie-version of Popeye suddenly sang out in her head—"He's Large"—and she almost giggled aloud.

Brandon took a few uncertain steps among the clothing racks, pausing to shrug his shoulders in an attempt to relieve his growing tension. He looked around uneasily at the wall displays of frilly little-girl party dresses. He didn't know if it was getting tangled up in that stupid mobile or the fact that the saleswoman was so damnably and distractingly attractive that made him feel so out of place.

Corey hesitantly followed him. "Is there something I can help you with, Mr...?" she asked in her very best unobtrusive, tactful salesperson's voice.

He swung around to face her, and she felt the same shock as before when his dark blue eyes met her wren-brown ones.

Inexplicably, she felt a need for some kind of support and reached out to cling to a clothing rack while pretending to rearrange the skirts hanging there.

She really was behaving like a dolt. Perhaps her friends were right when they accused her of hiding from men by burying herself in her store. *No,* she defended herself silently, *I'm not afraid of men; it's just this particular man is so, so—large!*

"Wolfe. Brandon Wolfe," he responded. "We're really here in Boise for the WILA show, but I thought while we were in town I could get the boys some new clothes," he said, nodding toward the children busily playing in the corner.

"WILA?" she puzzled.

"Western Idaho Llama Association," he replied absently. The hard lines of his face softened as he watched the older boy help the younger build a Lego tower. "You see, John starts kindergarten this fall. He needs just about everything. He grows so fast I can barely keep him covered, and he's so darned hard on his things there's not much left but rags for Robbie after John outgrows them. So Robbie needs some new clothes, too."

"Well, you've come to the right place then. We have lots of nice things for little boys," she said briskly in what she hoped was a business-like tone.

Her throat had tightened in a most unprofessional manner as she watched the play of strength and tenderness cross his rugged face. He was devoted to his children; that was evident in his expression and in the very fact he was the one who was shopping for them. Corey unconsciously pinched her lips together. Not like her ex-husband, who had made it very clear he thought the only purpose of children was to carry on the male bloodline and possibly to serve as slave labor on the ranch once they were old enough.

"But the problem is everything costs so much," Brandon said, a look of embarrassment and pain on his face. "I've been to half a dozen stores this morning, and it's the same everywhere. The prices on kids' clothes are jacked up sky high. Why, a little shirt no bigger than my hand costs more than what I pay for something for me!" he finished heatedly, his face hardening into a mask of angry frustration.

"That's exactly why I opened my store," she said, not adding she had also needed to earn a living and preserve her sanity after her divorce. "It's hard for most young families to make ends meet these days. Perhaps you didn't realize this is a resale store? Our prices are much lower than department stores."

"Oh, I realized all right," he said bitterly. "One of those snippy young clerks at the mall suggested I come over here after I balked at buying some of their overpriced stuff. But I don't want my sons wearing other kids' castoffs."

Corey hid a smile. Here was a raging case of pride battling necessity. She set to putting him at ease.

"We only accept clothing that is in excellent condition," she explained. "Some of our things have hardly been worn at all. A relative might send a gift that is too small or is in some other way inappropriate for the child; the parents don't want to hurt Auntie or Grandma's feelings by returning the present, so a whole outfit that is practically brand new ends up here. I sell the clothes on consignment. The parents can use the money to buy something for their child he or she really likes, and my customers get a great bargain. *Voilà!* Everybody is happy!"

Corey concluded enthusiastically with a little flourish and a brilliant smile, then faltered as she noticed how intensely the intriguing stranger was staring at her. Some of the self-assurance she had generated as she had warmed to her sales pitch ebbed away, and she turned hastily toward the boys' section.

"Here are the jeans. And here are corduroy pants. A local outlet was overstocked and discounted them for me to clear out their inventory. So they're actually new. Older boys think cords are unfashionable, but little boys still seem to like them, and they're nice and warm and soft when it gets colder. And on that table are the sweaters, and in this pile I have some long-sleeved T-shirts with TV cartoon heroes printed on them. They're really popular."

Goodness! She was chattering on like a ninny. What must he think of her? She loved helping mothers find the right clothes for their children; she mustn't let the fact that this time it was a man doing the buying unnerve her, even if that man was looking at her with an intensity most unbecoming to a husband and father. Corey took a deep breath and forced herself to slow down.

"Do you know what sizes the boys wear?" she asked.

"No," he admitted with a grin. Corey noticed with relief he was looking a little more relaxed by now. "I guess I never got past prices this morning."

Corey walked over to where the boys were playing. They were beautiful children. The older boy had very pale blond hair, almost white, and bright blue eyes like his father but lighter in color. The younger child also had blond hair but with more of a golden cast, and his eyes were hazel. Both boys had sturdy, healthy-looking little bodies and rosy, chubby cheeks. They wore shorts, T-shirts and sneakers with holes at the toes. Their clothes were rather shabby, Corey noted, but very clean. *Well,* she thought with satisfaction, *I can fix the shabby part.*

Corey smiled at the boys when they looked up at the adults. "So, you're going to start kindergarten, John. That's great. Stand up next to the giraffe so I can see how tall you are."

John jumped up from the Legos to stand next to the plywood cutout shaped and painted to look like a giraffe with inch and foot marks on the neck. He strained every muscle in his little body trying to look taller, thrusting his jaw up and stretching his neck until his face turned bright red.

"Wow! You're such a big boy. You're going to grow up to be really tall like your daddy," Corey said admiringly.

"I'm big, too," Robbie said, leaping up and down like a little frog in his attempt to reach the same level as John.

Corey smiled at the boys' antics, but she glanced over at their father and noticed he was frowning at his sons' performance. Not wanting to be responsible for behavior that might cause them to get a scolding, she quickly turned back to the clothing.

"I think a size six or maybe even a seven would be about right for John and probably a five for Robbie."

She efficiently gathered a selection of coordinated shirts and pants for both boys and handed them over to their father, exquisitely aware of the large hands accepting them. She tried to avoid any contact, but when her fingers grazed his hard, callused palm, she instantly felt all shivery in spite of the fact her small air conditioner was woefully inadequate for this hot August afternoon.

"Try these," she said a trifle breathlessly. "The changing rooms are over there. They're pretty small. I don't think the three of you will fit in one room. Maybe if you help Robbie, John can manage by himself."

"Course I can get dressed all by myself," John said indignantly.

His dad handed him his stack of clothes. He encircled them with his little arms in a mighty bear hug, crushing them against his chest, then marched importantly on short, sturdy legs into the curtained cubicle.

Robbie's father took him by the hand and led him into the fitting room next to John's. Brandon made short work of getting his younger son dressed in one of the new outfits. It fit the little boy perfectly.

Robbie obediently stood in front of a long mirror for inspection, but Corey noticed he spent more time glancing longingly at the toy corner than he did checking his reflection.

"I don't think he needs to try everything on. Just pick the things you like, and I can use this outfit to compare the sizes," Corey said.

Robbie gave her a grateful look and started to step out of the jeans right where he was standing, but his father firmly ushered him back into the cubicle to change. When he came out dressed in his old clothes, he skipped over to the toys and happily resumed playing with a dump truck.

Meanwhile, John had been cloistered in his changing room an inordinate length of time. "Do you need some help, Champ?" his dad called out.

"No," came the muffled response. "But something doesn't look right," he added in a plaintive tone.

"Come show me," Brandon said patiently.

A red face, topped with hair that seemed to have been arranged with an eggbeater, emerged from behind the zoo-patterned curtain. John walked out slowly, looking quite woebegone. Somehow he had managed to get his head through the long sleeve of a sweater. The whole length of the knitted sleeve was bunched up around his short neck, while one chubby shoulder protruded through the opening where his head should have been.

Corey and Brandon exchanged amused glances over the crestfallen little boy. "That's quite a fashion statement, John," Corey managed to say with a straight face.

The big man knelt down to carefully ease the sleeve over his son's head. He put the sweater right, then stayed down on one knee, his powerful hands gently squeezing the small shoulders. He smiled into the little boy's eyes until, reassured, the child smiled back.

Corey observed their interaction, admiring how Brandon understood his son's needs, but the tableau of man and boy created a wrenching pain deep inside of her as it reminded her of her own lost dreams. She had wanted children, a family, so badly.

She looked away, but that was even worse, for she could see all three of them reflected in the long mirror by the changing rooms. The golden strands in her light brown hair made her look as though she fit right in with the two blonds. Yes, it could be a happy family scene if you discounted the sudden shine in her brown eyes from unshed tears and the fact that her lips were compressed into a narrow line to stifle a half-formed sob.

Corey hoped the boys' mother realized just how lucky she was to have such a strong, yet tender, husband and beautiful children. It was exactly the kind of family she had always longed to be a part of.

For the first time, Corey questioned the wisdom of opening a children's store. It had seemed like a good way to satisfy the craving she had felt to be around children when she had finally accepted the painful fact she would never have any of her own, but now she wasn't so sure. Perhaps she had just chosen a method of rubbing salt into her wounds.

Corey turned away from the moving scene to straighten an already tidy pile of sleepwear. A few deep breaths and she had her emotions under control again. The boys' father would think she was certifiable if he noticed her getting teary-eyed just from watching him untangle his son from a sweater. She tucked her light green cotton shirt more smoothly into the white poplin
slacks she was wearing and turned back to her customers.

Brandon rose from his kneeling position, and soon he and John were engrossed in picking out which clothes they were going to buy. John tried on a few more items—this time with the help of his dad— when there was any doubt about the fit. He took a particular liking to a long-sleeved shirt with a garish imprint of hideous monsters who were the unlikely heroes of a popular children's TV show.

"This is really neat, Daddy!" John enthused, grabbing the shirt by one sleeve to wave it through the air like a flag. He quickly pulled it on, then went over to the mirror to admire his image. He contorted his face, trying to look as mean as the monsters, and puffed out his chest. "Can we get this one; can we, please?" he begged.

His father frowned at the shirt. "No, John, I don't want you wearing things like that to school."

John's face fell. Corey interceded for him.

"I live right across the street from an elementary school," she offered helpfully. "All the boys wear shirts like that to kindergarten. It wouldn't be inappropriate."

Brandon scowled fiercely at her. Who did she think she was, questioning his authority in front of his son? It seemed everyone he knew, from his own parents to strangers on the street, thought they knew more about raising kids than he did. He would put her in her place in a hot minute. He walked purposefully toward her.

So what if she saw a lot of kids and their clothes every day. That gave her no right to try to convert him to her way of thinking with a smile that could charm the skin off a snake. It was hard enough to enforce an unpopular decision without some adult encouraging a child to argue with his parent.

He looked at the shirt and at John's hopeful face. Perhaps the design really wasn't so bad, but if he changed his mind now, John would get the idea he could get his own way anytime he pushed hard enough.

He bent his head so that he was only a few inches from the pretty little saleslady's face and stared into her soft brown eyes.

Corey took a hasty step back, recoiling in surprise at the ferocity she saw in Brandon's face.

"I don't need you or anyone else telling me what's right for my children," he said in what was in reality a low voice, but somehow it seemed to hiss sharply through the room. He turned back to his son and commanded in a tone that allowed no room for further discussion, "Take it off, John. We're not going to buy that one."

For a few seconds it looked as though John might sulk, but he did as he was told and handed the offending shirt inside out to Corey. Corey straightened the garment, folded it, put it away and hesitated. Perhaps she shouldn't offer any more suggestions. She couldn't believe the way Brandon had changed so suddenly. He had helped untangle his son from the sweater sleeve with gentle concern for the child's feelings, but now he sounded like a domineering tyrant. If she had a terrific son like John, she would pay attention to his likes and dislikes and allow him to make his own choices whenever practical. She wanted to support John, but his father was so forceful, so opinionated, so... so mule-headed, she wasn't sure she should try.

Oh, fudge! She wasn't going to let any big bully intimidate her even if he did speak to her in a voice with the sting of a bullwhip. After all, the worst that could happen would be that he would stalk out of the store, and she would lose a sale. Resolutely, she skimmed through the remaining shirts and came up with one with a Buggs Bunny design.

Holding the shirt out for them to see, she turned and said brightly, "How about this one?"

Brandon stared at her with such heat in his dark blue eyes that she instinctively held the shirt up higher in front of her as though it were a kind of shield against his searing gaze. She had begun to waver and was going to put the shirt away when John broke in.

The little boy wriggled his nose, chewed an imaginary carrot, then said, "Eh, what's up, Doc?"

Brandon's tried to hide his amusement. Well, he hadn't actually said no to this particular one, and at least it didn't have a monster on it. He probably should turn it down, too, just for the principle at stake, but somehow he didn't want this lovely young woman, however misguidedly persistent, to think he was too unreasonable.

"It will do," he said quietly. "I think we have enough now. Let's add up the damage."

Corey tried to contain the little gasp of relief she couldn't quite hold back. She wasn't sure why the big man made her so uneasy—after all, what could he do to her?—but she was glad for John's sake she had stood up to him.

She helped John and his father carry the clothing to the cash register at the counter. Then John ran over to join his brother playing with the toys while Corey totaled the purchases. They had chosen a half a dozen pairs of pants with mix-and-match shirts and sweaters for each of the boys. She told Brandon how much the clothing was going to cost. When he heard the figure, his face lit up with a wide smile.

"That's more like it," he crowed. "They probably could have only had about one set of duds each for that amount of money at one of those high-priced stores."

Corey caught her breath. How quickly his moods changed. His wife surely must have her hands full trying to keep up with such a complicated man. But what a beautiful smile he had! Very white, evenly spaced teeth gleamed in sharp contrast to his deeply tanned face. Two little curved creases on each side of his mouth formed a double set of parenthesis around his lips. Corey felt a sudden sharp urge to reach up and trace the bowed indentations with a fingertip. Shocked at herself, she looked away and hastily started putting the clothing and the receipt into a large plastic bag.

Brandon pulled a checkbook from his back jeans' pocket and made out a check. Corey was unable to resist examining his face as he looked down at the counter. His eyelashes were light in color but unusually long for a man's and thick, like a brush. His chin and jaw line were square and too prominent, really, for conventional good looks. And though he didn't look old, in his early thirties probably, his face was already lined, perhaps from long hours in the sun, judging by his dark tan.

When he had first come into her store, he had overwhelmed her with his size and sheer presence, but she realized now you couldn't actually call him handsome, at least not in the movie star sense, though there was no doubt he did possess a magnificent body, and the navy eyes and thick gleaming blond hair were exceptional. *Still,* Corey thought, *what impresses me the most is the way his face changes when he smiles.* In repose, his face looked rugged, stubborn, possibly even arrogant with his chin jutting out at an I-dare-you-to-hit-me angle. But with a smile, his countenance exploded into unrestrained boyish glee.

Annoyed with herself, she shook her head ruefully. She had no right to speculate about some other woman's husband. *Though it would be wonderful to be the person who made a man smile like that,* she couldn't help thinking wistfully. Before she could contain it, she let a small, audible sigh escape. She couldn't remember even one time her ex-husband had ever smiled at her in quite that way.

At the sound of her sigh the object of her intense scrutiny glanced up with a quizzical expression on his face and handed the check over across the counter.

Brandon had what he needed now, but for some reason he felt reluctant to leave. It troubled him to think he would never again see those warm brown eyes that were as intensely focused on him as if he were the only man on earth. He suddenly realized that it had been a long time since any woman had paid that much attention to him, much less a woman as pretty and bright as a newborn day.

Whoa up there, he cautioned himself. He didn't have the time, money or energy to allow his thoughts to drift along those lines. And even if it had been the right time and place to meet a woman, this wouldn't be the right woman—not an uppity little thing who obviously thought she knew a lot more than he did even about his own kids.

Still, in a few days he would be back at his cabin, alone with his sons and his llamas. Who knew how long it would be before he could afford to enjoy a woman's company? Surely he could indulge himself in a wee bit of harmless flirting. A smile or two from this pretty little lady might have to last him a long while.

"I surely do appreciate your help," he said. "I was beginning to think the boys were going to have to run around buck naked this winter."

Corey examined the check and noted there was only one name printed on the account. She braced herself for the now expected jolt before looking up into his dark blue eyes. "I doubt if Mrs. Wolfe would be very pleased to see them in that condition."

He seemed to stiffen. "There isn't any Mrs. Wolfe," he said harshly.

Corey was ashamed of the flash of exhilaration that surged through her body. Where had it come from? How could any decent woman ever be pleased at the idea of a broken family? "I'm sorry to hear that," she murmured and tried to believe she really meant it.

He made a visible effort to relax as he turned to look at the boys happily engrossed in an entire village of Lego towers. He swung back around to face Corey again. This time his voice was light, conversational, with only a few swirls of sultry undertones. "Have you worked here long?" he asked.

Corey found herself reacting to the underlying sensuous timbre. Her throat tightened, and she found it hard to reply with the right touch for small talk. "I opened the store almost four years ago."

"So, it's your own business, then? Is there a Mr. to help out?"

Was she mistaken, or was the sensuous quality of his voice deepening? One thing she was sure about. Her friends were right; it had been too long since she had tried to talk to a man. She was letting her imagination run wild. It was hard not to stumble over her words.

"No. I'm divorced." After all these years she still hated to say it. "I opened Kids' Kloset after my husband and I separated."

The fine lines around his eyes crinkled as he smiled at her. Had he looked pleased when she told him she was divorced? He seemed almost playful now that he had outfitted the boys.

"I'm afraid I'm at a disadvantage. You know my name, but I haven't had the pleasure of learning yours."

"Corey. Corey Tierney."

He reached across the counter to take her hand as though they had just been formally introduced at some social function. "Corey," he said so softly she could barely hear him. "Corey," he said again a little louder, rolling the two syllables across his tongue as though he were trying them out, maybe tasting some unfamiliar fruit to see if he liked it. He seemed to come to a favorable conclusion, because he said more firmly, "Corey Tierney, I'm very, very pleased to meet you."

His hard, rough fingers were still clasping her smaller hand as the blue flame from his penetrating gaze scorched her soft brown eyes. Corey felt mesmerized. She couldn't move nor could she look away. *I'm being ridiculous,* she told herself. *He's a customer, nothing more.*

After what seemed like an eternity, but was surely only a few seconds, she finally managed to break away to pick up the large bag of clothing Brandon had purchased. She started to hand it to him, but he turned to walk down to the end of the counter and around it to take the package from her.

He was standing very close to her. Too close. Corey suddenly wished the wooden counter was still serving as a barrier between them. *I need protection,* she thought wildly, though she wasn't sure as to protection from what. He lightly grasped Corey's shoulder with one of his big hands, his palm warming her skin right through her thin cotton shirt.

"You run a real fine operation here," he said admiringly. "I'm glad Miss Snooty over at the mall told me about it."

"Tha... thank you," she responded shakily.

He grinned at her. "You should come to the fair. I'd like to show you what I do. Drop by the llama arena tomorrow; I'll be there all day. I might even treat you to some cotton candy." Then he added more softly as if he were only talking to himself, "Though it wouldn't be as sweet as you."

He dropped his hand from her shoulder, and Corey was surprised to realize she wished he would put it back. It hadn't been that way with her husband. By the time they had divorced, she had hardly been able to bear his touch.

Brandon wheeled around and in a few quick strides had collected the boys and was shepherding them toward the exit. She noted he took care to duck deeply when he reached the door. Both John and Robbie called out, "Bye," several times, and Robbie, though his dad held one hand, twisted around as he walked away to wave at her with his free hand until they had all left the store.

Corey looked around her shop. Yes, it looked the same. Coordinated outfits and accessories were still pegged to the walls, teddy bears were still attired in infant wear in the front display window, tables were still stacked with neat piles of sweaters, and racks of clothing were still aligned in orderly rows. Why, then, did she feel as though a tornado had whirled through the place and left her strangely bereft?

She took a deep breath and inhaled the last few lingering traces of Brandon's clean male scent. When he had touched her, he had been so close she could feel the heat radiating from his body and smell his unique fragrance made up of good plain soap, leather and well-scrubbed masculine body. She shivered as she remembered his hard fingers sliding over her shoulder, then she picked up some papers from the counter to fan her flushed face. She felt hot and cold at the same time.

What had he said? The fair. He had said he was in Boise for the fair. She hadn't been to the Western Idaho Fair since she was a little girl. She remembered delicious nose-tickling smells of hot grease and buttered popcorn and the pungent ammonia stench of the animals: fat pigs with curly tails, enormous bulls and soft, fuzzy, lop-eared rabbits.

But he had said llamas. That couldn't be right. She must have misunderstood. Had she been so befuddled by the mere presence of an attractive male that she couldn't hear the difference between llama and lamb?

Corey walked around the counter and paced restlessly through the store. She hadn't spent a day just on fun in ages. Tomorrow was Sunday. She always closed the shop on Sundays, but after church, where she sang in the choir, she usually spent the day sorting the mountainous piles of clothing people brought in for resale. It was a never-ending job. And there was all that bookkeeping she needed to catch up. And her house really needed a good cleaning.

He had said drop by, he would be at the fair all day. It hadn't been a real invitation, just a casual bit of flirtatiousness, a meaningless line thrown out without any serious intent. A handsome, virile man like him could never be really interested in a plain-Jane sort of woman like herself. She flicked an imaginary speck of dust off the display of baby bonnets.

Oh, fudge! I deserve a little time off, don't I? she thought a trifle defensively. Why couldn't she do something just for fun if she wanted to? And judging from the way she had practically fallen apart just because a man had turned up at her usually women-and-children-only store seemed to indicate it was about time she had a few casual encounters with the opposite sex.

Her closest friend, Kim, was always badgering Corey to go out. But to Kim going out meant going somewhere, most usually a bar, with the exclusive purpose of picking up a man. Corey hadn't wanted to because, as much as she loved her friend, she thought Kim chased men a shade too aggressively and indiscriminately to suit Corey's taste. And discriminating or not, Corey really hadn't wanted to meet any man since her divorce.

But that needed to change. She had made too big a deal of it. She really had been hiding from men by immersing herself in work and community obligations. It had been quite cowardly of her, actually.

Suddenly, it seemed very important to her to prove to herself she could be around a man without going all to pieces. Perhaps she had retreated from the world for a while after her awful marriage and divorce, but she was not afraid of men, not even a big, virile, opinionated, forceful man like Brandon Wolfe. She could meet him casually, just for the fun of it, if she wanted. Of course, he wasn't the right kind of man for her, but that wasn't the point. She just needed to show herself she could do it. It would be therapeutic.

Yes, Kim would go to the fair if Corey asked her. One of the things about Kim that made her a terrific friend was that she was always game for an adventure. She would be glad to spend a hot, sunny August afternoon with Corey at the dusty state fairgrounds. They could behave like kids again. It would be good for both of them. They would ride the Ferris wheel, eat caramel-covered apples, admire the blue-ribbon-winning loaves of home-baked bread, and if they just happened to run into Brandon Wolfe and his llamas, well, she could handle that, too. She was sure she could.

Two

Brandon saw Corey coming long before she saw him. She was wandering from pen to pen, admiring the elegant llamas. A woman, a petite blond, a real looker in tight short shorts and low-cut tank top, walked along beside her; but Brandon hardly gave the stranger a glance. Corey was the one who held his interest.

He lowered the pitchfork of hay he had been just about to throw into the pen for Tulip and Starshine, forgetting all about them.

He had spent a restless night thinking about the encounter with Corey at Kids' Kloset. Sleepless, he had tossed and turned on the narrow cot in his small travel trailer and listened to the peaceful breathing of the boys as he thought about soft, inviting lips and warm brown eyes. He couldn't believe how he had come on to her at her store, acting like a punk kid in a singles' bar. A good five years had gone by since he had approached a woman in any kind of way, much less with lust in his heart. Thank God he had only caressed her arm when what he had really wanted to do was pick her up, sling her over his shoulder and carry her off to his cabin in the mountains. If she had had any idea of what was going on in his mind, she would have run screaming out to the street to call the cops.

An insistent nudge to his arm and quiet but persistent humming reminded him of the business at hand. He resumed forking sweet-smelling grass hay into the enclosure for the hungry llamas.

"Sorry I forgot your lunch, ladies," he said apologetically. He gave Tulip and Starshine an extra fork full of hay to make up for neglecting them, but he couldn't get his mind off a very different lovely little lady.

He couldn't figure out what had triggered his uncharacteristic behavior with Corey. Maybe he had been isolated too long with only the company of kids and animals. *No. That wasn't it.*

There was something special about Corey. She pulled at him somehow, the same way a pristine mountain range beckoned to be explored. That was dangerous. He couldn't afford that kind of siren call right now. All the more reason he should have made certain he would never see her again. So what had he done? Asked her to come to the fair.

He didn't understand why she affected him that way. She had been friendly and helpful but in no way flirtatious or seductive. She had reminded him of a bright little wren flitting around in her nest, helping him feather his own fledglings. True, she had a wonderful soft, curvy body that would make a perfect armful for any man and lovely wavy silken hair that begged to be touched, but no matter how attractive, he knew better than to get involved with a woman. Any woman. He had too much to do, too many responsibilities. Women were trouble. They were expensive. And they always wanted to butt into your life and rearrange everything.

The weight of his responsibilities suddenly seemed very heavy as he watched the llamas bend their graceful necks to pick daintily at the hay. Hay he had to pay for, even when he hardly had two dimes to rub together. He hunched his shoulders against the tension, leaned on the pitchfork and peered through the wire mesh of the pen as Corey and her companion meandered ever closer to his spot in the cavernous llama barn. She looked terrific—cool and poised in spite of the August heat—in long walking shorts and a sleeveless top, her hair cascading down from a high ponytail. He was suddenly conscious of his own sweat-stained T-shirt and dripping face. Pulling a black and white bandanna from his jeans' pocket, he mopped his neck and forehead.

He had asked her to drop by the fair and then spent the whole night wondering if she would take him up on his invitation. It had been such a casual suggestion; he really didn't think she would come. She was obviously a very classy lady: a successful businesswoman, good with both adults and kids, self-possessed, educated, attractive. And what was he? An overgrown mountain man with two motherless boys and a llama ranch that had yet to make a penny. She had made it pretty obvious she thought she knew a whole lot more about what was right for kids than he did.

Still, he had wasted a lot of good sleep, hoping that she wouldn't show up and praying that she would. Disgusted, he rammed the handkerchief back in his pocket. He hated waffling around like this. Right or wrong, he always made quick decisions; anything that made him this uncertain couldn't be good. He was just getting ready to duck out the door at the far side of the barn when Robbie, who was sitting on top of a stack of hay bales with John, spied Corey.

"Daddy, look, it's the clothes lady, the one with all the teddy bears!" he called out in an excited, piercing voice that could have carried halfway to the next county.

Sure enough, Corey and her companion looked his way; and Robbie and John stood up, in spite of the strict instructions he had given them to stay sitting down on the high stack of bales, and waved wildly at the women.

Naturally, the ladies waved back, smiling, and started to walk directly toward him. *Damn!* he thought grimly. His once razor-sharp backcountry reflexes had deteriorated. He'd gone soft, living with the boys. He'd failed to make a timely escape. He stood rigidly tall and prepared for the onslaught.

Corey felt strangely giddy and light-headed as she approached Brandon. He hadn't been a figment of her imagination after all. She had thought perhaps the heat in her inadequately air-conditioned store had affected her brain. He was very real and as devastatingly attractive as she remembered. Towering over the exotic animals, a beam of dust-hazed sunlight turning his blond hair into a golden helmet, his sweat-dampened shirt clinging to his impressive musculature, a pitchfork in his hand, he looked like some kind of magical mythical being.

Corey glanced at Kim. Her friend's mouth hung open wide enough for a turkey to fly in it as she gaped at Brandon. *Maybe I should have come by myself,* Corey thought, noting how very brief Kim's shorts and top were and what a lot of skin they exposed.

Brandon put the pitchfork away, came out of the llama pen and swung first Robbie and then John down from the hay. They ran over to Corey to form a babbling chorus of confusion around her. She was touched at how pleased they seemed to be to see her again. She noticed they were each wearing one of the outfits she had helped their father select. They looked so cute; it made her feel proud to have contributed in a small way to their well-being.

Corey introduced Kim to Brandon and the boys. Brandon acknowledged the introduction courteously, but his gaze never left Corey's face.

"So, you made it to the fair," he said softly as he studied her face with an intense look Corey couldn't quite decipher. His expression made her feel elated and, at the same time, uneasy. She found she could only gaze into his eyes for a few moments before she felt compelled to look away.

"I thought I misunderstood when you said llamas," Corey said as she nervously twirled a lock of hair that had escaped from her ponytail. "I didn't know they were exhibited at the fair; I haven't been here in years. In fact, I don't think I've ever seen a real live llama before, only pictures on TV."

"The number of people breeding llamas here in Idaho has grown a lot over the years. What do you think of them now that you've seen the real thing?"

"Oh, they're wonderful! They're so graceful and elegant-looking, almost regal. Their fur is beautiful. They look very feminine."

Brandon chuckled at her enthusiasm. "It's not fur; it's wool. And what do you mean 'feminine'? I'll have you know they can carry a good fourth of their body weight; they're hard-working pack animals."

"Well," Corey said archly, "I don't see why feminine can't also mean hard working. But what I meant was the way they're shaped and their long eyelashes."

Brandon cocked a quizzical eyebrow at her, and Corey started to blush as she tried to explain. "I mean their hips. Well, I suppose they don't really have hips, just their back legs. They're curved like a woman's, wide at the top then taper down to slim little ankles."

Corey was relieved when Brandon didn't respond to her garbled description of the llamas' anatomy. There were plenty of men who wouldn't have been able to resist the perfect opportunity she had given him to make some kind of raunchy comment. He was either a first-class gentleman or more conscious than most men would be of the two sets of small ears in attendance.

"It just so happens Tulip and Starshine are females; I left my stud, Jester, at the ranch along with the other four members of his harem. Would you like to get acquainted?"

Corey nodded her head vigorously. "Oh, yes. I tried to pet some of the other llamas through the wire, but they wouldn't come over close enough. I guess they're a pretty aloof kind of animal."

"They just have the good sense to reserve judgment until they get to know you," Brandon said as he pulled open the pen's gate and stood aside so they could go through into the enclosure.

"No thanks," Kim said. "I like to keep my distance from anything that bites."

"Llamas don't bite people, just other llamas when they need to show them who's boss," Brandon said with a trace of irritation.

"They spit, too," John added helpfully.

"Only at other llamas," Brandon said firmly as he noticed Corey just perceptibly edging back toward the gate. "They're a little head-shy so put your hands behind your back and bend forward so they can sniff your hair and see your face. They're very face-oriented."

Corey did as she was told. The llamas were bigger than she had realized, actually quite a bit taller than she was. Their heads might reach almost six feet, she judged. Both llamas approached her, the white fluffy one in front. The long graceful neck arched down toward her face, and large soulful eyes looked into hers. The velvety lips twitched. Corey nervously hoped Brandon was right about llamas not biting people. She suspected those soft lips were stretched across some very large, hard teeth.

To Corey's surprise, the llama began to gently blow on her face. Then the sleeker red-brown llama came closer and also began softly blowing at her.

"The white one is Starshine and the red one is Tulip," Brandon said. "Blowing is their way of greeting you. Now you have two new friends for life."

The llamas went back to eating the hay. Her face shining, Corey turned to Brandon. "They're really lovely; can I pet them?"

Something inside of Brandon seemed to expand at the words of praise and the look on Corey's face. A woman gained a lot of points with him if she liked animals. He was just about to tell her how to touch the llamas when Kim interrupted.

"It's getting awfully hot and stuffy in this smelly old barn. Why don't we go get something to drink?"

Corey moved regretfully toward the gate. She had been enjoying the animals and their owner immensely, but she could see how restless Kim was getting. She really wanted to stay longer. *A lot longer,* she thought, as Brandon's strong arm reached around her to help when she fumbled at the wire latch. He was standing so close to her she could see the individual hairs gleaming like gold wire filaments on his corded forearm. Somehow, the sight made her feel all jiggly inside.

Brandon knew the fences at the llama arena didn't carry a current, but he could have sworn he felt an electric shock when his hand touched Corey's on the wire latch. His heart seemed to be beating in a strangely erratic way, too. Suddenly, he couldn't stand the though of her walking out the barn door without him. His brain had turned to mush. He struggled to think of a way to keep her with him just a little longer.

"I think I promised you a cotton candy. How about we make it my treat for the drinks?"

"Can I have a soda pop? Can I, Daddy?" John begged.

Robbie grabbed his father's hand and used it for leverage to vault up and down. "Me too; me too!"

Brandon smiled indulgently at them. "It's still quite awhile before supper. You can have sodas if you want."

"Oh, boy! Let's go," John said.

Robbie ran over to Corey. First ducking his head, then looking up, he grinned shyly at her, reached up to take her hand and tugged her toward the door. When Corey felt the small, warm fingers grasp her hand, it seemed as though he had taken hold of a little piece of her heart. With a lump in her throat, she willingly followed along behind him.

Robbie pulled her over beside his father so he could hold his dad's hand, too. By lifting both feet at once, he was able to swing between them as they made their way toward one of the open-air food booths that dotted the fairgrounds.

"Let go of Ms. Tierney. She doesn't want you hanging on her like that," Brandon told Robbie.

"Oh, I don't mind at all. He's having so much fun," Corey said and smiled up brightly at Brandon.

He frowned and started to say something else; but instead he released Robbie's hand, putting an end to the swinging. He wished Corey hadn't contradicted him like that in front of the children.

"Robbie, you don't have to call me Ms. Tierney, if you don't want to. My name is Corey."

Brandon's frown deepened.

He started to tell Corey he wanted his sons to address adults with respect, not by their first names, but just then Kim called out a greeting to someone she recognized.

"Can you wait just a minute for me, Corey? I want to say hello to Bob."

Before Corey could reply, Kim dashed off toward a display of antiquated fire-fighting equipment and old police cars where a heavyset young man stood waving in their direction.

"The restrooms are near here. I'll take the boys to wash their hands while you're waiting," Brandon said stiffly, then led the boys away.

What had happened to change his mood? Corey wondered.
He had seemed happy to see her, warm and welcoming when he

showed her the llamas. Now a shadow seemed to hover over them. Corey didn't have long to ponder the change. A little out of breath, Kim raced back.

"Bob and I are going to get some beers. You don't mind if I go on without you, do you? Kids and tall glasses always make me nervous anyhow; you never know when you're going to get a lapful of ice cubes. Anyway, you seem to be doing okay on your own making eyes at that gorgeous hunk of beefcake. It's about time, too. Well, don't wait around for me; we don't have to meet later. I'm pretty sure Bob will want to take me home."

Kim gave Corey a broad suggestive wink then leaned closer for a peck on the cheek and whispered softly with warm goodwill, "Good luck, honey. You deserve someone special in your life. It would make you forget all about that S.O.B. of a husband you had."

Corey affectionately watched Kim scurry off, though she was a little annoyed, too. It was just like Kim to jump to conclusions. Why, she had only met Brandon yesterday. She had just gone by the llama barn to say hello, and here Kim was acting like they were already an "item." They would probably never see one another again after today.

In fact, she thought uncomfortably, *maybe Brandon won't even want to share a drink with me since something seems to be bothering him.* She wished Kim hadn't abandoned her. There was safety in numbers. Maybe she didn't even want to go get a drink herself, come to think about it. Now that her friend was gone, Corey nervously realized just how much she had been relying on Kim to give her courage for this venture. Just as she was wondering if it would be too awfully rude if she just vanished into the crowd, Brandon and the boys reappeared.

"Kim went on with Bob," Corey told Brandon, shading her eyes against the sun to look up at him. He was so tall, so virile looking, so, so—male. A man like that could never be interested in her.

Brandon didn't seem in the least concerned about Kim's disappearance. He reached out, gently captured her hand and slipped it into the crook of his elbow to escort her along in old-fashioned gentlemanly style. "Right this way, Ms. Tierney. I spotted a stand that sells fresh-squeezed lemonade."

Corey's fingers trembled ever so slightly as she felt the smooth muscles of Brandon's arm. She wondered if she might be suffering a touch of heatstroke, for all of a sudden she felt strangely light-headed and breathless. "Lemonade sounds delicious," she murmured.

Brandon ordered two lemonades for them and colas for the boys. They sat on long benches at a wooden table, a little boy crowded close on either side of Corey, Brandon on the opposite side of the table from them. John and Robbie slurped away at the icy drinks and happily competed to see who could tell her the most about all the things they had seen at the fair.

Corey had to listen carefully to comprehend their funny stories. She sometimes thought children spoke in a special code; grown-ups had to pay close attention if they were to have any hope of cracking it. When one of the boys said something especially amusing, she would look across at Brandon to share a smile.

He was being awfully quiet, and he had a peculiar look on his face. It was strange, but his dark blue eyes seem to warm her more than the blazing August sun. Corey held the water-beaded lemonade container up to her cheek and slid it down along her neck to cool her flushed face.

Brandon watched Corey smooth the frosty cup over her skin. The lemonade cup left a trail of tiny drops of moisture along Corey's throat. Brandon longed to follow the dewy path with the tip of his tongue. He swallowed hard and looked away, afraid his eyes might reveal what he was thinking.

He hadn't heard a word the boys had said, but he could tell they were enjoying the conversation with Corey immensely. It was rare for an adult to pay that much attention to little kids. He hadn't realized how much he missed a woman's company. *Could the boys feel the same way?* After the first year, they had stopped asking about their mother. He had thought they were getting along just fine by themselves. He couldn't bear the thought his sons might need something he couldn't provide for them. The idea that his care might be inadequate made him so uncomfortable he felt like smacking the wooden table. Abruptly he rose to his feet.

John's insistent voice broke through to his consciousness. "Pigs do too race, don't they, Daddy?"

"I know there are always horse races at the fair, but pigs?" Corey questioned.

"John's right; there are pig races."

"Doesn't it hurt them? It's so hot for the poor things to be running around."

Corey thought of the immense hairless pink sows panting in the straw in the exhibition barns she had toured earlier that afternoon. Those gigantic globs of living lard hadn't looked like they could stand up, much less run.

"I suppose they go into training just like any other athlete," Brandon said, trying to get back into a relaxed mood. "They use the smaller varieties; they seem to do all right. We watched a race this morning."

"Can we show her? Can we, Daddy?"

"That all depends on whether she's interested. What do you say, Corey? Do you want to watch a Pork Chop Derby?"

Corey laughed and said, "Why, yes, I would. I'm sure it's fascinating. And the boys seem to want to see another show."

"All right then. Step right this way for the Swine Steeplechase."

Brandon led the way to a miniature grandstand and racetrack. They found seats and settled down. They didn't have long to wait before the next event took place, but in the meantime, the announcer told lots of pig jokes to get everyone in a jovial mood. At the sound of the gun, the rotund racers took off, squealing for all they were worth. The boys hopped up and down with excitement and cheered on their favorites. "Go, Piggy, go!" "Run, Porky! You can do it."

The bobbing curly tails and frantic stubby legs scurrying madly around the track struck Corey as being hilariously ridiculous. She laughed harder than she had in ages, collapsing into helpless giggles at each new absurdity.

When the last grand champion porker had eaten its Oreo cookie reward, Corey wiped tears of laughter from her eyes. "It's a good thing they're short races; I don't think I could have taken much more entertainment."

Brandon seemed pleased she was enjoying herself; but then he looked at his wristwatch and said regretfully, "I'm sorry, but I'm going to have to go. I'm showing Starshine this afternoon, and I have to check her grooming and get cleaned up and change."

Corey started to say goodbye, but Brandon seemed reluctant to let her go. He took her hand to help her down from the seats and continued speaking before she could say anything.

"If you have time to wait around a little longer, maybe you'd like to stay for the llama show," he suggested tentatively. "The competition starts in about an hour."

"I'd like that. Do you need the boys? If you don't, I could keep them for you until the show starts. I haven't been to the midway yet. I bet they would make first-rate escorts for a ride on the merry-go-round."

Robbie and John looked thrilled. Brandon frowned. "Those carnival rides are expensive. I don't think I have enough cash on me to cover more than a ride or two."

"Oh, don't worry about it. I did the inviting; I'll take care of it. It will be fun."

"Don't think we need any handouts, Ms. Tierney. I told the boys before we came to the fair we were here for business. They knew we weren't going to the carnival. I'm a long way from needing charity from anyone," Brandon said harshly, a scowl darkening his face with the swiftness of an unexpected thunderstorm.

But Corey wasn't paying any attention to Brandon; she was observing the crestfallen appearance of Robbie and John. She tried to think of something that would convince Brandon it would be okay for her to take the boys to the amusement center. She smiled up winningly at him.

"But I've been dying to go on the carousel all day. You don't know how silly a grown-up woman feels riding all by herself. You'd be doing me a favor if you'd let me take the boys along."

She was going to continue with her plea, but she finally realized the obstinate expression on Brandon's face meant she wasn't going to be able to sway him no matter how eloquent her appeal.

Brandon had no intention of giving in for Corey's sake, but he had seen how the boys' faces had gone from happy to sad to glad and back again as they had looked from one adult to the other as though they were following a tennis match. Angrily, he dug into his jeans' pocket and came up with a folded five-dollar bill. He grabbed Corey's shoulders and swung her around so his back was to his sons, and his body was between them and Corey. He spoke to her through stiff lips in an acid voice meant only for Corey's ears.

"If you have something to offer a child, it's a matter of common sense and common courtesy to ask for the parent's approval first."

He released her so quickly she stumbled. A nagging doubt suddenly pricked at him like a worrisome sweat bee. Maybe the clothes he had bought yesterday at Corey's store were priced a little unnaturally low. She had probably taken one look at him and figured he couldn't afford to pay much. *Does she get a tax-write off for welfare cases?* he wondered sourly. He picked up her limp hand and slapped the five-dollar bill into her palm.

"This won't go far, but it's all I have with me. I'll see you in an hour at the llama arena. Have fun on your merry-go-round ride," he ground out and disappeared with quick, furious strides, leaving an astonished Corey staring after him.

Whatever was the matter with the man? They had been getting along famously before he had blown up at her for no reason at all.

She pulled herself together for the children's sake. They were looking up at her in excited anticipation. She linked hands with them and set off for the midway. With false gaiety she chatted with them about what rides they would go on, but inside she was fuming. Who did he think he was, pushing her around like that? All she had done was offer to do him a favor, and he had behaved as though he were highly insulted. What kind of foolish male pride wouldn't allow someone to give his children a little treat?

Corey inwardly huffed through the carousel and Ferris wheel rides. It wasn't until the boys talked her into going on the giant swing that her attention was brought back to more immediate concerns—like not upchucking her lemonade. Head spinning, she let the boys ride by themselves on miniature airplanes while she prayed her stomach would calm down. Laughing when both Robbie and John waved at her every single time their airplane completed a circuit soon got her back on an even keel. Their beaming faces made her feel all was right with the world.

By the time the three of them returned to the llama arena, they were all in high spirits, discussing the relative merits of the Tornado, the Zipper and the House of Doom like longtime old friends. But as they approached Brandon's space in the llama barn, Corey noticed an increasing tension in her stomach that suggested she hadn't entirely recovered from the rides after all.

When the boys saw their father, they dropped Corey's hands and rushed ahead to tell him about their adventures. Feeling a growing uneasiness, Corey hung back and watched.

Brandon had changed into dark pleated trousers and a crisp white cotton shirt. A black leather string tie with a turquoise slide emphasized the strength and thickness of his neck. The pants hung beautifully over his lean, muscular hips. A black leather belt encircled a trim waist. There wasn't a hint of a paunch. Brandon was a giant of a man, and it was all pure muscle.

Corey was so enchanted with Brandon's appearance it took her a few minutes to realize what he was doing. He held a large leaf blower and was blasting Starshine's long white wool with it. Amazingly, Starshine seemed to be enjoying herself. She was leaning into the stiff breeze and had what looked to Corey like a llama grin on her face.

Brandon had turned the noisy contraption off while the boys were talking to him; but as soon as they ran off to play with some children they apparently knew, he switched it back on. Corey approached cautiously, afraid Brandon might snap at her again, but still curious to know what he was doing. Again he cut the motor, then picked up a wire dog-slicker brush and began combing out Starshine's coat.

"So, that's how you groom a llama," Corey said in what she hoped was a light tone, not wanting to betray her jitters.

Brandon didn't lash out at her, but he did seem nervous and distracted. "I wasn't planning on using the blower right before the competition, but she's been rolling in the hay. They love dust baths, but I didn't think she would roll in this little pen. The blower gets the worst of the debris out and opens up the coat, but it can tangle these longhaired ones. I was hoping to just do a little light combing right now."

"I think she's beautiful. I love all that fluffy wool."

Brandon grunted as he brushed furiously. "You and everyone else. I like the short hairs myself; they make better pack animals, but the long fleece is what's popular. That's why I'm showing Starshine. She's the only woolly llama I have."

Brandon pulled a handful of straw and tangled llama wool from the wire brush, threw the debris to the ground and attacked Starshine's haunches. "I've got to at least place in the show if I want to make any money in this business. You have to make a name for yourself, especially if you're just a small breeder like me. Hardly anyone knows my ranch, Moonmagic Llamas. I have to build a reputation. Fast."

"You aren't going to show Tulip?" Corey asked, wriggling her fingers at the red-brown llama through the wire mesh.

"No, I just brought her along as company for Starshine. They're sociable animals. I didn't want Starshine to feel lonely around all these strangers."

Brandon stepped back to inspect the llama's coat. The beautiful sheet of fluffy white wool cascaded almost to the ground.

"Well, I guess that'll have to do. They just called our class. Now Starshine's groomed to the nines, and there's no time for her owner to comb his own hair."

Brandon nervously ran his fingers through his thick blond hair, pushing it back from his forehead. He snapped a lead onto Starshine's halter and walked her out of the pen.

"Wish us luck."

"She looks as glamorous as a movie star," Corey said encouragingly. "I'll give you the traditional theater opening-night good-luck wish—break a leg."

Brandon groaned. "Don't say that; one of us probably really will."

Corey stood on tiptoe to push an unruly lock of Brandon's hair in place. She was a little surprised at herself for risking such an intimate gesture. Not usually a touchy-feely kind of person, it seemed slightly audacious to make such a personal gesture to someone she hardly knew. She had reached out without thinking, wanting Brandon to do well in the competition and trying to help in some small way; but the outcome left her shaken.

Holding Starshine's lead in one hand, Brandon used his free hand to lightly grasp the soft flesh of Corey's upper arm. He swooped down and—in a movement so fast she hardly realized what was happening before it was over—dropped a quick kiss on her parted lips.

"Now that's a much better way to wish someone good luck, I think," he said, looking very satisfied with himself.

He grinned rakishly at her and led Starshine away to the center of the arena to join the other llamas being shown.

How strange. Her legs actually felt so weak she thought they might give way beneath her and deposit her in the dust on the barn floor. *Well,* she thought ruefully as she made her way shakily to the closer of the two bleachers set up on both sides of the arena, *the man is certainly full of surprises.*

Corey climbed up high in the bleachers where she had a good view of the proceedings. John and Robbie soon joined her, along with the older children who had been playing with them.

It seemed to Corey the judges took a long time to come to a decision. With frequent stops for close individual inspection by each judge, the llamas were led round and round the small arena area.

The crowd that had gathered for the judging was quiet and subdued. Having no idea what the judges were looking for, Corey couldn't even guess at which llamas would place; but Starshine, stepping daintily and haughtily indifferent to both crowd and judges, looked magnificent to her. Not to mention the man leading her around the circle. Brandon stood tall, broad-shouldered and confident, perfectly turned out in spite of his last-minute stage fright. He looked as regal as Starshine.

Into the hush, Corey whispered to the boys, "What makes the judge think a llama is a winner?"

Both boys mulled her question over for a minute or two. Robbie quickly decided it wasn't worth puzzling over. He stuck his thumb in his mouth and nuzzled into Corey's side. With a lump in her throat, Corey put her arm around him. His little body felt so good, so right, cuddled next to her.

John was still struggling to come up with an answer to her question, his face scrunched up in a thinking-hard expression. Then his face cleared. "Straight front legs," he said importantly. "Daddy says they carry most of their weight up front, so they need straight legs to carry big heavy packs. They can't carry little boys, though," he finished mournfully.

Corey had a sneaking suspicion that last bit of knowledge had come from lots of discussion and perhaps even a bit of debate. She hid a smile and gave him a quick consoling hug.

It looked like the judges had finally come to a decision, for the llamas and their owners were lined up facing the judging table.

When the judges announced Starshine had taken first place, Corey thought she would burst with pride. Delighted with the outcome, she applauded enthusiastically and hugged the boys.

Wait, slow down, she scolded herself sternly, suddenly realizing how caught up she had become in a stranger's triumph. *How could I have formed such a feeling of attachment so quickly to Brandon and his children? This was supposed to be just a little outing for me to get used to the idea of relating to men. I shouldn't be feeling so close to Brandon's family; I won't even be seeing them after today.*

Nevertheless, when a beaming Brandon led Starshine away from the ring, and she and the boys scrambled down from the bleachers to congratulate him, she couldn't help feeling as elated over his accomplishment as if she had personally contributed to the victory.

"You won! How wonderful! I'm so happy for you."

"Yeah. It will make a big difference. Now when Starshine has babies, I'll be able to get a lot better price for them. We just might make it, yet." The sound of pride, relief and hope were all mixed up in his voice.

"This calls for a celebration—along the lines of a caramel apple at the very least. My treat." Corey was fairly dancing along side of Brandon, she felt so happy.

"Oh boy! I want a hot fudge sundae," John said.

"And I want cotton candy," Robbie echoed.

Brandon stopped abruptly and faced Corey. "It's too close to supper time for sweets," he said firmly with a trace of tension underlining his words.

Still feeling excited over Starshine's first place, Corey totally missed the undercurrents. "Oh, there's plenty of nourishment in an apple or a frozen banana. Let's celebrate," she said gaily.

"Is it your hearing or your ability to understand that's lacking, Corey? I told you earlier you don't offer a child a treat without getting permission from his parent first. I say the boys don't have dessert before supper. I'm their father, and what I say goes," Brandon thundered.

Corey stepped back hastily, shocked at his fierceness. "I didn't mean... I only thought..."

"You didn't think; that's the problem," Brandon growled, turning his back on her to put Starshine in the llama pen.

Hot tears stinging her eyes, Corey rushed away before anyone could see. She knew she shouldn't leave without saying good-bye to the boys, but she couldn't bear for Brandon to see her cry. She was nothing more to him than one of many chance acquaintances he had made while he was in Boise for the llama show. She didn't want him to know what an effect he had had on her, just how very much he had hurt her feelings. She liked to do things for people, she always had; it was just a part of her nature, but it seemed he had deliberately misunderstood her good intentions.

Brandon Wolfe was a devastatingly handsome, intriguing man who could be tender and charming when he wanted to be; but he could also be bossy and mean-spirited, full of false pride, unwilling to take the tiniest suggestion from anyone, possessive and unfairly strict with his children. She had certainly picked a fine man for her first friendly encounter when she had decided to break away from the self-imposed cloister of her store.

When Corey reached the parking area, she had to walk up and down the long rows of cars for quite a while, too angry, hurt and distracted to remember where she had parked. When she finally found her car, she yanked open the door and leaped in, only to burn her legs on the hot vinyl. She yelped, then gave a bitter little laugh at herself. What a sorry state she was in.

She had come here to prove she didn't need to hide from men, that she had recovered from her painful divorce and was capable of a relaxed, casual visit with an attractive male. Dashing the tears from her eyes to clear her vision for the drive home, she decided if she had worked a lifetime on it, she couldn't possibly have come up with a more dismal failure.

Three

Corey rinsed out her coffee mug and set it on the drain board to dry. She had stayed home today, determined to get her account books up to date. Consignment checks were paid out once a month; October's payments were due next week. Fortunately, she had a bevy of grandmotherly types who were always glad to mind the store for her when she needed time off. They welcomed a change in their usual routines and a chance to earn a little extra income.

Corey sighed. She had arranged for a whole day of uninterrupted bookkeeping—now if she could only concentrate.

She liked to be busy—she sang in the church choir and taught the third and fourth grade Sunday school class in addition to attending to all the demands of her business—but lately she seemed to be spending an inordinate amount of time mindlessly wandering from room to room in her home, more often than not ending up here in the kitchen, staring out across the tree-lined street at the children playing in the elementary school yard.

She had put a lot of time and thought into making her small cottage warm and cozy. Usually, she enjoyed working or just puttering around at home. Why did her little house now seem so hollow and echoing?

In the first few months after her husband had left her, she had felt numb—alone and lonely—but she had taken the generous divorce settlement and started a business all on her own. She had bought and furnished her home. She had made friends. Little by little she had built a busy and complete life. So why, after almost four years of hard-earned contentment, did she suddenly feel so empty?

Corey grabbed a dish towel and vigorously rubbed the already dry coffee mug, then yanked open the ivy-stenciled cupboard door and put the mug away with a hard thump. Here it was already late afternoon, and she hadn't accomplished much of anything. It was time to quit moping around and get down to work.

She took one more quick glance out the window toward the school. She noticed a small figure sitting slumped at the curb. She looked again. The child seemed familiar.

Could it be?

The little boy had his chin tucked down into his jacket, but Corey was quite sure now it was John Wolfe. The white-blond hair was unmistakable.

What was a five-year-old doing there alone? School had let out long ago; all the other children were gone. And Brandon and his sons didn't live in Boise anyway. John shouldn't be at this school. Corey watched the children so often she recognized a great many of them. She certainly would have noticed if John had been among them.

Corey grabbed a sweater and went out quickly to cross the street. The little boy was pushing brightly colored fallen leaves with the toe of his sneaker and didn't notice her approaching.

"Hi, John. How are you today?"

John scrambled to his feet at the sound of her voice, obviously startled and perhaps a little fearful. His face lit up when he saw who it was.

"Oh, hi, Ms. Tierney. I'm awful glad you're here. My daddy is real late. He said to wait right here for him, but everybody went away and left me all by myself, and he hasn't come yet."

A host of questions sprang to mind, but Corey didn't want to overwhelm the child with a cross-examination.

"I'm glad I'm here, too. See the little white house across the street with the green shutters?" John looked in the direction Corey was pointing and nodded yes. "That's where I live. Did you move into town?"

"No. We still live at Roby Creek."

John picked up two of the leaves from the sidewalk and tried to tie the stems together. Now that he had some company, he seemed to be completely unconcerned with his dilemma.

Well, Corey thought with wry amusement, *I'm not doing very well as a detective.*

A chill breeze caused her to shiver and pull her cardigan together across her chest. It was already getting pretty nippy these late October afternoons. She was glad to see John was wearing a warm-looking parka. His hands and cheeks were red, but unlike Corey, he wasn't shivering. With only the light sweater as a wrap, she was definitely going to freeze before she found out what was going on.

She hesitated. She would like to ask John to come to her house where he could be warm and comfortable while waiting for his father, but she wasn't sure she should get involved. Brandon Wolfe was obviously a man with strong opinions about what was right and wrong for his children. There was no way to tell how he might react if she took his son into her home without permission.

She rubbed her hands together to warm them. It embarrassed her to think of how she had tracked him down at the fair. She realized now she had been fooling herself when she had decided to drop by to see him on the pretense of a casual, friendly hello. The feelings

Brandon aroused in her were anything but casual. He made her wish for things she thought she had given up on long ago. She just had to accept that she wasn't meant to have a family.

And it wasn't only that seeing Brandon with his sons revived her painful longings for a husband and children; there was also the disturbing physical reaction she had when she was near the man. He had only to look at her to set her atwitter like somebody's maiden aunt. Perhaps she should be grateful to have discovered it was possible for her to respond to a man the way a woman was surely meant to; but why, oh why, did the first man to ever stir her that way have to be a stubborn, opinionated crank like Brandon Wolfe?!

Corey almost felt like stamping her foot in frustration at the thought, but she saw that John had thrown his leaf chain down and was shyly reaching for her hand. Her own slim fingers seemed warm and strong compared to the reddened, cold little hand that slipped so easily into her protective clasp. At the touch of the small fingers, a wave of tenderness swept over Corey, followed by a feeling of resolve.

John had to get in out of the cold. She would be darned if she would let a stiff-necked ogre of a man intimidate her when a child was in need. Fudge! She was going to take John in and give him a cup of hot chocolate even if Brandon had her arrested for kidnapping.

Corey smiled at the little boy. "Would you like to come over to my house and have some cookies and cocoa? You could eat them by the window so you could watch for your daddy."

John's face brightened. "I'm glad you're not a stranger 'cause I'm awful hungry."

Hand in hand they crossed the street. It seemed doubly warm inside Corey's home after being out in the crisp autumn air. Corey hung her sweater and John's parka in the closet in the entryway. Corey kept a potted fern on an old-fashioned plant stand next to one of the smaller windows in the living room. She put the fern on the coffee table and moved the little plant stand next to the large window facing the street, so, with a footstool to sit on, John would have a comfortable place to eat while looking out at the school.

Fortunately, in anticipation of Halloween, Corey had spent several evenings baking and decorating cookies as a treat for her Sunday school class. They were waiting in the freezer. It only took a few seconds to defrost several in the microwave while Corey mixed up a saucepan of cocoa from scratch.

John was studiously watching the street when Corey returned with the plate of warm cookies and steaming mug of hot chocolate. She put them down on a place mat in front of him.

"Careful, the cup is hot," she warned.

Corey's efforts were more than adequately rewarded with John's expression of delight. His eyes and mouth widened into three big Os of surprise and pleasure.

Corey stood behind John while he ate so she could watch for his father. She was getting really worried. It would be dark soon. She wondered if she should try to call Brandon. Would he be listed in the phone book? Would John know his telephone number?

She was glad John didn't seem upset. He was enjoying the snack immensely, carrying on a running conversation with the cookies as he gobbled them up. "You can't boo me, Mr. Ghost; I'll bite your head off." And he did.

Corey smiled. It made her feel good to see a child enjoy the treats she had fussed over, trying to make them look scary.

"John, if you live out at Roby Creek, why do you go to the school here?" she asked, deciding the direct approach was the only way to get information from the little boy.

"I went to a diff'rent school first. On a big yellow bus. It was fun. But Daddy had a fuss with the teacher," John said through a mouthful of cookie. He picked up a witch on a broomstick and zoomed her through the air.

"And then what happened?" Corey prodded gently, only feeling slightly guilty at encouraging the child to tell tales behind his father's back.

"Daddy said he didn't want any son of his—that's me," John said, thumping himself on the chest, "going to any school where all they did was cut out paper dolls all day. So now he drives me here. But he forgot to get me today, I guess."

Well, Corey thought, hiding a grin, *fussing with the teacher seemed to fit with what she knew about Brandon Wolfe.* Then she sobered. But she never would have thought he would be so irresponsible as to leave a five-year-old waiting on the sidewalk all alone.

John took a big drink of the cocoa. With a wide chocolate mustache adorning his upper lip, he said seriously, "But it's okay now, 'cause you're taking care of me."

Touched, Corey impulsively bent down to give him a hug. It was then she saw a car pull over to the curb across the street. Brandon and Robbie got out, and the car drove away.

"Look, John. There they are. Quick, let's go tell them you're here."

Corey grabbed her navy pea jacket and John's parka from the closet. She helped him into his coat, zipping it up snugly to his chin. She thrust her arms into her jacket as they hurriedly crossed the street.

Brandon was walking with long, swift strides away from them toward the entrance to the school. Robbie was trotting along behind, rapidly losing ground, in a vain attempt to keep up with his father.

"Daddy! Here I am," John called out.

Brandon whirled around at the sound of his son's voice. Even at a distance, Corey could see the deep lines fear had etched around his eyes and mouth. When Brandon saw John, his face lit up like a flashbulb. John started to run toward his father, but Brandon closed the gap between them so fast it almost seemed to Corey as though he just materialized in front of her. Brandon scooped John up, crushed the child against his broad chest and buried his face in the thatch of white-blond hair. When he raised his head to stare in bewilderment at Corey, she was disconcerted to see what looked suspiciously like moisture beading in the corners of the dark navy eyes. She hoped relief, not anger, was what made his voice sound so harsh when he spoke to her.

"What are you doing here?" he asked, his voice demanding an answer.

Really! That was gratitude for you. She was getting ready to stalk home without even bothering to explain, when John started wriggling in his father's arms.

"Daddy, let me down. You're squashing me," John gasped out in a choked voice.

Brandon loosened his hold on John and lowered him to the sidewalk. "Sorry, Champ. I was afraid the next time I saw that chipmunk face of yours it would be looking back at me from a picture on a milk carton."

John looked a little puzzled, then his face brightened. "The clothes lady made me some yummy cocoa with a carton of milk. She has spooky cookies, too. She lives right over there," he said, pointing across the street.

"I saw John sitting on the curb *all alone*," Corey said, emphasizing the words "all alone" with an edge to her voice, "so I asked him to come in out of the cold and wait at my place."

Well, at least Brandon finally has the good grace to look contrite, Corey thought.

"The truck broke down," he said wearily, scrubbing his hand across his forehead. "There isn't much traffic out to Roby Creek. I was already too far from a phone—don't have a cell—to be able to call before the school office closed, so we walked to the main highway to catch a ride into town."

"I got to ride piggyback," Robbie piped up.

So that was what happened, Corey thought, forgiving him at once. He had walked, who knew how many miles, carrying a child, to get here. And intensely worried all the while, judging from the emotion she had seen on his face.

Then Brandon surprised her by stepping forward and taking both her hands in his. "I appreciate your taking John in," he said with what looked like heartfelt sincerity, his eyes warm and friendly. "Thanks for helping out."

The look Brandon gave her and the heat from the big hands enveloping hers made Corey feel as though a blast furnace door had suddenly opened before her. She nervously thought she might just melt into a puddle at his feet right there on the sidewalk, but she managed to say defiantly, "I gave him cookies before suppertime."

Brandon released her hands and grinned at her. "You could have given him a whole candy store, and it would have been okay with me. I'm just glad he's safe."

The sky was beginning to darken. A sudden gust of chill wind rattled the dry leaves in the gutter. Corey noticed Brandon wasn't wearing a coat—just a wine-and-black-plaid wool Pendleton shirt buttoned over a black turtleneck sweater.

"Well," he said, "I guess we'd better get going. I've got to find a service station that's willing to send somebody out that far to help me get the truck running."

Corey hesitated. She was attracted to this man, there was no way to deny it; she wouldn't try to lie to herself again. Four years had certainly been long enough to mourn her dead marriage. If he were the only one involved, she might go with her feelings and see what would become of it, but there were the children. Already the little imps tugged at her heart, and she had only seen them a few times. Such a long and painful part of her life had been spent trying to have children. What would become of her if she got to know these two special little boys better, and then they dropped out of her life? She didn't think she would be able to bear it.

She started to say goodbye, but the words died on her lips. They were in a difficult situation. It was wrong to selfishly think only of protecting herself when someone needed help.

"You can use my phone to call, if you like," she offered hesitantly. "When you find a repair place, I could drive you there. It would save a lot of time and walking."

"Thanks," Brandon said, grudgingly grateful. He hated accepting aid from anyone ever, but it especially irked him that the assistance was coming from Corey Tierney. For reasons he couldn't pinpoint, he didn't want to appear incompetent in her eyes. He had known for quite awhile the pickup needed work, but there was never enough money to take care of all his expenses. Now that he had neglected the truck until it had actually broken down, the cost would probably be twice as high to fix it as it would have been to service it when he should have.

"That would be a big help," he admitted reluctantly. "That is, if you don't mind all of us tromping around in your house. I'd go on if it were just me, but I hate to drag the boys all over town."

Corey looked up at him and then down again, feeling unexpectedly shy as she realized, whether he really wanted to or not, Brandon was actually going to enter her personal territory. "I think my house can stand a little tromping. Come on over. You must be freezing without a coat."

Brandon raised one thick dark blond eyebrow and grinned at her roguishly. "Nope. I'm not cold at all. I'm a pretty hot-blooded man."

His response brought a sudden naughty image before Corey's eyes and a quick stain of pink to her cheeks. To cover her confusion, she shooed the boys across the street and into the warmth of her home.

While Corey hung up her pea jacket and the boys' parkas in the entryway closet, Brandon stood in the living room and looked around admiringly. He had no real understanding of interior design, so he didn't take in each of the little details Corey had artfully planned; he just knew the overall effect made him feel welcomed and happy to be there.

"Well," Corey said briskly, rubbing her hands together to warm them, "the telephone is right over there. There's a phone book, too. I'll just clear these dishes away while you're calling."

She bustled over to gather up the remains of John's feast. She paused with the dishes in her hands and said to the boys, "You know, I think I have a brand new box of colored marking pens just waiting to make some pictures. Would you like to come into the kitchen with me and draw while your dad is phoning?"

John and Robbie enthusiastically followed her toward the kitchen. Corey paused at the doorway and called to Brandon, who was already leafing through the yellow pages of the phone book, "It's getting close to suppertime. I'll bet you're hungry, especially after that long walk. I don't have anything fancy, but I could make us some soup and sandwiches."

Brandon frowned and said in a gruff voice, "You've already done more than enough. We'll pick up something later." He started to dial a number, then apparently as an afterthought added, "But don't let us mess up your schedule. If you're hungry, go ahead and eat. We'll be out of your way pretty soon."

Now Corey felt like frowning, too, but she had the good manners not to let it show. As if she would sit down and eat in front of two hungry little boys! She had noticed how Robbie eyed the crumbs of cookies left on John's plate. She bet he was starving. Maybe she could slip him a sandwich while Brandon was on the telephone.

Corey found the colored pens and some large sheets of paper and set the boys up to draw at the kitchen worktable. While they happily scribbled away, she got out a loaf of bread, butter and cheddar cheese and started buttering slices of bread to make grilled cheese sandwiches. The children interrupted frequently for her to admire their masterpieces in progress. They were all having a great time when Brandon entered the kitchen. Corey guiltily stepped in front of the cutting board so he couldn't see how many pieces of buttered bread were lying there.

Corey's cozy little kitchen seemed dwarfed by Brandon's giant size. She had always felt so comfortable puttering with her pots and pans; now the whole kitchen seemed to shrink until it reached dollhouse proportions. Brandon had unbuttoned his wool shirt, and his black sweater stretched across an endless expanse of chest. *He is sucking up all the air in the room,* Corey thought crossly. That must be why she felt so suddenly breathless.

Brandon ran his fingers through his hair, causing it to stick up in little golden tufts of exclamation all across his forehead. Corey had an inexplicable urge to go smooth it in place. She gripped the edge of the counter tightly just to be sure she didn't do anything foolish.

Brandon sighed. "I found someone who'll work on the truck, but I'm afraid it won't be for another couple of hours. They're too busy to go right now." He looked at the boys sitting at the table and said as though he were talking out loud to himself, "I guess we could find a cafe or something close to the service station and wait there until they're ready." Then he turned to Corey and grinned sheepishly. "But if that offer for some soup still goes, I'd sure appreciate it."

"Yippee!" Robbie whooped.

Corey hid a small, triumphant smile. "Of course. If you don't mind canned."

"The way my stomach is rumbling, it could be petrified and it would taste good to me."

"Oh, I think I can do better than petrified," she assured him smoothly. "If you would please set the table for me, I'll have the food ready in no time. The plates and bowls are in the cabinet next to the refrigerator, and the silverware is in the drawer by the sink."

While Brandon took a stack of dishes into the dining room, Corey opened three cans of chicken noodle soup, put the contents to heat in a big pot on the stove and went back to buttering bread and slicing cheese. When everything was ready, Brandon helped her carry the platter of sandwiches and tureen of soup to the table.

Corey hid a smile when she saw her big oak dining table. Evidently Brandon wasn't well versed on the finer points of table setting—at least his arrangement of the pieces followed no pattern she had ever seen. Still, she felt pleased he had been so willing to help with the preparations for the simple meal.

Corey went back into the kitchen to get a pitcher of milk. "If you want to wash up before supper, the bathroom is just down the hall," she told Brandon.

"Okay. Come on troops, let's march. Hup two three four."

Giggling, John and Robbie scrambled down from the kitchen chairs and strutted after their father, Robbie trying, but never quite managing, to get in step with his brother.

When Brandon turned the light on in the bathroom, he paused in something approaching awe to look around at the riot of greenery, frilly towels and fancy soaps and sponges.

He whistled softly. "Whew. It sure doesn't look much like our bathroom at home, does it?"

John wrinkled his nose and sniffed the perfumed air. "Nope. It doesn't smell right."

"Let's hurry up and wash our hands before all the grub gets cold. I think we're supposed to use the soap that looks like seashells in that little flowery bowl. Grab a shell and scrub up."

It was more than hunger making him anxious to get out of the bathroom—the feminine smells and female bathing accoutrements made him feel restless and irritable. When he looked at the old-fashioned lion-paw bathtub, he saw a startlingly vivid image of Corey standing there after her bath: rosy, dewy and very, very nude. It had been hard enough working with her fully clothed in the close quarters of that ridiculously tiny kitchen of hers; if he started mentally undressing her, he was lost.

After the boys dried their hands, Brandon made a halfhearted attempt to fold the lace-edged, peach-colored towel back the way they had found it. Exasperated, he tossed it on the freestanding linen rack, where it hung crookedly next to its dainty comrades in what looked to Brandon like silent reproach. How he wished he and the boys were back at the ranch. Men didn't fit in with all of this disturbing female frou-frou.

"Let's get out of here," he said crossly.

Back in the dining room, Corey stood waiting for them by the table, her eyes alight with welcome. Her warm, smiling eyes instantly soothed Brandon's jangled nerves. *Ah, those eyes! A man could drown in their soft brown depths if he weren't careful.* Brandon stood frozen staring at her, the ladder-backed chair he had pulled out suspended in midair.

"Daddy, I can't sit way up there," Robbie complained, tugging on the chair leg.

Embarrassed, Brandon put the chair down on the hooked rug with a loud thunk, but he was relieved when Corey didn't seem to notice anything unusual.

"I'll get a cushion for you to sit on," she said and bustled around making everyone comfortable, passing sandwiches and filling soup bowls.

"You sure are a good cooker," John said after taking a huge bite of grilled cheese.

"Don't talk with your mouth full," Brandon reprimanded automatically.

"I like to see a child enjoy his food. Manners will come with time and practice; a good meal is more important," Corey said and smiled indulgently at John.

There she goes again, Brandon thought with annoyance. Just when he started to feel a little more comfortable with her, she had to butt in and question his authority. She reminded him of his parents. "Do this for the boys; be sure you don't do that. They need more discipline. Don't be so rough on them." A constant stream of unsolicited and sometimes contradictory advice.

And his parents weren't the only ones. Society was supposed to support equality of the sexes these days, with husbands changing diapers and requesting paternity leave, but what people said they believed and how they acted were two different things. As soon as anyone, male or female, learned he was raising his children alone, they seemed to think it was their duty to give him childcare suggestions. He would be willing to bet Starshine's firstborn that if he were a woman, all the butt-in-skis would assume he knew what he was doing.

It had its humorous side, he supposed, but right now he wasn't feeling particularly amused. Corey obviously thought he could benefit from some advice, but he knew what was best for his sons. He didn't need any help raising them, especially not from a little slip of a woman whose only credential, as far as he could see, was that she owned a kids' clothing store.

Brandon absently spooned up the last of his soup, hardly tasting it, his thoughts distracting him. You could have knocked him over with a feather when he had seen Corey standing by John at the school. He'd had a weird sense of unreality as though he were awake in the midst of a dream. Probably because Corey had starred in so many of his fantasies since he'd met her. Not that he should have been so surprised to see her there. He remembered now she had said she lived across from a school. That was her other qualification for being an expert on child rearing.

The woman posed a real threat to him. He hadn't been able to get her out of his mind. He was attracted to her, but she was the wrong woman at the wrong time. He had to get his business off the ground before he could even think about courting any woman, and when the time was right to seek female companionship, he would look for someone who respected his decisions and wasn't always trying to point out the error of his ways.

Not that he deserved to ever have a woman in his life again after the way he had failed the boys' mother.

Corey barely noticed how little Brandon spoke through the rest of the meal; she was too busy entertaining and being entertained by the boys. She seldom had anyone over to eat with her. Her family—her mother and father and several brothers and sisters, all of whom had children of their own—lived in the Twin Falls area. For their family get-togethers, it always seemed simpler for Corey, as a single woman, to go to them than for all of them to come to her.

But even though it was unusual to have two lively children at her table, clamoring for more soup and vying for her attention, it felt so natural and right that by the time she served up the rest of the

Halloween cookies for dessert (her Sunday school class would just have to make do with store bought), she was fairly bubbling with good spirits.

After supper Corey turned on the TV in the living room for the boys to watch while she and Brandon cleared the table. It was then when they were alone in the kitchen that she noticed how silent Brandon had become. She tried to strike up a conversation, but all she could get from him were terse, monosyllabic replies.

"What do you think is wrong with your truck?" she asked as she rinsed plates and stacked them in the dishwasher.

"Not sure."

He was lounging in the doorway, leaning against the frame, looking impossibly tall, relaxed and—male. He made her nervous. Drat! She had put the package of butter in the oven. She took it out quickly and put it away in the refrigerator, hoping Brandon hadn't noticed.

He probably didn't want to discuss the problem with the truck because he thought she, being a woman, wouldn't know anything about automotive repairs. She would try to start a conversation about the boys; that was something they could both talk about.

"John and Robbie really seemed to enjoy the cookies I baked; they must not get too many homemade things," she said brightly.

He sprang from the doorjamb so fast it made her think of a lion on the attack. She shrank back against the sink, not understanding why she felt frightened, for he took hold of her arm gently.

"Look, you're an attractive woman." He leaned down closer to her, his breath warming her face, his dark blue eyes mesmerizing. "No, a very attractive woman, and I know you mean well, but there's something we have to get straight."

There was a loud jangling; the phone was ringing. Wondering why she felt as though she had been saved, Corey slipped away from Brandon to answer it.

He watched her leave the room, still smarting with resentment that she so clearly thought he didn't provide his children with everything they needed.

"It might be for me; I gave the garage your number," he called after her.

She was back in a few moments. "It was the service station. They have a tow truck ready to take you to Roby Creek so they can pull your pickup back to the garage if the mechanic can't fix it on the spot."

Brandon groaned. "Don't even say a thing like that. I can't afford to have it towed. If it's that bad, I'll get the llamas and pull it myself."

Corey chuckled at the mental image she conjured up of llamas towing a truck but stopped laughing abruptly. Maybe he was serious. Perhaps this breakdown would cause him a real financial hardship. She wondered if there was anything she could do to help.

They went into the living room to round up John and Robbie. Corey retrieved their pint-sized parkas, and Brandon bundled the boys up while Corey collected her coat, car keys and purse.

The short ride to the service station was quiet except for Brandon answering the boys' questions about tow trucks and explaining what would probably happen when they got to their own pickup. When they arrived at the garage, Brandon seemed strangely reluctant to leave Corey's car. John had unfastened his own seat belt and helped Robbie undo his. Impatient to get on with what they seemed to perceive as an adventure, both boys were excitedly hanging over the front seat between Corey and Brandon.

"Sit down," Brandon told them sternly. "We'll go in just a minute." The boys obeyed, but they were still fairly dancing in the back seat. "First we have to thank Ms. Tierney for all she did for us."

Brandon slid across the seat closer to Corey and took her hand. Corey's heart rate accelerated, and she felt a little light-headed as though she had run from her home to the garage instead of merely driving her car.

"I don't like to owe anyone, but I can't think of any way to repay you for all your help."

"Yeah," John piped up. "Grandma always says you shouldn't be beholden to nobody."

Brandon turned his head to grin at the boys. Corey had a feeling he had heard that particular homily many times.

"Well, what do you think we should do to thank Ms. Tierney?" he asked them.

"Peoples always like to come to the ranch and pet the llamas," Robbie suggested.

"Yeah. And we could cook for her like she did for us. Daddy could make beanie weenies," John agreed.

"And she could bring more cookies," Robbie added hopefully.

Brandon dropped Corey's hand as quickly as if it had suddenly scalded him and moved away until his back was against the car door. "I guess we could have her out to the ranch," he said hesitantly.

Corey had a strong suspicion a visit to his ranch wasn't what Brandon had had in mind; but charmed by the boys' invitation, and reacting partly in defiance of his obvious reluctance, she made a snap decision to say yes.

"Why, I would love to see the llamas and eat beanie weenies," she said sweetly with just the slightest touch of irony in her voice.

Brandon hastily opened the car door and uncoiled his long frame to get out as fast as if something were chasing him. He leaned down to say, "Well, all right then; it's all settled. You'll come out this weekend. I'll call you with directions."

He opened the back door and hustled the boys almost at a run over to the tow truck to lift them up into the high cab. He looked to Corey like a predatory animal, strong, but temporarily defeated, beating a hasty retreat.

Feeling strangely self-satisfied, Corey hummed gaily to herself all the way home. She could hardly wait to see Brandon and the boys again. Not once did she remember her resolution to protect herself against getting hurt.

Four

Brandon paced nervously from window to window, looking out at the winding graveled driveway leading up through the forest from the main road to his cabin.

How did I ever manage to get myself into such a fix? All that silly talk, asking the boys what they thought they ought to do to thank Corey for helping them out. He knew John and Robbie could be charming; Corey certainly seemed to be taken with them, so he had thought they would say something cute to thank her, and that would be the end of that. He never could have guessed the little scamps would invite her to the ranch. And what could he say then? Because they did owe her, and he always paid his debts.

After they had finally gotten the pickup running and were back home, he had allowed himself a small span of peace of mind by pretending he wasn't going to call her with directions to the ranch. But he had said he would, and he always kept his word, so he did.

Her voice over the phone was as melodic and soothing as a mountain stream murmuring over mossy stones. The conversation had been brief. He had cheated just a little by making the directions more obtuse than necessary. Perched high up on a mountainside, the log cabin was difficult to find at best. Perhaps she would just give up in disgust and go home. Now why did that thought make him feel so bad?

Brandon pulled the collar of his navy turtleneck away from his throat. For some reason the usually comfortable sweater seemed to be choking him today. He stopped wearing down a path in the wooden floor and paused to lean against the frame of the window with the best view of the drive, his face close enough to the windowpane for his breath to fog the glass. He wiped the window clear with his elbow and sighed.

Maybe subconsciously he really had hoped something like this would happen. It was a fact that there in Corey's home it had strained his self-control to the limit to keep his hands off the woman. She had a wonderful round bottom that positively made a man's palms itch to cup all that luscious womanly softness. The way her old worn denims had outlined her curves was an absolute sin.

But still, he was sure he didn't want her here on his own turf, nosing around in his home and butting into his life. She could take over the whole place if he weren't careful. It was clear she never took no for an answer. He had seen her making all those sandwiches after he had told her not to fix them. He sure didn't think a little thing like her planned to eat all of them herself. Never mind they had ended up having supper with her. She should have waited until he had accepted the invitation.

She was nothing like his wife, Jane. Now there was a woman who minded her own business and did what she was told. He hadn't appreciated her when he'd had her. Well, there was nothing he could do about that now. The only way he could make up for his past neglect of Jane was to take good care of her sons now. And get rid of a potential troublemaker like Corey as fast as he could. This was the second time he had made the mistake of encouraging her, but it wouldn't happen a third time.

He squinted through the clear patch in the foggy window and saw Corey's small blue sedan creeping through the trees. Feeling disgusted with himself, he started toward the door. He was beginning to think like one of those people who seemed to enjoy endlessly analyzing their own motives and debating with themselves about what they should or shouldn't do. He wasn't like that. He always knew exactly what he wanted. And it definitely wasn't Corey Tierney.

The boys must have been watching for Corey, too, from their loft bedroom, because they came tumbling down the stairs and out the door before he could do anything but yell after them to put on their coats. They had heard him, he would be willing to wager, but chose to ignore him, in their eagerness to greet their guest. There, he knew it, she was already disrupting his usually firm discipline, he grumbled to himself. The boys had even broken the standing rule to always close the door behind them.

He decided to take his time going out, pausing to pick his oldest red flannel jacket from the row of wooden pegs driven into the wall by the door. He could see Corey sitting behind the steering wheel and noticed, with perverse pleasure, his dog was making a tremendous racket, barking ferociously and pacing back and forth in front of Corey's car door, so she was afraid to get out, though John and Robbie were trying to reassure her Whiskey wouldn't bite.

Brandon sauntered out to the car, rocked back on his boot heels, stood with thumbs hooked in his jeans' pockets, arms akimbo, and commanded, "Sit, Whiskey."

The noise stopped instantly. Whiskey dropped to her haunches at Brandon's feet, her tongue lolling out. *Good,* he thought with satisfaction, *at least somebody still knows who's boss around here.*

Corey climbed out of the little blue car. *Lord! She looks wonderful.* She wore a close-fitting sweater that, for some inexplicable female reason, was cut short enough to expose a sliver of bare skin, and wool pants. *She sure has a great body. And her face!*

She looks as fresh and radiant as an alpine meadow at dawn. It's going to be awfully hard to get rid of her in a hurry, he thought grimly, *when just looking at her makes me feel so good I want to hop up and down just like the boys are doing.*

"What an unusual-looking dog," she said in her lovely musical voice and bent down to stroke Whiskey's multicolored, speckled coat.

Whiskey's whole body began to shimmy in delight, and she slobbered all over Corey's hand.

"Traitor," Brandon said under his breath. "Whiskey's an Australian shepherd," he said aloud to Corey. "A blue merle Aussie."

Corey cocked her head to one side and shut one eye, then the other. She looked to Brandon like an inquisitive little sparrow. He thought for a moment she was winking at him, but then she said, "I hate to tell you this, but she has one brown eye and one blue. She isn't wearing contact lenses, is she?"

Brandon chuckled. "Nope, it's a characteristic of the breed. Whiskey earns her dog biscuits by patrolling the fences and keeping predators out of the llama pastures."

Corey gave a little shiver. "Predators? There aren't any wild animals around here, are there?"

"Only bears, coyotes and wildcats," Brandon said slyly. *Maybe she'll get so scared she'll jump back in her car and go home right now,* he thought hopefully.

"Mostly Whiskey just barks at other doggies to make them go away," John piped up. *Another traitor,* Brandon thought glumly. It looked like he had a general mutiny on his hands.

John and Robbie were standing on tiptoe to look in the window of Corey's car. "Is that pie for us?" Robbie asked.

Corey smiled and went over to them to open the back car door. "It's cherry. I baked a chocolate cake, too, in case you don't like pie."

She bent over to retrieve the desserts from the back seat. Brandon looked hastily away from the heart-shaped curves formed by her beautiful backside and swallowed the boulder-sized lump that seemed to have suddenly formed in his throat. She straightened and handed him a covered cake plate.

"Would you carry this for me, please?" She turned to delve in the back of the car again and came up this time with a stack of jigsaw puzzles with large pieces for little fingers.

"And these are for you," she said to John and Robbie. She handed each of them several puzzles. With whoops of delight they took the gifts and tore off for the cabin.

"What do we say?" Brandon shouted after them.

"Thank you," drifted back from the disappearing small forms.

Corey shut the car door. "I'll carry the pie," she said happily.

Brandon frowned. "It was supposed to be our turn to do something for you. You shouldn't have brought anything."

"Oh, this isn't anything," she said airily and started walking toward the cabin.

Displeased but resigned, Brandon fell into step beside her. "Did you have any trouble finding the place?"

"I made a few wrong turns, but it's so lovely out here I enjoyed the drive anyway."

I'll bet she took more than a few wrong turns, Brandon thought smugly, remembering his garbled directions. Then he felt a stab of guilt at deliberately misleading someone who, no matter that they hadn't asked her, had done quite a bit for his family.

"Lunch is ready. We held off eating to see if you would show up."

"Oh, I'm so sorry I'm late," she promptly apologized. "I hope the boys aren't too awfully hungry."

Now he really felt bad. She was apologizing for something that was actually his fault. He balanced the cake plate on one hand and held the door open for her to precede him into the cabin.

Corey looked around with interest. The ground floor of the cabin was essentially one big room with about half of the space devoted to a cooking and eating area and the other half a living room. A loft came out over the kitchen, but the living room space soared up the full height of the cabin. A skylight flooded the room with sunshine, causing the pale, smooth logs to glow with a mellow sheen.

"Why, this is really nice," she said, reaching out to trace the smooth curve of one of the huge light yellow logs that made up the walls.

Now, why does she sound so surprised? Brandon wondered contemptuously. *Does she think we live in some kind of filthy hovel?*

Corey put the cherry pie down on a long scrubbed pine table in the kitchen area. She realized the open, spacious feeling of the cabin was heightened by the fact that there was very little furniture. The usual kitchen appliances and the pine table and chairs stood in the cooking area. A large metal box, containing a stack of split firewood, and a wood-burning stove, with a long black stovepipe that stretched almost to the roof before exiting through an opening in the wall, dominated the living area. A roll-top desk with a captain's chair sat in one corner, and a plain brown corduroy couch was pulled up in front of the stove.

That was it. There were no curtains, rugs, pictures or other decorations except for some drawings by the children held in place on the refrigerator door with magnets.

Everything was very clean and very bare. The only redeeming factors that kept the house from looking too austere were the gleaming pale golden wood tones of the magnificent logs and the crackling, welcoming red glow behind the door of the potbellied stove.

John and Robbie were lying on their stomachs on the floor near the stove, putting their new puzzles together. The table was set with paper plates and napkins and plastic tableware, and there was an unmistakable smell of hot dogs and pork and beans in the air.

"Ummm, something smells good. Do I detect your famous beanie weenies?" Corey asked.

Brandon grinned. "Actually, we cooked them in separate pans this time in honor of our visitor. Boys, show Ms. Tierney where the bathroom is and then we'll eat."

Corey put one hand out tentatively to touch Brandon's arm. He moved toward her, and she could feel the smooth, hard biceps contract under the soft, faded red flannel of his jacket. Her hand trembled slightly. "Please. Won't you call me Corey?"

Brandon looked into her eyes for a long moment. "Corey it is then," he said in a deep, husky growl.

Brandon cleared his throat. Corey thought he was going to say something more, but instead he walked over to a coat rack by the door to remove his jacket, and the boys descended on her to lead the way to a small bathroom tucked away under the stairs.

Lunch was a noisy, gay affair. Nobody could decide between pie and cake, so they all had a little piece of each. After they had eaten, everyone helped to clean up. Corey was impressed at how even little four-year-old Robbie automatically, without being told, carried his own used paper plate to the trash and helped John take the hot dog condiments to the refrigerator and put them away. It seemed to her that John and Robbie were about the best-behaved little boys of their age she had ever seen. *Brandon must be doing a good job of raising them,* she thought, *even if he does seem too strict some of the time.*

"Paper plates are really convenient, aren't they?" Corey said, following Robbie to toss her own dirty plate into the trash.

"'Cept they use up all our timber," John said solemnly. "Daddy said we'd have to sacrifice a tree so we could have company."

"'Cause we only have three regular plates," Robbie added.

Corey stole a quick glance at Brandon, up to his elbows in suds at the sink where he was washing the pots and pans. She didn't think it was the hot water that caused the faint flush under his deep tan.

"Okay, guys, it's naptime. Take your puzzles upstairs to put away and hop into bed," he growled.

Both boys ran over to Corey and gave her a quick hug then walked more slowly, reluctantly, to gather up the jigsaw puzzles and head for the stairs. Corey didn't think children, especially boys, were usually so demonstrative. *Perhaps they're just more outgoing than most, or maybe...* Corey looked over again at Brandon, now drying his giant hands, thick wrists and powerful forearms on a tea towel, the sleeves of his navy sweater pushed up above his elbows.

Corey swallowed hard and looked away quickly. Brandon was a tough disciplinarian, but maybe he wasn't so good at other things children needed. Perhaps John and Robbie were simply starved for affection.

"I want to get the boys settled down for their naps. I'll be back in a few minutes, if you don't mind waiting." He draped the tea towel over the pans drying in the dish drainer, pulled his sleeves down and followed the boys to the stairs.

Corey sat down on the couch and stretched her hands out toward the stove, enjoying the warmth, but after a few minutes she got up, feeling strangely restless. She could hear a faint, faraway murmur coming from the loft. She tiptoed up the stairway, even though she felt as though she were acting like a spy.

The loft was divided into two partitioned rooms. When Corey reached the top of the stairs, she could see the first area was the boys' bedroom, furnished with bunk beds, bookshelves and toy boxes. Through the railing that edged the loft, she could look down into the living room, and across the loft she could see through an open door into what was probably Brandon's bedroom.

Brandon was sitting in a large, cushy easy chair by the bunk beds, reading *The Three Little Pigs* to the boys. John was nestled up to him, tucked under the arm holding the storybook. Robbie was sitting on Brandon's lap, a thumb stuck in his mouth, his other hand reaching up to grasp Brandon's earlobe. They were all so engrossed in the story they hadn't noticed Corey's ascent up the stairs.

She paused, still standing on the stair steps with only her head above the level of the loft floor, not wanting to disturb them. Brandon was reading, "...and I'll huff and I'll puff and I'll blow the house down..." in a dramatic, growly wolf voice. John snuggled closer to Brandon, and Robbie tightened his grip on Brandon's ear.

In an involuntary gesture, Corey's hand flew up to her chest. She felt as though a giant fist were squeezing her heart. *How could I think the boys aren't getting enough affection? She* suddenly felt a wave of shame at spying on them. She was an interloper here. They didn't need or want her.

She had seen the spark of desire in Brandon's eyes, felt the current of sexual attraction and thought it meant more than it really had. She had tried so hard to have children; she had wanted a family so badly. She realized, on some hidden level, she had thought she could slip into their lives and fill an empty space, but she had no business here. They were complete, a unit. They didn't need her at all. They might accept her as a friend; Brandon possibly desired her as a lover, but she wanted more. She was going to get hurt, badly hurt.

Almost in a panic, Corey fled down the stairs as quietly as she could manage. She rushed to the kitchen to retrieve her pie pan and cake platter. She found the paper plates in the cupboard and unceremoniously dumped what was left of the desserts on two of them. *They'll just have to sacrifice another tree*, she thought. She was reaching for the doorknob to leave when Brandon came down the stairs. She saw a look of concern cross his face when he took in her distressed appearance.

He crossed the room swiftly to come to her. "Corey, what's the matter? Is something wrong?"

Corey tried to compose herself. She gave him a somewhat shaky smile. "No. I thought I'd take my things out to the car. I'm sure you have lots to do. I'd better get home. When they wake up, would you say good-bye to the boys for me?"

Brandon scanned her face. Something had happened; he was sure of it, but he couldn't imagine what. Something had changed in just the few minutes he had been gone.

"Don't go yet. There isn't anything I have to do today. I wanted to show you the llamas."

Now why did I say that? The words had just popped out of his mouth. He could have kicked himself. Hadn't he been scheming all morning on how to get rid of her in a hurry? Now, like an idiot, he was practically begging her to stay.

Corey looked up into Brandon's dark blue eyes. He seemed sincere. It would be childish to run away as though she had seen a ghost. Well, she had seen a ghost—a ghost of her lost dreams—but she could still behave like an adult. Besides, she had run away without saying good-bye to the boys at the fair, and they had seemed so glad to see her today; she didn't want to risk hurting their feelings. She had come to tour a llama ranch, so tour she would. Then she would go home, dignity intact, and give up her foolish dreams for good.

"All right. I would like to say hello to Starshine and Tulip again." She tried to smile once more; it was a little easier this time.

"You'll be too cold in just that sweater. Let me get you one of my jackets."

"That's okay," she said quickly. She didn't want to wear anything of Brandon's. It seemed far too intimate. "I brought a coat along. It's in the car. I'll go put these things away and get it."

Brandon walked along with her to the car. When she had donned her coat and gloves, he took her mittened hand and tucked it into the crook of his arm to escort her toward the buildings behind the cabin. As they walked, Brandon's hard thigh brushed against Corey's hip. The whole side of her body next to him seemed to be buzzing as though a swarm of bumblebees had taken up residence there. It was hard for Corey to keep up with Brandon's long strides. That had to be why she seemed so short of breath.

They arrived at a medium-sized, barn-like structure with several smaller outbuildings clustered nearby. Brandon slid back the barn door so they could walk through to the paddocks on the other side. A half circle had been fenced on the far side of the barn to form six enclosures. The pens were shaped like the pieces of a pie with the widest part of the wedges away from the barn, the points funneling into one lot containing a watering tank, salt block and feed troughs. Beyond the pens, a large fenced meadow spread out toward the peak of the mountain.

Corey could see all but one of the llamas were in the larger pasture. A dark brown llama was confined in one of the smaller enclosures. Brandon opened a gate for Corey to enter the pen.

"This is Soft Touch. She's due to have a baby any day now, so I have her close by where I can keep an eye on her." Brandon unbuttoned the flap on the pocket of his flannel shirt and pulled out several carrot sticks. "Here. You can give her these. She loves them; she thinks they're candy."

Now that she was close to the llama, Corey noticed her bulging sides. "Poor thing. She looks like she's about to burst. Do you think she's going to have twins?"

"No. I wish she could; I'd double my profits; but llamas hardly ever have twins; and when they do, the babies rarely survive. Her cria—that's another name for a llama baby—could weigh up to thirty-five pounds, though, so she has good reason to be so big."

Corey fed Soft Touch the last of the carrot sticks. She did seem to enjoy them.

"Come on," Brandon said. "Let's go visit the others. The two outer pens have gates through to the field. We can walk straight through here to get to them without climbing a fence."

Soft Touch followed them as they walked toward the meadow. When Corey stopped to wait for Brandon to open the far gate, the llama put her muzzle on Corey's shoulder and breathed moistly on her neck. Corey wished she had more carrots for the soon-to-be mother.

The little herd of llamas stopped grazing when they saw the visitors and drifted toward them. Soon the inquisitive animals surrounded Corey and Brandon. A large red, brown and white llama with a long mane greeted Corey with a snort like a hard sneeze right in her face. Startled, it was all she could do to keep from jumping back.

"Mind your manners, Jester," Brandon scolded. "That's my stud. He gets a little carried away with his hellos sometimes. Lacy is the white and gray one, the caramel-colored one is Plie, and the black one with the white legs and face is Guinevere."

"I already know Starshine," Corey said, reaching out to tentatively pat the llama's beautiful long white wool.

"And there's Tulip." Brandon pointed to a red-brown llama with black points, who was edging through the herd to get her share of attention.

"They're all so lovely and elegant, but I think Starshine is my favorite." Corey stopped stroking the fluffy wool and looked more directly at Brandon. "I'd never even heard of raising llamas before I met you. It seems like a rather, well, unusual occupation. How did you get into it?"

When she saw the sudden stab of pain in Brandon's navy eyes, Corey was sorry she had asked. He looked away toward the mountaintop, and for a moment she thought he wasn't going to answer her. But then he began to speak, still gazing at the mountain peak. He spoke in such a far-away voice, Corey had to strain to hear him.

"I've always loved the forests, the wilderness. I guess it would be fair to say it's all I ever really cared about. I was forever getting into trouble for going camping when my father thought I should be working."

Brandon bent down to pick up a twig. He snapped it in two and threw the broken pieced back to the ground.

"He's a farmer—grows potatoes," he continued, his voice twisted with pain. "When I was old enough to leave home and go out on my own, I didn't need much for myself. I made enough as a guide on backcountry treks to get by. Then I met Jane."

He fell silent. All was quiet except for the whisper of a gentle breeze through the nearby pines and the high-pitched humming of one of the llamas.

"She's the boys' mother?" Corey prodded gently.

"Was," he responded grimly. "She died two years ago in an auto accident. John was three and Robbie was only two."

"How awful," Corey said with a sharp intake of breath. She had wondered a million times about the boys' mother but hadn't wanted to ask. She had never imagined their mother might be dead. "It must have been terribly painful for you."

"It was, but not the way you think." Brandon turned to stare directly into Corey's eyes, and he clenched his prominent jaw with a stubborn look as though he were determined to tell her the truth whether it was palatable or not. "I hardly knew Jane when we married, and I didn't know her much better when she died."

"I don't understand."

"Jane lived with her parents and worked as a waitress at a cafe in a little place up north. There wasn't much there—just the cafe, a market and a gas station. It's a major wilderness area, so I did a lot of camping nearby. I'd always stop in and say hello to Jane when I went through town. She was pretty and friendly, and one night I took her to the nearest burg that had a movie theater."

Brandon shifted uncomfortably from one foot to another and kicked at a clod of dirt. "Well, what can I say? The night was warm, the moon was out, and we got carried away. That's when John was conceived. So we got married."

Corey wondered at the finality of the way Brandon said they had married, as though he were reciting a commandment. "But if you really didn't know one another, didn't you even consider any other alternatives?" she asked curiously, though she knew it was too personal a question.

Brandon clamped his strong jaw down even harder and stared at her with a look of reprimand in his navy eyes. "Like what? There aren't any alternatives as far as I'm concerned. I fathered a child, so I took care of my son and his mother."

Suddenly his face split into a grin. It looked as though a beaming sun had popped out from behind a dark thundercloud, and Corey marveled again at how his face changed when he smiled.

"Come to think of it, that's probably the only thing my father and I ever agreed on. When I was just getting into my teens, he told me about a thousand times, 'You can have all the fun with the ladies you want, but if you get one of them pregnant, you marry her.' And he was right."

Corey thought maybe the ladies in question might have something to say on the subject, but she didn't want to argue with Brandon. The llamas seemed like a safer topic. "That's when you started raising llamas? When you got married?"

"No." The glowing sunshine of his smile disappeared. "I kept right on camping and leading treks. I was hardly ever home. Though I guess I was there often enough, because Robbie was born just one year after John," Brandon said ruefully.

"It was about that time I first came across llamas. I was hired to help with a big hike in Oregon. I was really surprised when I found out the organizers of the trip planned to use llamas for packing. I wasn't too crazy about the idea at first, but by the time we got back, I was a true believer. Llamas have a very low impact on the environment."

Brandon gestured for Corey to follow him as he walked toward Plie. "Come over here. I'll show you. Llamas have a two-toed foot with a leathery kind of pad that makes them really sure-footed and doesn't leave much of a print, probably not as much as a hiker's boot."

Brandon bent down and picked up Plie's foot so Corey could see the toes. She removed one glove to touch the soft, springy pad. Brandon dropped the llama's foot, straightened and brushed off his hands. Corey enjoyed seeing his enthusiasm; Brandon radiated an aura of excitement when he talked about llamas.

"They can go anywhere you can—like over downed wood in a forest or across boulders—and they don't need nearly as much to eat or drink as horses or mules. They mostly browse along the way, taking a little bite here and a nibble there, so they don't kill the plants. They wait patiently at camp; they're safe with people, even kids; and they can pack eighty to one hundred pounds, at least a quarter of their own weight."

Brandon paused, apparently realizing he had launched into a lecture. "Well, anyway, I liked the llamas a lot, but I didn't suppose I'd ever have much to do with them after that trek. We were having a hard time of it. It's really tough trying to support a family on a guide's income, although Jane never fussed about it much. My father did though. He couldn't believe a grown man, with a wife and two children, still spent most of his time hiking around in the woods and sleeping in a tent. Then it happened."

"The accident?" Corey asked, alarmed at Brandon's look of despair.

"Yes. I never even got to say good-bye. I was trekking. I almost missed the funeral; they had to send a helicopter to search for my party to tell me she had died."

"What a tragedy," Corey murmured, thinking of two little boys deprived of their mother and the huge responsibility suddenly thrust upon their father.

Brandon ran rough, agitated fingers through his thick blond hair. "The worst of it was when I started thinking about how little I had ever done for them. Jane was a good woman, a good mother. She took care of everything when I was gone, and I respected her, but I was never there for her, or for the boys either, for that matter. So I decided I had to make it up to them; I had to give up trekking and stay home to take care of them.

"Didn't you have anyone to help you?"

Brandon stiffened as though he had been insulted and said proudly, "I didn't need any help. You sound like my parents. They wanted John and Robbie to live with my sister. I would never agree to that. She does everything our parents tell her to, including working in a bank at a job she loathes. She probably even asks them before she goes to bed with her husband. And she's raising her own daughter the same way. I want my sons to know who they are just like I know who I am. If Sandra had them, they'd turn into little clones of my father."

Corey sensed they were getting into dangerous territory again, judging from the angry expression on Brandon's face. She was gaining fascinating information about his life, far more than she had thought he would reveal to her, but she decided now she should try to steer the conversation in a safer direction.

"So you haven't had the llamas very long?" She could see him visibly relaxing just at the mention of the animals.

"No. We had managed to keep up payments on our insurance policies through all the rough times, thank God. When I started searching for some way to earn a living that would allow me to stay home with the boys, I remembered what the owners of those llamas in Oregon had said. How llamas didn't cost much to raise after you had the breeders, how easy they were to take care of and what high prices they could bring. I did some more research. The more I learned, the more it seemed like the answer. So I used the insurance money to buy this place from my father, and then I got the llamas."

Brandon gave a short bark of angry laughter that caused the llamas drifting away to perk up their banana-shaped ears and stare haughtily at him. "The joke was on him. He'd been using the cabin as a rental to doctor-and-lawyer types. A mountain retreat for vacations. He sold it to me way below market value—probably thought I was going to get a real job in Boise, day care for the boys, and commute. The winters can be pretty bad up here. It might even have been in the back of his mind that after a winter isolated in a cabin with two little kids, I would be willing to let Sandra raise them. Maybe he thought I would eventually really settle down and help him grow potatoes. Anyway, I didn't think it was necessary to tell him about my real intentions," he concluded with a smile that was more of a grimace.

"So what did he say when he found out about the llamas?"

"He was fit to be tied. It's a common reaction. There's a little restaurant in Gooding not far from my father's farm where a lot of ranchers and farmers go for a cup of coffee and to catch up on the local news. My dad said when he told his cronies his son was raising llamas, they nearly laughed him out of the place."

Brandon took Corey's hand and started walking back toward the barn. "Let's go. I need to check on the boys."

Corey took a last look at the peacefully grazing animals. "Goodbye, llamas," she called to them. "I think they are wonderful. I don't see why anyone would object to you raising them."

Brandon shrugged. "It's hard for some people to accept new ideas. It's never mattered to me what anybody else thinks about something, if it's what I want to do. I like to do things my own way."

They reached the gates. Brandon waved his hand to indicate the enclosures. "The barn was already here when I bought the place, but I put in almost all of the fencing myself. It's New Zealand, five feet high with thirteen strands of wire, electrified top and bottom," he said proudly.

"I turned the current off before we came out here," he added when he saw Corey step hastily away from the fence.

"You must have worked very hard, especially taking care of the boys, too, without any help," she said, admiration glowing in her eyes.

He basked in her obviously sincere appreciation of his efforts. "It wasn't all that hard. Now, if we just have lots of healthy female baby llamas to sell, everything will be just fine," he said, looking toward the very pregnant Soft Touch, a trace of worry in his eyes.

They entered the dim, quiet interior of the barn. Dust motes floated in a golden slice of sunlight filtering through a crack in the barn wall. The hushed atmosphere made Corey think she should tiptoe through, almost as though she were in church. Brandon had to be feeling the same way, she thought, because when he spoke to her, his voice was just a raspy whisper.

"It was good of you to listen to me, Corey. Jane's death is something I hardly ever talk about."

Even in the faint light, Corey could see the intense longing on Brandon's face. Her body began to quiver. When Brandon took her in his arms, she was shocked to discover his great, powerful body was also trembling.

He lifted her from the barn floor and pulled her close to him, crushing her against his massive chest. It felt so good to be held in his mighty arms; she felt as though she were enfolded in a magic circle formed by his strength. She lifted her hands to stroke the back of his neck, a hard, thick column of corded muscle.

She could barely understand what he was saying as he lowered his lips to hers. She only heard his deep, husky voice caressing her name. "Corey, oh sweet Corey."

Then nothing existed but the feel of his firm lips, the abrasion of his rough cheek, the warmth and wetness of his tongue invading her mouth. She parted her lips for him, and he caressed her tongue, her teeth, the deep recesses of her mouth. She vaguely heard a low, guttural moan torn from deep in his throat.

Brandon let her slowly slide down the length of his body, and she became aware of the hard, tangible evidence of his desire. He set her feet gently on the barn floor and cupped her bottom in his large palms. He slid his hands up under her coat and sweater to bare skin. His ungloved hands were cold. The shock of his cold, calloused fingers against her warm back returned her to reality—where they were and the significance of what they were doing.

"Brandon, no. I can't... please," she stuttered.

His hands stilled. He took several deep shuddering breaths, slipped his hands out from under her clothing and stepped away from her.

"Right. You're right," he ground out and walked toward the barn door.

His voice grated on her sensitized nerves. All the tenderness and warmth were gone. She blinked rapidly and took several shallow breaths, trying to adjust to the change in mood. She thought she might cry, but she lifted her chin, squared her shoulders and stepped out of the barn with as much dignity as she could muster.

Brandon walked her to the car and opened the door for her, but not once did he look her in the eye, not even when he said goodbye.

Corey managed a shaky thank you for his hospitality and asked him to give her thanks to the boys, feeling sad and regretful that once again she was running out on them without saying goodbye. Then her blue sedan was bumping over the ruts in the driveway toward the main road. She wasn't sure who was steering the car, because her thought were concentrated elsewhere.

She had learned a lot about Brandon today. She thought she might even know a few things about him he didn't know. He might be perfectly capable of raising his sons alone, but if he thought he didn't need anyone else in his life, he was wrong.

Corey had heard need in his voice, seen it in his face, felt it in his body. Someday, a strong, determined woman would teach him just what he needed, but that woman wouldn't be Corey, for she had learned some things about herself, too.

She had discovered that just one kiss could set her afire and make her forget all reason.

She had recovered from her husband's rejection. She had come to terms with the fact she would never have children of her own. She didn't think she'd be able to bear another failure.

Her reaction to Brandon was far too intense. Without even trying, he had already cracked her shell of self-defense. Not seeing him anymore would cause her pain, but if she tried to teach Brandon about love and didn't succeed, she knew she would never be able to put herself back together again.

Five

Corey paused at her desultory clothes sorting when the telephone rang. "I'll get it," she called to Mrs. Gordon, her sixtyish gray-haired assistant who was waiting on a customer.

She walked listlessly to the phone and made a real effort to sound cheerful or, if she couldn't manage cheerful, at least businesslike. "Kids' Kloset. May I help you?"

"Corey, it's Brandon."

At the sound of Brandon's deep voice, all her senses went on immediate red alert. Her muscles tensed, her eyes dilated, and her heart hammered painfully in her chest.

She had told herself over and over, until it had practically become a litany, that her feelings for Brandon were merely a trifling infatuation. She had convinced herself she believed it, too, except perhaps when she lay sleepless late at night, watching her digital clock's glaringly bright numerals advance. So why now was her stomach clinched into a tight little knot while blood pounded at her temples?

A whole month had gone by, not that she was counting, since she had visited Brandon. She hadn't seen or heard from him since, though when she was at home, it had taken fierce self-discipline to restrain herself from peering through the windows facing the grade school at the times Brandon might be dropping off or picking up John. *The desire to see him was bound to fade eventually, so why did he have to call now, after so much time had passed, and stir things up again?* she wondered resentfully.

Today Brandon's voice held a note of urgency she had never heard in it before. "I hated to call you, Corey; but I couldn't think of anything else to do."

Thanks a lot, Corey thought huffily. Here was a man who really knew how to ruffle a woman's feathers.

"Soft Touch is having her baby, but it doesn't seem to be going right, and I'm afraid to leave her. It's almost time to pick up John, and I don't have anyone else to get him."

Brandon paused. Corey could almost hear him swallowing his pride before he actually asked for help. "I know you're at work. I really hate to bother you, but is there anyway you could... what I mean is... do you think you might be able to...?"

Another long pause. Corey suddenly realized, to her horror, she couldn't manage to squeak out a single word.

Brandon sighed, then said in a dejected voice, "Oh, hell, I shouldn't have disturbed you. Just forget I ever called." There was a loud click then a hum.

Corey slowly replaced the telephone receiver. She hadn't intentionally refused to answer him, but it was no doubt for the best. He would find a way to deal with his crisis. Anyway, it wasn't her problem.

But still she remained standing by the telephone. She closed her eyes and willed herself to walk away and go back to work. Two quick scenes flashed behind her closed lids: a little boy sitting all alone on a sidewalk, and an animal in trouble trying to give birth.

Corey opened her eyes and looked out the storefront windows at a blanket of white flakes. She had been sorting clothes in the back storage room and hadn't realized it had started to snow.

Corey took a deep breath. *Oh, fudge!* She absolutely, positively could not ignore someone who needed help, no matter what the cost might be to her. She reached for the telephone, called directory assistance, then dialed Brandon's number.

"Hello, Brandon? I, ahm, had a little frog in my throat. Of course, I'd be glad to pick up John. You just took me by surprise. I'm sorry I didn't answer you more quickly. One of my helpers is here today, so it's no problem with the store. I'll leave right now and drive him home.

It made Corey feel good to hear the relief in Brandon's voice. "Are you sure? It's snowing pretty hard. Do you think you can make it out here? You might need chains on your tires."

"Don't worry about a thing," Corey said with confidence. "I'm an old hand at driving the back roads in rough weather. We'll be there soon."

"Thank you, Corey. I can't tell you what this means to me. I'll call the school and let John's teacher know you're going to pick him up. Since that time the truck broke down, I made an arrangement with her to keep him in the classroom until I get there. I'll be watching for you. Bye for now."

Brandon's voice had deepened to such a warm, inviting register it caused a quiver of anticipation to dart along Corey's spine. *Oh, dear Lord, what have I let myself in for?*

Mrs. Gordon willingly agreed to stay late to close up the store, though Corey made her promise to call her husband to see her safely home through the snow. The customers she had been helping had left in time for Mrs. Gordon to observe, with a rather speculative look on her wrinkled, plump face, the last bit of Corey's telephone conversation. Corey found herself unaccountably blushing when she explained to Mrs. Gordon why she needed to leave early.

Shame on you, Corey scolded herself, *you're not some schoolgirl getting ready for a date; this is an act of pure Christian charity.* Nevertheless, she took the time to put on a little lipstick and brush her hair before setting out to get John.

Corey drove cautiously across the slippery street to the elementary school, checked in at the main office, found the kindergarten room and introduced herself to John's teacher, a tall, striking brunette dressed in a fashionable, short skirt. Miss Daugherty looked Corey up and down with a rather cool, appraising stare.

"Yes, Mr. Wolfe called to say he was sending someone to pick up John. Such an intelligent man and so involved with his son's education. I'm sure that's why he has requested so many parent-teacher conferences."

Corey had a sudden uncharitable and definitely un-Christian urge to step squarely on Miss Daugherty's high-heeled instep. She refrained from any such unladylike display and concentrated instead on greeting John, who was delighted to see her. Corey helped him into his parka, tying the hood snugly under his chin. She noted with amusement two giant safety pins securing each mitten to a sleeve.

She hustled him out to her little blue car and carefully helped him fastened the seatbelt on the passenger side. She noticed he thoroughly examined the back seat before allowing himself to be buckled up and, once seated, looked across the street toward her green-shuttered house where the roof was already frosted with snow.

"Didn't you bring any cookies?" he asked, his voice sounding disappointed.

Corey smiled at his woebegone little face, wishing she had some sort of a snack for him. "Not today, I'm afraid. But I'll bake some for you soon, I promise. Maybe gingerbread Pilgrims since it's almost Thanksgiving time."

That perked him up. "I'm gonna be a turkey in the Thanksgiving program. Wanna hear me gobble?"

John chattered nonstop all the way to Roby Creek, frequently interrupting himself to practice his gobble. The snow was coming down thicker now, greatly hindering visibility. Corey was immensely grateful for her new all-weather tires as she negotiated the treacherous highways, but it still took her almost an hour and a half to make a trip normally requiring only about forty-five minutes.

She didn't think the car was going to make it up the final steep drive to the cabin, but the little sedan surprised her by biting through the now deep snow to the gravel underneath and clawing its way all the way up to Brandon's doorstep.

Corey's shoulders slumped in relief when she finally turned off the ignition. As much as she enjoyed John's company, she wasn't used to having anyone in the car with her, much less someone who never stopped talking. She realized now what a strain the drive had been.

She looked out the window and saw Brandon carrying Robbie slung on one hip, striding, in spite of the handicap of child and snow, at a great pace down from the barn toward the car. *He must be wearing seven-league boots,* she thought, smiling tenderly at the welcome sight.

He had made a few concessions to the cold, she noticed. A navy knit cap, dotted with large white snowflakes, was pulled down to his thick dark blond brows, and he wore a heavy jacket but still no gloves. To think it had been such a simple thing as a lack of gloves that had saved her from herself the last time she was here. *Maybe I should buy him a pair for Christmas,* she thought wistfully.

When Brandon reached the car, he yanked the door open impatiently. He spoke so rapidly his words seem to tumble out of his mouth. "Corey, come quick. Soft Touch needs help."

Corey squeezed her eyes shut for a heartbeat. What a painful irony that someone expected her to know what to do at a birth. But she had to try to help. She scrambled out of the car and immediately sank into the soft snow. Fortunately, she had worn boots today under her best pair of gray wool slacks, but they were her good black leather dress pair, not exactly the right outfit for a barnyard. Oh well, helping was what was important, not what happened to her clothes.

"What about the children?" Corey asked as Brandon used his free hand to steady her as they tramped through the snow to the passenger side of the car. The strength of his firm grip sent darts of excitement all up and down her arm. She shivered, but it wasn't from the cold.

Corey helped John out of the car. It looked to her like the snow was already deep enough to get into his little red rubber boots.

Brandon bent to pick up John. "I can carry both of them, if you think you can make it. I have a warm place for them in the barn."

"Go ahead. I'll follow you."

"Try to step in my tracks; it will be easier going."

Corey realized with alarm that the snow was falling so thickly now it was hard to see more than a few feet ahead. Even weighted down with a child on each hip, Brandon took long strides. Corey had to leap from one footprint to the next in order to follow in his path. By the time they got to the barn, she was winded. Brandon wasn't even breathing hard. Corey stamped her feet and brushed at her pants legs and coat to rid herself of the clinging snow. Brandon put the boys down.

"Come on, John. Come see the fort Daddy made for me," Robbie said, tugging on John's sleeve.

John resisted. "Is Soft Touch gonna have her baby? I wanna see it."

"The baby isn't here yet. You can see it when it comes. I want you and Robbie to stay in the fort. It's warmer there, and you can eat raisins and bananas and peanut butter sandwiches. I don't think we're going to be able to have a regular supper."

"Oh, boy," John said, his face brightening at the mention of food.

Corey admired the way Brandon patiently took the time to settle the boys down in spite of his anxiety about Soft Touch. A small electric heater was warming one of the stalls in the barn. Bales of hay and old blankets made the "fort" at the far end of the small enclosure. Sandwiches and fruit were packed in a knapsack. The boys were soon happily playing soldiers while munching on their rations.

Brandon came out of the stall hurriedly, shutting the half door behind him. He stopped abruptly, as though frozen on the spot, and stared at Corey as she took off her black wool beret and shook her hair to loosen the last few snowflakes. She smiled at him, wondering why he had such a strange expression on his face. She couldn't see herself as he did: her face glowing pink, the softly flowing gold-touched brown hair, her bright eyes radiating warmth and something more. Suddenly, there was a sort of grumbling hum from one of the stalls. The sound seemed to release Brandon from his trance.

"That's all a man needs when there's work to be done—a beautiful woman to make him want to start spouting compliments," he muttered.

"What did you say?" she asked in confusion.

He ignored her question and gestured toward the stall from where the noise had come. "She's been humming like that for quite awhile now. It's not her normal sound. And she's been up and down all day. I thought I saw a foot coming out when you drove up. Maybe she's already delivered," he finished hopefully.

Brandon went over to the stall and opened the door. Corey followed timidly. She'd never been around animals giving birth, not even a cat or a dog. She peeked around Brandon and saw Soft Touch lying in the straw, both back legs off to one side. A tiny, sac-covered hoof protruded from the llama.

"Nothing has happened," Brandon said grimly. "It's taking way too long. Llamas are supposed to have easy births. All the books said the deliveries should go very quickly."

"I guess Soft Touch didn't read the books," Corey said, feeling a little giddy.

"We have to do something. Corey, can you reach in to find out what's wrong?"

"Me!!" she sputtered in shocked disbelief.

In a lightning-fast move, Brandon grabbed her wrist and held her hand up to his, palm to palm. Even enlarged by black leather driving gloves, her hand looked tiny compared to his giant paw.

"If you were having a baby, whose hand would you want to do the exploring?" he asked.

Corey swallowed hard. "Okay. What do I do?"

"You need to wash up. The water is freezing cold out here, but I don't think you should take the time to go inside. Do you think you can stand it?"

Corey nodded numbly, incapable of speech.

"Good. After your hands are clean, you put on the surgical gloves I have in my birthing bag."

Brandon smiled encouragingly at her and slipped her gloves off slowly, holding both her hands in his for a brief moment before letting them slide through his fingers in a gesture that seemed intensely sensuous. He turned away to check his supplies, leaving Corey staring blankly at nothing at all. How was it possible for just the touch of his hands to make her feel as though she were sizzling on a tropical beach instead of shivering in a barn in the midst of a blizzard?

Brandon directed Corey to the faucet at the watering tank and poured liquid soap on her hands while she scrubbed them under the freezing water until they were red and numb. She wondered how she would be able to feel anything at all. Brandon helped her don the surgical gloves, and they reentered the stall where Soft Touch lay.

Corey knelt in the straw, holding her hands out in front of her as though they belonged to somebody else, and looked up at Brandon beseechingly, silently begging for help.

"The head and front feet are supposed to come out first," he instructed. "Just reach inside and tell me what you feel."

Corey gingerly slipped one hand inside Soft Touch who, to Corey's amazement, didn't seem to be paying any attention to them at all.

"I think I can feel the other foot," Corey said hesitantly. "It seems to be bent backwards."

"Good. You're doing just fine. Try to straighten it so it's parallel with the one we can see."

To Corey's surprise the foot moved quite easily when she tugged on it. "It's straight," she told Brandon.

"Okay. I don't know anything else to do. I don't think we should pull, at least not yet. We'll just have to wait now, I guess."

Corey pulled off the rubbery gloves and stood by Brandon. Both of them seemed to be holding their breath as they staring at the laboring Soft Touch. In a short while, a nose appeared.

Brandon grabbed Corey's shoulders and squeezed hard enough to hurt, but Corey hardly noticed, for she was as intensely concerned over the llama as he was. There were a few more contractions, then, with a slithery slide, a baby llama dropped to the straw.

Brandon pulled Corey from the stall, picked her up and whirled her around in the air as easily as if she were a child. He set her down, his face ablaze with happiness, and hugged her to him.

"You did it; you saved her," he said in a choked voice. "Corey Tierney, you are one terrific lady."

Corey felt inordinately pleased at his praise, though she wasn't so sure she'd had all that much to do with it.

The boys came tearing out of their stall. "Has the baby come? Can I see it now?" John cried excitedly.

Brandon pointed to the new baby flopping around in the straw.

"Yuck! It's all slimy like a snake," John said in disgust.

Robbie didn't say a word just stared round-eyed in silent awe.

"Would you mind staying inside the house with the boys for a while, Corey? I want to dry the baby off a little since it's so cold; llamas don't have an instinct to lick their babies. And I should dip the umbilical cord in iodine. It needs to nurse, too, before we're really out of the woods. I want to watch until it gets started."

Corey readily agreed. Brandon helped them to the cabin. Corey was grateful for his assistance. She wasn't sure they could have made it by themselves. She had read stories about country people getting lost between the barn and the farmhouse and freezing to death in the blinding snow only a few feet from their own doorstep, but she had never imagined she could be in a situation even remotely similar.

Once snugly inside, she helped the boys with their coats and boots and got out of her own wraps while Brandon fought his way back to the barn. She found an old-fashioned percolator in the dish drainer and made coffee, feeling sure Brandon would want some when he came back into the cabin.

It wasn't until she was comfortably curled up on the couch, sipping scalding hot coffee and contentedly watching the boys playing by the stove, that the thought occurred to her. She was stranded at the cabin! There was no way she could possibly drive down the mountain in this storm.

Stunned, she sat immobilized on the couch. Why hadn't she realized her predicament earlier? She had been so caught up in the exciting role of midwife that she hadn't given a thought to her own well-being. She should have beat a hasty retreat the minute she had seen John safely home when the roads just might still have been passable. Now she was stuck.

She got up and put her cup in the sink. She couldn't swallow another drop. She began pacing nervously back and forth in the kitchen area. What was she going to do?

She took several deep breaths and forced herself to calm down. After all, she and Brandon were adults. He could hardly kick her out in the snow after she had helped him. He would just have to put her up for the night, even if it inconvenienced him. She was sure he would behave like a gentleman. But she knew it wasn't really Brandon's behavior she was worried about. It was her own.

There was a banging at the door, and Corey ran in her stocking feet to open it. There stood Brandon so covered in snow he looked like a giant snowman. He was carrying the
little llama wrapped in old towels. Corey gaped at him.

"Quick. Let me in. You're letting all the warm air out."

Corey jumped aside. Brandon carried the baby llama to a corner of the cabin not too close to the stove, and Corey quickly shut the door against the frigid blast of wind-driven snow. The boys crowded around their father to watch as he unwrapped the towels and put them on the floor for the baby to lie on.

"It's a boy," Brandon said in such a comically disgusted voice that Corey almost giggled in spite of her worries.

"Does it really matter? I thought your line was supposed to be it didn't make any difference as long as he was healthy."

"Of course it matters," Brandon snapped. "I can sell a female for a much higher price than a male. And besides that, he may not even be healthy. He hasn't nursed yet, and it's been way over an hour since he was born. He's not even curving his neck up looking for milk like he's supposed to."

"What can we do?" Corey asked, alarmed now, too, for the little baby animal she had helped to bring into the world.

"He just kept getting quieter and moving less all the time. That's why I brought him in here. I think he's smaller than he should be, and it's so cold. I guess I'll try to milk Soft Touch and bottle feed him."

"Is that possible?"

"It had better be," Brandon said grimly, "I can't afford to lose any babies."

He went to the kitchen cabinets, quickly rummaged about until he found a small metal pail and then started toward the door. The snow had melted on his jacket and hat, and his clothes were steaming now in the warm room. Corey ran after him.

"Wait! Warm up a little before you go back out. I made coffee. You could at least take a few minutes to drink a cup."

"Thanks," he said, not even pausing to look at her. "I'll have some after I get the milk."

She clutched at his sleeve. "Be careful, please. It's really bad out there."

He turned and registered her concern. One of those quick dazzling smiles lit his face. "Don't worry about me. I'm an old mountain man. I've been out for days in a lot worse than this with just a sleeping bag."

Worried now about Brandon's welfare in addition to her own dilemma, but with no means to resolve either of their problems, Corey wandered over to join John and Robbie where they were watching the baby llama. She sat down cross-legged on the floor next to the little llama, and the boys nestled up to her.

"Can I pet him?" John begged.

"I don't really know. Maybe we'd better just look until we can ask your daddy."

The baby was dry now, fluffy and utterly adorable with its graceful neck, pert little nose and curved-in-a-smile mouth, alert banana-shaped ears and long, stiff eyelashes. The body, short tail and back legs were light brown, the front legs and neck were white and the head was dark brown. Corey wanted to pet him almost as much as John did.

The little creature stared right at Corey with his bright button eyes, and she could almost imagine he wanted to thank her for helping him out into the world.

She sighed regretfully. Birth was truly the universal great miracle in both the animal kingdom and for humankind. She tried to always keep her thoughts in the present and not dwell on disappointments from the past, but it was impossible now not to remember her own struggles to have a baby.

She had been so impressed with Wayne when they had first met at a party at her parents' home in Twin Falls. He was several years older than she was—thirty-two to her twenty-one at the time—and had a successful law practice. Her father had gone on and on about how fast Wayne had risen in their field.

Corey had been quite flattered by the attentions of the older, accomplished man, and though she was initially surprised when he proposed only a few months later, it didn't take her long to accept his offer of marriage. After all, even though she was in her third year of college at the time, her real goal had always been to be a wife and mother, and Wayne, with a beautiful home, financial security and declarations of undying love, seemed as though he would make a perfect husband and father.

Corey sighed again, long and gusty, and the baby llama stretched his neck toward her. Corey couldn't resist running her fingers along the white fluff, but even as she delighted in the newborn's charm, the past tugged at her.

She should have known better than to have married for such prosaic reasons, for she had recognized, even with so little experience at twenty-one, that what she had felt for Wayne wasn't love. She had thought love would come later. How could she have been so foolish?

Still, the first year or so had gone smoothly. Wayne had made it clear from the very first he wanted a son as soon as possible. Corey had delighted in fitting out one of their spacious home's large, sunny rooms with the best nursery furniture and accessories money could buy. She had been rather like a little girl playing with a life-sized dollhouse, she thought wistfully.

Wayne had sometimes embarrassed her in company by bragging about what a great little baby maker he had married. He would grab her by the hips and squeeze her playfully while telling everyone she was shaped perfectly to spit out babies. She had forgiven him then, thinking his intentions were good, even if his form of expression was in extremely poor taste, but now the very memory made her shudder.

Her own family had been subtler but just as persistent, inquiring, in one way or another every time they saw her, when she was going to announce she was expecting. She was the youngest of three older sisters and two brothers, all married with numerous children of their own. They all believed in large families, and she hadn't faulted them, because it was what she believed in, too.

And then the pain had started. Deep inside her body, eventually so excruciating she couldn't bear even the thought of being touched. She had tried to hide it for months, thinking it was just her imagination. She had always been disgustingly healthy; she had even managed to miss most of the common childhood ailments, so she had thought the pain had to be a sign she had turned into a hypochondriac.

But it had become so bad she couldn't keep it a secret. When she had told Wayne, he had rushed her to the doctor. Her life had become an endless round of appointments, tests and examinations. Laparoscopy had finally confirmed the doctor's diagnosis. A tube with a special light and lens had been inserted into her abdomen. She had endometriosis: the lining of her uterus was growing where it didn't belong—on the ovaries, fallopian tubes and connecting ligaments. When she was menstruating, these spots of tissue would bleed, too, but there was no place for the blood to go, so the bloody cysts had formed that had caused her so much pain.

The treatment had been almost as bad as the disease. First, the doctors had tried a hormone therapy that had caused her to gain weight until she had hardly recognized herself. Then later, surgery had been recommended to rid her of the adhesions, followed by more drug therapy to prevent reoccurrence. Finally, the doctors had pronounced the treatment a success. She had been infertile, they had said, because her eggs had been unable to get to the uterus, but now there were no obstructions, though there were no guarantees there would be no regrowth.

Wayne had stood by her through all the painful and expensive treatments, but after they were over, their relationship had deteriorated rapidly. Wayne had become a driven man, absolutely determined to impregnate her as quickly as possible. Lovemaking became as clinical as a doctor's appointment. She had come to hate what she had begun to think of as just a continuation of her treatment. Sex was an unpleasant duty to be gotten through as hastily as possible.

But still no baby. After another year of trying, Wayne had told her he wanted a divorce.

She had felt betrayed, devastated by his rejection. But part of her had felt he was right; she had failed to provide him with an heir, which had been the reason, the only reason, he'd married her.

Her self-esteem at an all time low, she had left the beautiful house she had thought was her home, not planning to ask for anything from Wayne. But her lawyer father had insisted she get an attorney to represent her at the divorce proceedings. As it turned out, her lawyer had had little work to do. Wayne had voluntarily given her a more-than-generous divorce settlement. She was sure it was because he had pitied her; he had thought she was worthless since she couldn't have children.

Corey's mouth twisted in a bitter smile as she remembered, and a tear trickled down her cheek. Startled out of her painful memories by little fingers patting her face, she almost jerked away before she focused on John kneeling beside her, his childish features a mask of sympathy as he worriedly studied her with big, round eyes.

"Does your tummy hurt?" he asked anxiously.

"Why, no, John," she said, managing a shaky smile. "I was just being silly. I guess I got too excited over the new baby."

He pointed at her fist gripping a handful of llama wool. "You said we couldn't touch," he said reproachfully.

"You're absolutely right. I'm sorry; I forgot."

She loosened her unconsciously clenched fist and gave John a reassuring hug, though whether it was meant to comfort him or her she couldn't have said.

Then a blast of cold air swept through the cabin, and Brandon entered, triumphantly swinging his little metal pail, a gleeful smile stretching from ear to ear.

Six

"I got the milk," Brandon crowed.

Corey scrambled to her feet and went to the door to greet him, dabbing at her eyes, hoping her bout with the past didn't show on her face. Brandon handed her the pail to hold while he got out of his snow-encrusted boots and coat. The bucket was still slightly warm from the milk.

"Boy, was that a job. Soft Touch screamed bloody murder when I milked her. She didn't seem to mind all the poking around you did. I don't see why she made such a fuss with me, but I won anyway," he boasted.

He looked wonderful to Corey as he gloated over his victory—his lean Nordic face was ruddy with cold and radiant with pleasure over his success, his dark blue eyes snapped with excitement, his golden hair haloed his head in a crown worthy of a king. Brandon raised his arms in a long stretch. Corey caught her breath at the sight of taut muscles along the whole long length of him. He was so intense about everything he did. When she suddenly realized she was wondering if he made love with the same intensity, she looked away hastily.

"Now we have to find a way to get the milk down the little critter," he said, more subdued now as he apparently realized there was still another challenge to be met.

He looked over at the llama and saw Robbie had fallen asleep on the floor beside it. He looked hesitantly back at Corey. "I hate to keep asking you to do things for me, but do you suppose you could manage just one more chore?"

"What?"

"Well, I want to feed the little one right away. I saved a box of John and Robbie's baby things when we moved here. I think there might still be a baby bottle in it. Do you think you could get the boys upstairs and into bed while I try to do the feeding?"

"Putting John and Robbie to bed wouldn't be a chore for me," she said quickly. "I'd be glad to help."

He seemed surprised she had agreed so readily. He looked her up and down as though he were judging the strength of a pack mule. "I don't know; now that I think about it, you look pretty puny to me. Robbie is asleep already, and he's heavy. I don't know if you could make it up the stairs with him," he said rather uncertainly.

Corey burst into laughter at his ridiculous assessment, though his frank appraisal of her physical abilities had made her flush hotly. "Don't be silly. Of course I can carry a four-year-old child. And as I said, I would enjoy taking care of them. Go ahead and feed the baby. I'm worried about him, too."

Brandon still seemed to hesitate as though he doubted her ability to handle the boys. Corey stepped forward, intending to give him a playful push to get him started looking for the baby bottle, but the moment she laid her hands on the solid wall of his muscular chest, she knew she had made a serious tactical error.

Brandon caught both her wrists in one of his large hands and pulled her up against him. He encircled her with his free arm and pressed her tightly to his body. Every part of him she touched was rock hard. She could feel the rapid, rhythmic throbbing of his heart like a great engine against her palms.

For a few minutes she relaxed against his strength. Her flesh felt soft and malleable as though it might melt and flow until it molded against him, but her heart was fluttering in a wildly erratic way against her rib cage. She began to struggle.

Feeling ashamed, Brandon immediately released her. He clamped his arms tightly against his sides and fought to suppress his surge of desire. Every time she was near, the desire to touch and hold her grew until he was afraid it would overpower him, but when he felt her struggle in his arms, it reminded him of a caged bird. He had never been able to bear seeing wild things captured. If she didn't want him that way, he would have to control himself if it killed him.

Corey backed away, staring at him with wide, frightened eyes. She opened her mouth but couldn't think of a thing to say, so she turned toward the children and fled.

Brandon sucked in a great lungful of air and let it out slowly, trying to calm his racing pulse. It was unnerving the way this thing he felt for Corey would strike when he least expected it. He would be resolutely going about his business when a glance at her lovely face and soft body would zing him like the sting of a rattler. And when she touched him, it was more like a wolf at his jugular. She was strong stuff, and he'd best beware.

Now she was struggling to lift Robbie. He smiled admiringly at her determination when she managed to rise unsteadily to her feet under the weight of the limp, boneless deadweight of the sleeping child. She probably had had no idea of how heavy even a small boy could seem when he was asleep. He quelled his own strong urge to go to her aid. It wasn't safe to be near her until he got himself back under control.

And he had something he was supposed to take care of, didn't he? *What was it? Damn!* He had forgotten all about the baby llama. It still hadn't been fed. His investment was wasting away while he stood here like a fool mooning over a little bit of a woman who didn't even want him to hold her.

He couldn't afford to lose a single cria. He had to raise one big enough to sell soon, or his whole business would crumble. Then how would he take care of his sons? Go get a job he hated? If he could even find anyone to hire him—he didn't know anything but mountains. Run begging to his father? He ground out a curse at the very idea and resolved for the thousandth time to succeed at breeding llamas.

He hastened to the closet where he thought he had stored the baby things. When he found the box, he rummaged through the jumbled contents until he unearthed a bottle and a somewhat disreputable-looking nipple. He ran his thumb over the nipple, flexing it back and forth. Fortunately, the rubber hadn't crumbled away; the nipple was still sound.

He debated about boiling the nursing equipment but decided Soft Touch's teat wouldn't have been sterilized so surely a wash in good hot water and soap would do.

As he hurriedly prepared the bottle, he couldn't prevent his thoughts from returning to Corey. He remembered her face when she had helped Soft Touch. She had been uncertain and fearful, but she had gritted her teeth and gotten on with it. She was quite a woman. She would make a wonderful partner for a man. She was more than equal to facing all the trials of life with courage and spirit.

When he realized just where his thoughts were leading, Brandon almost spilled the hard-won milk he was pouring from the pail into the bottle. He had absolutely no right to be thinking like that. Corey was a successful career woman who owned her own well-established and apparently profitable business while his own new enterprise had yet to make a dime. He had nothing to offer a woman.

As abhorrent as the idea was to him, the truth of the matter was his livelihood still came from his poor dead wife. He gripped the bottle so hard his knuckles turned white. How could it be that he, who hated to be dependent upon anyone for anything, was living off a woman?

I should have found a way to handle this situation today without running to Corey for help. There were probably dozens of solutions to my dilemma if I'd just used some logic to think of one. Oh hell, I might as well admit it; I just wanted to see her. Well, I've seen her, and she's made me forget everything that's important. And now she's stuck here with snowdrifts outside the size of the Big Horn Crags.

A slow, lazy smile drifted to his lips. Somehow, good idea or not, he just couldn't resist reflecting on all the possibilities that brought to mind.

Upstairs, Corey was trying to cope with the bittersweet pleasure of tucking the boys into bed. This was the career she had dreamed of, prepared for her whole life. Never once when she was growing up had she imagined her future would be childless.

Seeing all the children in her store helped some—that was why she had used her divorce settlement to set up the resale shop. It helped assuage her craving to be around children and allowed her to help their parents at the same time—but it was nothing like the joy of parenting.

With great self-importance, John was explaining the bedtime routine. He pulled back the covers on the lower bunk for Corey so she could put Robbie down. He fetched Robbie's and his own pajamas and struggled out of his clothes while Corey eased Robbie's limp arms and legs out of sweater and jeans and into flannel PJs. John insisted on tucking his brother in all by himself, though in his enthusiasm to help, he covered Robbie's whole head with the blankets. Corey quickly corrected the overzealous tucking when John turned his back to lead the way to the connecting bathroom between the two loft bedrooms.

In the bathroom John pointed out where his toothbrush and the toothpaste were stored and vigorously showed Corey how you were supposed to brush your teeth until the whole lower half of his face was covered with foamy bubbles. He looked rather like a child version of a mad dog, but Corey managed to maintain a respectful attention, though it took intense self-discipline to keep from laughing. It wasn't until he wanted to demonstrate how his daddy had taught him big boys use the potty that Corey declined, suggesting big boys might need a little privacy.

Corey waited for John in the overstuffed chair by the bunk beds. When he came marching out of the bathroom, his bright blue eyes lit up when he saw where she was sitting.

"That's the reading chair. Daddy always reads us stories before we go to bed."

Corey smiled. "All right. I see you have lots of books on your shelves. Pick your favorites."

John peeked up slyly at her through the long, thick lashes that looked so like his father's. "Daddy always reads ten stories," he said, clearly fibbing.

"Ten! How about two?"

"Maybe five," he countered.

"Three. And that's my final offer."

John considered solemnly. "Okay," he agreed.

Negotiations completed, Corey settled back and enjoyed the colorfully illustrated children's books. John was nodding by the time she finished the third story, his eyes half closed, and made no protest when she tucked him into the top bunk. Corey brushed his white-blond hair away from his forehead and kissed his cheek before she carefully fitted the safety rail in place.

Then she took a deep breath and smoothed her cream cable-knit sweater down over her gray wool slacks. There was no telling what might be waiting for her downstairs.

Corey crept down the stairs just in time to see the baby llama lustily suck down the last few drops of milk. Brandon heard her approaching and turned to grin at her. He gently pulled the nipple away from the hungry llama and wagged the empty bottle back and forth to show Corey all the milk was gone.

"It worked," he said proudly. "I'll go see if I can get some more milk in a few hours. Then if he's up on his feet by morning, I'll take him back out and introduce him to his mother. Maybe he'll be able to nurse by then."

Brandon got up from the floor, took the bottle to the sink, then went to the couch and sank down wearily. He scrubbed at his forehead with one hand, causing his hair to stick up at odd angles, then noticed Corey was still standing, just watching him. He patted the couch cushions beside him.

"Come sit down. It's been quite a day. You must be tired."

Corey joined him on the couch, easing herself down gingerly in the corner as far from him as possible. She didn't trust herself for a minute. She had the strangest urge to run her fingers through that messy golden hair, throw herself against him and cover his face with kisses. She had never dreamed she had such a talent for erotic fantasies. Some of the things she imagined them doing were truly shocking, coming from her conservative Sunday-school background. But then, it was part of the great design for a man and a woman to come together. She had just never been with the right man to bring out that part of her nature.

Trying to take her mind off her lascivious thoughts, Corey looked over at the baby llama still lying in his nest of towels but now arching his neck up, looking for more milk. He looked so sweet and so very vulnerable.

"You're not going to take such a little thing out in the snow, are you? It's really cold even in the barn. Come to think of it, why was he born now in November, anyway? I thought the stork brought all the baby animals in the spring."

Brandon smiled at her, feasting his eyes on her fresh, innocent face and warm, caring eyes. He focused resolutely above her neck, not daring to look any lower. Maybe if he concentrated on the llamas, he could keep himself from grabbing her and kissing her until she was breathless.

"Llamas are native to the Andes; they're used to the cold. I just brought this one in because he wasn't nursing and didn't seem very strong. And they can be born anytime of the year."

She followed him attentively as he talked. She made him feel like an expert, as though he knew everything in the world worth knowing. Her soft, moist lips were parted slightly; he could see a tiny gleam of white teeth. He longed to press his mouth against hers. *Llamas. I'm supposed to be thinking about llamas.*

"Soft Touch was my first llama; she'd just been bred when I bought her. It's been almost a year now; the gestation period is usually about three hundred and fifty days. Jester serviced the rest of my females. They're all due in the spring and summer."

"But if the bottle feeding is successful, maybe you should keep him inside for a few days anyway, just in case. He's such a little bit of a thing."

Brandon watched the way the perfect pink bow of Corey's upper lip danced above her soft, full lower lip when she talked. He wanted to kiss those lips so badly he could already taste them. He definitely didn't want to sit there discussing animal husbandry. On the other hand, as long as they were talking about llamas, instead of, say, what tonight's sleeping arrangements were going to be, they were probably safe.

"That might make a good name for him, 'Little Bit.' No, sounds more like a female. You can name him, if you want, since you delivered him."

"Oh, thank you. It would be fun to give him a name. I'll ask the boys for suggestions tomorrow. I think they're more imaginative than I am. But I still don't think you should put a baby out in the snow."

"I don't want to bottle feed him any longer than I have to. He needs to bond with his mother and the other llamas. If a baby is over-handled before he's six months old, he can imprint with the people feeding him."

"But that wouldn't matter, would it?"

"Yes, it could. When he grows up, he would think humans are the same as llamas, and he might spit at a person to show dominance or knock someone down. It's worse with males. I'd probably have to geld him if I kept him inside much longer. There's even a name for it—'the berserk male syndrome.'"

Corey broke into peals of musical laughter. "I think that's a really excellent term. I believe I know a few men we might apply it to."

Brandon smiled easily along with her, no need to take offense at her anti-male sentiments; he liked making her laugh. He started to reach along the couch to pull her to him but stopped himself in the nick of time and turned the reach into a lazy stretch. A hollow rumble from his stomach reminded him of another chore he needed to take care of. Plus, it would get him away from the close-quarters danger zone of the couch. He stood up.

"I don't think I've had anything to eat since morning," he said. "I bet you're hungry, too. I'll see if I can rustle us up some grub."

Corey trailed after him to the kitchen area. "Can I help?"

"No, Corey," he said firmly as he opened the refrigerator door. "This is my kitchen; I do the cooking here. Sit down at the table and have a cup of that coffee you made. Unless you think it'll keep you awake," he added, then said, as though it were the first time it had occurred to him, "I guess you've realized by now you can't drive home tonight, haven't you?"

"Yes," she said in a faint little voice, looking down at the scrubbed pine tabletop. It wouldn't be caffeine keeping her awake if she tried to sleep in the same house with Brandon.

"You can sleep in my bed. I don't have a spare room. I'll use the couch." His voice sounded a little choked.

"Oh, no. I couldn't put you out of your bed; I'll use the couch." Somehow the idea of sleeping in Brandon's bed was quite alarming even if he wasn't going to be in it.

"No way. I'm sorry I got you stuck up here; the least I can do is give you a decent bed."

"But…"

"I don't want to hear anymore about it," he said forcefully. "Now, will sausage and eggs do for supper? It's the quickest thing I can think of."

"Eggs are fine. Whatever is easiest for you."

Brandon put sausage links in a cast iron skillet to fry, broke eggs into a bowl, added milk and salt and pepper and began beating the mixture with a fork. There was a rather strained silence.

Corey cleared her throat. "How will I get out tomorrow? Surely the highway people don't clear the roads all the way up here."

Brandon put a plate of steaming scrambled eggs, toast and well-browned sausages in front of Corey. He poured mugs of coffee for both of them, then sat down across from Corey and began to eat.

"No problem," he said. "I barter for a lot of the things I need. I did some work last summer for a neighbor. In exchange he promised to blade my drive to the main road all this winter. He has a nice little bulldozer that will take care of those snowdrifts in no time."

"Oh. That's good," she said weakly.

She couldn't think of another thing to say. *Well, aren't I just the sparkling conversationalist?* She couldn't remember when she had ever felt so ill at ease. The eggs and sausage were quite tasty, but she couldn't seem to get them down. She had really only stirred them around on her plate. All she could think about was the inevitability of spending the night in Brandon's home.

Brandon didn't seem to be suffering from any such discomfort. *He probably has women sleeping at his place all the time.* He took the last bite of plump brown sausage and then used his fork to point at the baby llama.

"Look. I think he's going to be all right."

The little llama wobbled to his feet just as Corey looked over at him. He took a few tentative steps, then walked more steadily toward them. He poked his nose into Corey's sweater.

"Oh, isn't he cute? I think he's the sweetest little animal I've ever seen. Do you think he's looking for milk?"

"Probably. I'd better get back to his mama. Why don't you go on upstairs and make yourself at home? There are some new toothbrushes in the medicine cabinet. I bought them for the boys, so they're kind of short and have Mickey Mouse all over the handle, but they ought to do in a pinch. I don't know what else you might need, but feel free to use anything you want. You're such a tiny little thing; you could probably use one of my flannel shirts as a nightgown."

Maybe he was having a little trouble with this situation, too, Corey thought when Brandon looked away and flushed at the mention of nightgowns. Perhaps he was more uncomfortable than she'd thought.

She gave the llama a little pat and got up from the table. "I'll just wash up the dishes first."

"No. Leave them. You've already done way too much for me as it is," he said gruffly. He stalked over to where his outside clothes were drying, yanked them on and was out the door in a matter of seconds.

Well, whatever got into him? she wondered, feeling a little grumpy herself. Even if it was his house and his kitchen, she had no intention of paying any attention to a command issued in that tone of voice. He still had to feed the baby llama tonight—maybe several times before morning—she had no idea what kind of a feeding schedule a llama should be on, and the boys would probably be up early tomorrow. She would just tidy up the dishes before she went to bed, then at least one chore would be taken care of for him.

While she washed the dishes and scoured the skillet, Corey hummed an upbeat sort of tune, trying to establish a feeling of normalcy to replace her unease at being stranded with Brandon. At a nudge to her leg, she glanced down and saw the little llama looking up alertly at her. Of course, humming was how llamas communicated. Did the baby think she was trying to talk to him?

"You and I make a fine pair, don't we? We're both in quite a pickle," she murmured softly to the little creature as she stroked his back.

She started toward the stairway and noted with satisfaction how vigorously the baby scampered across the floor. He seemed to be getting stronger by the minute. But when she was halfway up the stairs and saw the baby trying to follow her, she paused, frowning in concern. She was afraid he would fall if he continued his efforts. He was already up two risers.

Corey went back down and tried experimentally to lift the cria. He was actually quite easy to carry and didn't seem to mind being held, so she decided he would be safest if she took him with her. She slipped quietly through the boys' bedroom and put the baby llama down in the bathroom on a fuzzy throw rug. The cria seemed to be content there for the moment, so Corey shut the connecting door to the boys' room and began looking around for what she would need to get settled for the night.

Brandon's room was as neat and unadorned as the lower part of the cabin. Corey looked apprehensively at the plain dark maroon comforter on the double bed. She knew she would never be able to sleep a wink in Brandon's bed.

She hurried to the closet and searched through the orderly, sparse array of clothing for something to sleep in. A subtle fragrance wafted her way as she moved the hangers. Her stomach clenched with nervous jitters, and a prickling sensation raced from the top of her head to her toes. She felt Brandon's presence from his unique scent as strongly as if he were standing beside her.

She selected an old flannel shirt that must have been red once upon a time but had faded with many washings to almost pink. She held it to her cheek. The shirt was soft enough to use for baby bunting. She took it into the bathroom to change.

Downstairs, Brandon entered the cabin, got rid of his outer clothing and took the pail of llama milk to the sink. He frowned when he saw the clean dishes in the drain rack. There she went again. That dratted woman only followed directions when it suited her. He looked around and realized neither the baby llama or Corey were to be found. What was going on? Where was the cria?

Still clutching the wire handle of the pail, Brandon took the stairs two at a time. He entered his bedroom just as Corey came out of the bathroom attired in his flannel shirt. He could see the llama lying on the bathroom floor. That solved one mystery, but he now definitely had other things to worry about.

Corey looked utterly charming even in the voluminous flannel. All he could see of her bare legs was the delicious curve of her calves and the delicate turn of trim ankles, but that hinted at enough to stop his breathing. Even her toes looked like a delicacy that could be nibbled.

Apparently startled at his sudden appearance, Corey's face, neck and—showing at the deep vee of the partially unbuttoned shirt—a bit of cleavage flushed a rosy pink. She glanced up at him once through the tracery of long lashes then looked down shyly. Brandon swallowed a lump in his throat the size of the Bogus Basin.

"Wha... what's the cria doing up here?" he finally managed to stammer, feeling like an incoherent fool. What he wanted to tell her was that she was the most beautiful woman he had ever seen, then coax her to his bed and show her how much he wanted her.

"He tried to follow me up the stairs. I... I was afraid he would fall." Corey knew she must look like an idiot standing there in the ridiculously oversized shirt, stuttering and blushing, but she couldn't seem to control her response to Brandon.

With great effort Brandon forced himself to look away from Corey and take a step toward the baby llama. He felt as though he were staggering under the weight of a two-hundred pound backpack.

"I'll take him down and feed him, then maybe I can find something to block the stairway."

"I want to help; let me carry the milk."

Brandon silently handed over the pail, went into the bathroom, scooped up the little llama and carried him down the stairs. Corey followed.

Brandon let Corey give the cria his bottle, and the baby was soon contentedly humming as he sucked hungrily at the nipple. The fun of feeding the baby animal gradually restored Corey's self-confidence. When the llama had taken all the milk, Brandon turned off the lights, and they watched the inquisitive little beast toddle about exploring the cabin in the soft moonglow spilling down through the skylight. By the time the little creature was nodding off in his bed of old towels, she felt quite comfortable curled up on the couch with Brandon. Until she turned from watching the sleeping llama and saw the hunger in Brandon's navy eyes.

Her heart began to trill in her chest so loudly Brandon must surely hear it. She put her hand over her heart as though her touch might calm the rapid beating and drew in a shuddering breath. She needed air; she felt light-headed as though she might faint. *The wood must be burning too rapidly in the stove,* she thought in a daze. *The room is much too hot and stifling.*

Brandon slowly reached for her. It seemed to take a very long time; the moment stretched on and on as though he were moving in slow motion. She held her breath until he touched her.

Grasping both her arms, he pulled her up against him. She marveled at the strength in his hands, the solidness of his flesh.

He bent his head to kiss her—her forehead, eyelids, cheeks, lips, neck. She threw back her head to bare her throat. *Yes, it must be the stove,* she thought in confusion, for his lips were burning hot, and his kisses left a trail of tiny brush fires that instantly spread and threatened to engulf her whole body.

Brandon loosened his hold on her long enough to reach up and pull off his sweatshirt. Even that brief absence made Corey lonely for the feel of his body pressed against hers, and she wanted to snatch him back, but she was rewarded for her patient waiting by the sight of his magnificently muscled chest and arms. A golden pelt spread across his chest, then narrowed and darkened to a line of sable that disappeared into the waistband of his jeans.

Brandon tossed the sweatshirt to the floor. Corey was trembling, and her eyes were large pools of liquid brown, but he sensed no resistance, so he began unfastening the buttons on the flannel shirt one at a time, kissing each new patch of creamy skin as it was revealed.

Corey gasped when the burning kisses reached the very tip of her bare breast. He circled both dusky, rose-colored buds with his tongue until they tightened into knots of exquisite sensation. Then the fiery path of kisses went lower, across the seemingly fragile ridges of her rib cage, over her softly rounded belly, down to the center of her pleasure.

Brandon nuzzled the soft fluff of light brown hair, gently parted her legs, then ran the very tip of his tongue along the delicate petals of her flesh. Corey cried out in ecstasy, arched her back and dug her fingers into the dense muscles of his neck and back. A deep moan was torn from Brandon's throat. He rose to stand by the couch and started to unfasten his jeans.

Suddenly he froze, and a deep frown furrowed his face. "No," he groaned.

"What's wrong?" Corey asked in alarm, half sitting up on the couch and clutching the flannel shirt together over her chest.

"I'm so sorry, darling, but I don't have anything to use for protection. I'm not prepared. We don't want another little Robbie on our hands."

Corey squeezed her eyes tightly shut at the sudden stab of pain. A little Robbie was the one thing in the world she wanted most, but it could never be.

"Don't worry, Brandon. It's all right; I can't have children. We don't need anything."

A brief spasm that Corey couldn't decipher crossed Brandon's face, and he hesitated for a moment longer, then he began to push his jeans down his lean hips. At that moment a long wail sounded from the loft.

"What the...?" Brandon ground out and jerked his pants back into place. He was halfway up the stairs before Corey's befuddled senses even took in what was happening.

Corey slowly buttoned the flannel shirt and tried to calm her painfully raw nerves and quickened breathing. She'd had no idea a man's kisses could feel so wonderful or that she could react so wildly and with such abandon to anyone's touch.

Even in the first months of her marriage when everything had still been all right between them, her husband's lovemaking had never excited her. She had thought it was just her inexperience and that sex would get better as time passed. Instead, it had steadily worsened until Wayne had seemed absolutely repugnant to her, and she had had to grit her teeth to get through their "appointments" trying to conceive.

From the loft, she could hear a childish voice shrill with distress and Brandon's much deeper, soothing rumble. It wasn't long before a hush settled over the cabin, and Brandon returned to her side. He took her in his arms again, but this time without passion. He cuddled her in his lap and sighed.

"It was Robbie. He doesn't have nightmares very often anymore. They were almost a nightly thing right after Jane died. I'm sorry about the interruption. I think it may be the very first time I ever wanted to wring his little neck."

"Don't apologize," Corey said, feeling blissfully content just snuggled up against his broad chest. "I would never think of a frightened child as an interruption."

They sat there companionably for a few moments, listening to the crackling of the burning logs, Brandon gently stroking Corey's hair. She felt peaceful and relaxed, no longer fearful of what the evening might bring. Brandon was so quiet, almost as though he were listening, waiting for her to speak, receptive if she had anything she wanted to say.

"You have beautiful children, Brandon. My husband and I wanted a family. We tried for a long time to have a child," she began hesitantly.

She paused. The reassuring caressing of her hair continued.

"After we had been married for a while, I started getting these really bad pains." She crossed her arms over her lower abdomen, hugging herself, remembering the agony.

"The doctors said I had endometriosis. There was tissue growing inside me that prevented pregnancy. They said it was treatable. I took medicine for a long time and finally had surgery, but nothing worked," she said sadly. "My husband was so disappointed he didn't want to stay married anymore. So—well, he divorced me." The ugly words came out brokenly.

The poor little thing, Brandon thought, pulling Corey closer to him. *What kind of a man would treat a woman like that, abandoning her after she had endured such pain and unhappiness?*

Suddenly he froze as a horrible thought crossed his mind. He had wondered why such a classy lady would be interested in him. Now he knew; he wasn't what Corey wanted. He felt a gut-wrenching twist of pain and humiliation.

Brandon had stopped stroking her hair. Somehow his body no longer felt comforting. Corey moved away and looked into his face. His eyes looked flat, hard, his face forbidding.

"You can't have my sons, Corey," he said in a dull voice.

Corey's eyes widened in shock. Her hand flew to her mouth to stifle a hurt cry. *How could he be so cruel?* She had poured out her heart, had told him secrets she could hardly bear to think about much less discuss, had shared the worst part of her life with him. He had totally misunderstood.

Corey leaped up from the couch and darted toward the stairway. Upstairs, she crawled into Brandon's bed, huddled under the covers and sobbed into the pillow long into the night until a fitful sleep finally blotted out her troubled thoughts.

She was awakened early the next morning by a grumbling roar. She got up wearily and walked listlessly to double doors that lead out onto a balcony. A fairyland stretched out before her. It looked as though a treasure chest of diamonds had been scattered over every tree and bush. But Corey saw the mountain's blanket of sparkling crystals through a haze of tears.

A clanking, small yellow bulldozer rumbled up the mountain, clearing a path through the snow. *Thank goodness!* She desperately needed to escape. She couldn't stand to breathe the same air as Brandon for another minute. He was, without a doubt, the most insensitive, selfish, cruel, bossy, pigheaded man on earth. And somehow she had managed to lose her heart to him.

Seven

Christmas Eve, and I'm all alone. Serves me right, Brandon thought glumly, *after the ugly thing I said to Corey.* The minute the cruel words had rolled off his thoughtless tongue and he had seen the stricken expression on her face, he would have given anything to have taken them back.

He had spent a long month thinking about that evening. He alternated between triumph when he recalled her gasp of pleasure at his touch and despair when he remembered her cry of anguish at his words.

He wasn't sure what had prompted him to say such a thing. Had Corey ever given any indication she wanted to snatch his children away? Brandon snorted at such a ridiculous idea as he lowered a new mineral block into place for the llamas and walked out of the feedlot, closing gates behind him. Of course not. Did he think she wanted to marry a practically penniless, tactless mountain man like himself just so she could rear his motherless sons? Not bloody likely. It had been pride that had spoken—pure, unadulterated, raging male ego and injured pride.

Brandon entered the cabin, and in spite of his gloomy mood, the corners of his mouth quirked up when the baby llama zoomed over to greet him. For the first time, he was almost glad the baby had never learned to nurse properly. At least the llama would be a little company while the boys were gone.

The place seemed terribly empty without them. Perhaps it had been a mistake to allow them to spend all of the Christmas holiday with Jane's parents. He probably wouldn't have let them go if he didn't feel so damned guilty about her death.

Brandon tried to shrug off the uneasiness that had been nagging at him ever since the boys had left for the visit with their grandparents. The Thorntons seemed different to him in some sort of way he couldn't quite put his finger on. They seemed like a mere shadow of the once vigorous couple they had been.

He had gotten along with them reasonably well when he and Jane were married. They must have noticed John had arrived a little early after the wedding, but they'd never said anything to him about it. And if they'd thought he had been gone from home more often than a good husband should have been, they had made no comment.

Opening the microwave, Brandon put a bottle in to warm for the baby llama. The cria was taking regular milk now, so at least he didn't have to milk Soft Touch anymore. The microwave went "ding," and the little llama ran into the kitchen and pranced in circles around Brandon. The baby had already learned the signal that meant he was going to be fed.

Brandon sat in one of the kitchen chairs and held the bottle for the llama, who was soon humming happily in a high-pitched mew. But Brandon couldn't stop worrying. Surely the Thorntons didn't blame him for Jane's death. True, he hadn't been home, but even if he had been there, how would he have known Jane shouldn't drive for groceries that day?

The baby llama slurped the last of the milk and tried an exploratory nibble at Brandon's sleeve.

Brandon sighed, got up and put the empty bottle in the sink to soak. Perhaps they just resented the fact that he was still alive when their only child was dead. He might have feelings just as irrational if anything ever happened to John or Robbie. *Thank God the Thorntons had been babysitting, and the boys hadn't gone to the store with their mother on that awful day!* Brandon broke out in a cold sweat just thinking about it.

He wished he could talk over some of these disturbing thoughts with Corey. He remembered the look of shared suffering on her face when he had told her about Jane's death. Her lovely warm brown eyes were so expressive. He'd felt comforted and restored after talking to her. Usually, he didn't like to discuss feelings. When he felt uneasy about something, he would grab his backpack and head for a wilderness for a few weeks. By the time he returned to civilization, he would have forgotten all about whatever had been bothering him.

But it had helped to talk to Corey. And how had he returned the favor? By insulting her when she had trusted him with her own past grief. Brandon slammed his fist down hard on the kitchen counter. He might as well face it; he was just no damned good at this relationship thing. He liked Corey—he liked her a whole lot more than he was prepared to admit—and he wanted her so badly his whole body ached. Just remembering the beauty of breast and hip touched by moonlight, her soft lips, her body opening for him, caused him to stiffen with frustrated desire.

But he was no good for her. He had nothing to offer her. He had already failed one woman. He didn't want to do the same thing to Corey.

And even if she was a good listener, when it came time to make decisions, she had made it perfectly clear she made her own. She was one of those females who only listened to a man when she chose to do so. He didn't know how to deal with a woman who was so independent. And really, did he want to?

No. He didn't. Brandon stalked across the kitchen toward the stairs to go up to his bedroom to change. It was Christmas Eve. The boys were gone. He was a bachelor again for a week.

He remembered seeing a cowboy bar near the fairgrounds in Boise. There were bound to be some singles out celebrating tonight. He didn't need a difficult, complicated woman like Corey Tierney who made him think too damn much. He just needed a woman, any woman, to ease the ache in his groin.

An hour later his pickup roared to a stop in front of blinking neon. He paused inside the bar to get his bearings. The bar was dimly lit, but at a glance Brandon saw it was packed from wall to wall with noisy celebrants. A country-western band was twanging out a Texas two-step at an ear-splitting decibel level for cowboy-booted dancers on a little patch of a dance floor.

Brandon's vision was somewhat obscured by fog-like cigar and cigarette smoke, but it didn't prevent him from observing several women who had been inspecting him hopefully from the moment he had come through the door.

Brandon shifted his weight uneasily from one foot to the other. Even though he knew some women considered him attractive, he had never thought of himself as a ladies' man. When he was younger, his friends had often tried to talk him into accompanying them on their nighttime prowls to help them pick up girls. They were amazed when Brandon, more often than not, chose to go home alone. Even as a young man, he had felt sharing his body with a stranger was some kind of sacrilege, and one of the few times he had broken his own rule, it had changed his life forever.

But now he was here on a mission. He had spent entirely too much time wondering and worrying about Corey Tierney. He wanted to wipe out all thought of her. He was sure an encounter, no matter how meaningless, with some other woman would serve his purpose.

Brandon studied the expectant faces turned his way. There was a redhead who didn't look too bad. But somehow her hair seemed harsh and brittle—not at all like Corey's gold-shot, flowing brown waves that were as soft to the touch as a squirrel's tail.

Well, farther down the bar a cute, little, chubby lady stood with one elbow jauntily propped against the bar rail. Brandon started to walk toward her, then he noticed the immodest cut of her fringed cowboy shirt. Why, she was practically popping out of the blouse, her plump breasts exposed for all to see. He frowned with distaste. Corey would never wear anything like that. She would save her charms for him.

Brandon exhaled sharply in disgust. It was no use. There were plenty of attractive and, no doubt, perfectly nice women here tonight who more than likely would be willing to spend an evening or more with him, but he just wasn't interested. They weren't Corey. He wanted Corey. Only Corey.

He stalked out of the bar, got into his truck and started it with a roar.

~ * ~

Corey sat in her darkened living room, the only illumination the twinkling of the Christmas tree lights. She couldn't remember a time when the holiday had given her less pleasure. Business was brisk at Kids' Kloset. Usually, Corey enjoyed helping little girls pick out red velvet dresses and bows for their hair, but this year she felt nothing but pain. When she rehearsed the moving and beautiful Christmas hymns with the church choir, it was all she could do to squeeze back the tears.

Stacks of gaily wrapped presents were piled under the tree, ready to take to her nieces and nephews tomorrow at the family celebration at her parents' home. She sighed deeply. She dreaded going; she didn't see how she could possibly get through the day.

Exasperated with herself, Corey decided it was time to take control of her feelings. She would just have to put on a happy face no matter how much it cost her. She certainly didn't want to worry her parents. They already acted sometimes like they felt sorry for her since she was the only one in the whole bunch without a partner.

Well, the first thing to do is to stop sitting here in the gloom, she thought. *It's foolish and morbid.* She had just risen from the couch to turn on some lights when the doorbell rang.

She hurried to the entryway and peeped through the little viewer. Her visitor was so tall she couldn't see his face, but Corey knew instantly—with a shock as sudden and violent as if she had plunged through ice into frigid water—it was Brandon.

Corey rested her forehead against the cold wooden door and shut her eyes. For a moment she considered not opening the door. The lights were off; he would think nobody was at home. The bell rang again, clanging through her head as she leaned against the door. Corey held her breath. Surely he would go away soon. Another peal. Corey sharply exhaled the air trapped in her lungs, straightened her shoulders and put her hand on the doorknob. *Oh, fudge! How can I be such a coward, refusing to open my door to someone on Christmas Eve?* She twisted the knob.

Brandon had just turned away and started back down the sidewalk. He swung around toward Corey at the sound of the door unlatching. Corey flipped on the entry light.

For a long frozen moment they stood staring at one another.

Brandon noted Corey's wide eyes and pale, strained face. She was dressed in a deep purple flannel robe and slippers. It wasn't very late yet—not even ten. Brandon wondered if he had caught her changing for a date or if she were just making an early evening of it.

At the thought of Corey out with another man, Brandon's fist clenched spasmodically, further crushing the already wrinkled wrapping on the gift he was carrying. He caught a glimpse of pale pink lace where Corey's robe overlapped across her bosom. Surely that was some kind of nightdress. She must not have been getting ready to go out. He relaxed his death grip on the squashed package.

Lord! She looks beautiful. The robe she was wearing was a modest design, obviously intended more for warmth than seduction, but the way it draped softly all along the length of her lovely body hinted more enticingly at the luscious curves beneath the deep purple fabric than more blatant peek-a-boo or see-through lingerie. Brandon swallowed hard.

"I didn't see any lights; I didn't think you were at home." His voice sounded unnaturally loud in the frosty, still night air.

Silence. Brandon uncomfortably shifted the package from one hand to another.

"I probably should have called before I came over, it being Christmas Eve and getting kind of late and all."

More silence. Damn the woman. Surely she doesn't expect me to apologize!

"Well, I just thought I might as well drop by since the boys are gone for a little visit with their grandparents, and I didn't have anything else to do."

"How flattering!" Corey said scathingly, outrage apparently loosening her tongue.

Brandon sighed in exasperation. He had about as much tact and charm as a grizzly bear. He had better get away from here before he made a bigger fool of himself than he already had.

"I brought you a present. Merry Christmas."

Brandon thrust the crushed package at Corey, wheeled around and stalked off down the sidewalk. His boot heels rang hollowly against the frozen concrete.

Corey watched his broad back retreating. She felt as though he were taking a huge chunk of her heart with him. If he left, she would feel utterly empty inside. She knew she was making a terrible mistake, but she couldn't bear to see him go.

"Wait," she called out.

Brandon turned around again and stood silently scowling impatiently at her.

"I just thought... well, it's so awfully cold out. Would you like a cup of hot cider?"

A flash of square white teeth appeared, and his impossibly blue eyes lit up. Brandon's whole expression was instantly transformed.

"I thought you'd never ask," he said, grinning so boyishly all six feet five inches of him looked almost as young as John.

He strode right past Corey and into her home as confidently as if he owned the place. *He captured my heart just as easily,* she thought resentfully, as she followed him and shut the door.

Corey put the bedraggled package down on the coffee table. "I served refreshments all day at the store," she said. "I kept some cider simmering in the crockpot in case any of my neighbors dropped by this evening. It's still hot. Sit down; I'll get you a cup."

She fled to the kitchen, leaving the grinning Brandon to spread his lanky frame on the couch. She desperately needed a few minutes respite from his unnerving presence to pull together at least a semblance of calm. Her hands shook as she ladled out a mug of steaming mulled cider.

If Kim or any one of her other friends had told her a few months ago a man could have this kind of effect on her, she would have laughed in her face. Brandon made her senses reel. Whenever she was around him, she couldn't think clearly. The memory of the way she had revealed her body and soul at that last stormy-night encounter made her flush with embarrassment until her face was as pink as her nightgown.

She removed the plastic wrap from the tray of homemade cookies and candy—rum balls, divinity and double fudge—she had kept ready for any unexpected guests who might drop by on Christmas Eve until she had given up on the possibility of company and prepared for bed, hoping to get some sleep. She was known in the neighborhood for her warm welcomes. Everyone knew they would be greeted with cheer at Corey's door. But it was straining her hospitality to the limit to entertain this most unexpected guest of all.

She had not spoken a civil word to Brandon that snowy morning before she escaped from his cabin the moment the road was cleared. She'd been hurt and angry right down to her toenails. How dare he suppose she wanted him because he'd had the good fortune to have children and she hadn't! She was outraged he would jump to such an unjust conclusion after she'd confided what she considered her life's greatest disappointment.

Then she had calmed down and analyzed her feelings with brutal self-honesty. She had to admit she'd had many happy daydreams featuring herself as a part of Brandon's family. Certainly, she had never consciously intended to imply she wanted to be Brandon's wife and his children's mother, but perhaps—and it was so humiliating to finally admit this to herself—she had somehow betrayed her little glimmer of hope without realizing it.

When she was able to admit Brandon might have had some grounds for his conclusions, she had hoped he would call her so they could talk things over, but as the weeks dragged by, she realized what she had deduced once before and conveniently forgotten the minute Brandon had asked for her help with John—he just didn't care about her as much as she cared about him.

It hurt. It hurt so much her heart was squeezed into a tight little painful pebble in the middle of her chest. It felt like Santa had left a lump of coal there for her Christmas present.

Corey picked up the tray of confectioneries and mug of cider and carried them to the living room. She paused in the doorway and looked at Brandon, relaxed and comfortable, sprawled on her couch. It infuriated her to see him so at ease when she felt like her insides had been frozen into a rock.

She walked over to the coffee table and set the tray and mug down with a considerably louder thump than was called for by the dictates of courtesy. Brandon didn't seem to notice her tension. He wrapped his big hand around the warmth of the cup, inhaled the fragrant, spicy-sweet steam with obvious satisfaction, reached out with his other hand to pop a large square of fudge into his mouth, then leaned back against the couch's soft cushions and breathed a sigh of contentment.

Corey wanted to scream, thinking how he had dropped in because he just happened to think of her when he didn't have anything else to do, while he hadn't been out of her thoughts for a moment since she had last seen him.

"Aren't you going to open your present?" Brandon asked, nodding toward the crushed package lying on the coffee table.

Corey picked it up. "I'm sorry. I don't have anything for you," she said stiffly.

"That's okay. I didn't expect you to," he replied easily. "Go ahead and open it."

Corey unwrapped the elf-patterned paper. Inside lay what looked like hand-knit gloves and a matching soft wool hat in lovely muted earth tones of gray, brown, white and black with a design of tiny stylized llamas prancing around the cuffs of the gloves and brim of the hat. Corey put one hand in one of the gloves and stroked the fluffy wool with her other hand.

"They're beautiful," she said sadly, a tear threatening to trickle down her cheek as she though of Soft Touch and her baby and all the other llamas.

Brandon watched the play of emotion cross Corey's lovely face. She seemed quite overcome with his gift. What a lucky break he had already loaded the cab of his pickup with his family's Christmas presents before he left home for the bar. *It was a stroke of genius to give her the package I'd intended for my sister,* he thought smugly. He only hoped the tag he had removed with Sandra's name on it was the only one on the present. Before he had left to spend Christmas Eve with his grandparents, John had helped Brandon wrap the gifts, and the little scamp liked to fasten stickers all over them.

"There're from Peru. I traded raw wool for them to a weaver who makes wall hangings and also imports gloves and blankets and such from South America."

Corey examined her fingertips, which were poking through the ends of each finger of the glove. She wriggled her fingers.

"Why are there holes in them?"

"I don't really know. I'll have to ask my weaver friend. I suppose it makes it easier for the Peruvians to do things out in the cold. They're pretty hard workers."

Brandon eyed Corey speculatively for a brief moment, trying to judge her mood. He rose from the couch and stood towering over her as she sat huddled in her chair.

Corey's pulse rate instantly accelerated until her heart was thudding painfully against her rib cage, and she was breathing in shuddering gasps, unable to get enough air into her lungs. She felt trapped. Now she knew how a baby rabbit must feel crouched at the hunter's feet. She fervently wished he would just go away.

Brandon knelt on one knee beside her. He captured her gloved hand and slowly, glancing at her averted eyes after each caress, kissed one by one each rounded, pink, nakedly exposed fingertip protruding from the woolly glove.

Each finger tingled deliciously as it waited for its turn. To Corey, it was the most erotic sensation imaginable. As the kisses continued, the tingling spread across her hand, along her arm, through her whole body. Corey sighed, and with the shuddering release of that breath, she felt the hurt and tension of the last month flow out of her body. Her muscles unclenched, and she relaxed. She felt light and floaty and dreamy. And very receptive.

Brandon gently grasped her chin and turned her head until he could look her in the eye.

"I never meant to hurt you, Corey. I'm pretty rough around the edges, and sometimes I say things without thinking, but I didn't mean to spoil things between us.

"I... I think I understand," she stammered.

He flashed her a grateful smile and bent his head to give another uncovered fingertip a kiss.

"I think the Peruvians knew what they were doing," Brandon murmured against her hand, his breath tickling her fingertips.

He slipped the glove off and with the tip of his tongue traced a little circle in her palm. Corey moaned softly. Brandon pushed the loose sleeve of Corey's robe up her arm, exposing the faintly blue-tinged tender flesh of her inner elbow. He kissed his way along her arm, sending prickles of excitement to every cell in her body.

Tugging gently, Brandon pulled the robe down from Corey's shoulders, revealing Corey's creamy breasts molded by her nightgown's lacy bodice.

"Perfect. You're perfect, Corey. So very, very beautiful," he whispered softly.

The wide lace straps of the gown followed the robe in a descent to the chair, so now Corey was surrounded by a little puddle of purple and pink fabrics. Brandon leaned forward to smooth his lips over her rounded shoulders. Corey shut her eyes and let her head fall back, and Brandon kissed the swanlike curve of her neck. He cupped one of her breasts in each of his hands and lowered his head to delicately tease first one then the other puckered bud between his teeth.

Corey gasped and began to writhe in the chair. Brandon stood and pulled her up against his body. Corey's nightclothes slithered to the floor. She could feel Brandon's shirt buttons and belt buckle branding her tender flesh as he pressed her tightly to him, but she perceived no pain and met his fevered kisses with an eager passion of her own.

Brandon groaned deep in his throat and released Corey only long enough to strip off his own clothes in a moment's time. As he turned to flip off the switch for the overhead light, Corey trembled at the sight of his magnificent aroused body. He was even more beautifully male than she'd imagined.

After spreading an afghan from the couch over the carpet in front of the Christmas tree, Brandon laid Corey down and knelt beside her. He ran his big hard hands all up and down her body, causing her skin to quiver with excitement.

"So beautiful, my sweet, sweet Corey."

He said the tender words in a voice that was rough and harsh. The sinewy muscles of his thighs and the big rounded muscles of his biceps were tensed in anticipation as though he were preparing to run a marathon or fight in a sparring match. He started on the same long, delicious journey of kisses all along Corey's body that he had begun in his cabin a month ago. That blustery night the exploration had ended in frustration and hurt, but there was no one to interrupt them now, and no thoughtless words were spoken.

Corey lost all sense of time and place. All of her body—her skin, her flesh, her bones—strained toward Brandon's caresses.

Shyly, tentatively at first, she began to return his touches, stroking his long, muscular body. Emboldened by his growling, guttural moans, Corey intensified searching out the mysteries of his beautiful male physique until Brandon could bear no more. He eased himself deeply into her welcoming body. As a multitude of tiny points of colored light played over their joined bodies, Corey found herself answering Brandon's every cry and meeting him thrust for thrust until there was a blaze of light behind her eyelids far more brilliant than the twinkles cascading over their entwined bodies.

As he uttered one last strangled roar, Brandon's body stiffened at the final great rush of release. Spent, his mighty arms trembling, he lay close beside her until his ragged breathing steadied to a point where he could speak.

"It's never been like that for me before, Corey. You're an amazement."

Corey flushed with both embarrassment and pride at his words. She refrained from telling him she hadn't even known it could be like that. Her only other lover had been her husband, and she had never experienced anything with him that had even come close to what she had just shared with Brandon.

After a bit, Corey's sweat-dampened skin felt the chill, and she began to shiver. Brandon tried to wrap the afghan over her, but it was too small.

"You're freezing. Do you suppose we could move to the bedroom? I'd like to tuck you under some warm blankets," he said.

Corey rose slowly, languorously to her feet. Chilly or not, she would have liked to stay just where they were forever. She took his hand and led him through the living room and down the hall to her bedroom.

Brandon paused hesitantly at the doorway. He looked from Corey to the bed. It was piled high with every kind of white lace, tatted and embroidered pillow imaginable. It was edged with an immaculate white eyelet bed skirt and peeking out from under the mounds of white pillows was a white crocheted bedspread.

"Can we really lie down on all of that?" he asked doubtfully.

Corey raised her arms above her head and arched her body in a long, luxurious stretch—the movement of a supremely confident woman: fulfilled, sexually satisfied, replete—but capable of infinitely more.

With an inward, secret smile of self-satisfaction at Brandon's sharp intake of breath when she stretched, she replied, "Oh, we most definitely are going to lie down on it."

Eight

Corey hummed happily as she sped over the salt-and-cinder-crusted highway. Soon, spring showers would wash away these last reminders of winter. Mentally, she counted up the Sundays she had spent at the cabin with Brandon and the boys since Christmas. Amazing! Almost three blissful months of increasing intimacy.

She laughed softly to herself. Not that Brandon would ever admit they were growing closer. Several days during the week he would hang around town after picking up John from kindergarten until it was almost time for her to close the store. Since he "was in the neighborhood," he would drop by the store just as she was locking up, and she would invite them all to supper. Then toward the end of the week, with a surprised sort of expression on his face as thought the thought had just occurred to him, Brandon would invite her to spend her day off at the ranch.

She would hesitate as though she were mentally reviewing her appointment calendar, carefully not revealing how eagerly she had been awaiting the invitation all week, and then graciously accept.

Corey almost giggled aloud as she pulled to a stop in front of the cabin. Brandon's style of courtship, if that was what they were truly engaged in, was as ritualized as the water minuet performed by mating terns that Brandon and the boys had watched on public television at her house one weekday evening after supper.

Two bright little faces appeared over the rise between the barn and the cabin. The boys were leading Hot Shot, Soft Touch's baby. Corey chuckled at Hot Shot's attire. He was wearing a bright red sweater, his front legs thrust through the sleeves. Corey knew Brandon was trying to acclimatize the little llama to outside temperatures after it had spent the winter inside in the warmth of the cabin. He had hit upon the idea of using one of his largest old sweaters for Hot Shot's walks outside. The red cable-knit sweater had fit pretty well when he had first tried it on Hot Shot, but now the growing llama was bursting through the seams. Soon, he would be able to join the other llamas in the meadow.

Corey had been touched to discover on her first visit back to the ranch after helping deliver Hot Shot that Brandon was still just calling the llama "baby." He had held true to his promise that she could name the new cria since she had assisted with his birth. Corey had taken one look at the little creature, a month and a half old, running and leaping all over the cabin as if he owned the place, and she had immediately come up with the name Hot Shot.

The boys waved excitedly at Corey and came tearing down the hill, Hot Shot, in his halter and lead, cavorting along beside them. *They're probably anxious to find out what kind of goodies I brought them,* Corey thought with amusement. Brandon grumbled occasionally she was spoiling them, but Corey ignored him, noticing with satisfaction he gobbled up the treats just as eagerly as the children.

What a delight it had been to spend time with John and Robbie. She had been able to see the world anew with all the wonder and awe of fresh unjaded eyes. She was experiencing life from a brand-new perspective.

Of course, the boys always had to be considered; you couldn't just snap your fingers and make them disappear for your own convenience. Their presence often frustrated Brandon and Corey's ever-increasing desire for one another. Still, the secret, meaningful glances, the little touches, the brief, stolen kisses all built towards a shattering crescendo when they did manage to find an hour or two of privacy.

Corey gave a little shiver of anticipation. Whatever else Brandon felt for her, she had absolutely no doubt he delighted in her body. She had never felt so desired, so much a woman.

Carrying the pan of butterscotch brownies she had baked that morning before church, Corey started toward the cabin door just as John and Robbie came panting up to greet her. Corey lifted a corner of the foil covering the baking pan so the boys could peep inside.

"Yum," Robbie said, licking his lips.

"I'm awful glad you're here," John said a trifle anxiously. "Daddy's real grumpy, and you always make him feel better. He's got an awful tummy ache—only it's up here," he said, pointing to his forehead.

Instantly worried, Corey let John have the honor of carrying dessert so she could hurry inside.

Brandon was hunched over the desk in the living room, staring at a stack of papers. The sight of Corey wiped the scowl off his face, and he rose to greet her. A hug from Brandon always lifted Corey a few inches from the floor, and even though she knew something was wrong, she couldn't help but enjoy the strong, solid feel of his body and the arms that supported her. He set her down gently.

"You look busy," Corey said, trying not to sound anxious. "Would you like for me to take the boys upstairs and read to them for a while so you can concentrate?"

"It wouldn't do any good," Brandon said shortly. He stalked over to the couch and slumped down in one corner.

Corey followed slowly. Now she was really worried. Brandon was a man of many moods, but despondency wasn't one of them. Perhaps John's diagnosis was correct, and he just had a very bad headache. She sat down cautiously next to Brandon on the couch.

"Is there something I can help you with?" she asked softly.

"No," he barked at her, then leaped up from the couch and paced vigorously about the cabin, scrubbing his forehead and thick blond brows with one large hand.

Corey carefully hid a little smile. That was more like it. Cranky or not, this was the man of action she knew and loved. She had felt a pang of fear when she had seen him crumpled listlessly in the corner of the couch.

The boys came in, and John set the brownies down carefully on the pine table in the kitchen. One look at his father and he decided, with five-year-old wisdom, it would be a good day to play upstairs in the loft. He took the lead off Hot Shot's halter and hung it by the door on the lower coat rack their father had installed for Robbie and his use, then the two boys and the little llama all scrambled up the stairs at breakneck speed.

Brandon was so intent on his thoughts he didn't even seem to notice. Corey knew Brandon normally would have made the boys come back down and walk up the stairs more slowly. Finally, he began to speak, and the words came tumbling out as though he couldn't contain his worries any longer.

"It's just bills, Corey. Plain, old, ordinary bills. Vet, hay, mineral supplements, electricity, insurance, gas—not to mention the fact the boys and I have to eat. The bills keep pouring in, and I'm running out of operating capital."

He ran his hands roughly through his hair until it stuck out in little points all over his head. Streaming down from the skylight, sunshine glittered on the shards of hair, making him look like he was crowned with a coil of golden barbed wire. In spite of the fact there were still patches of snow outside on the mountain, Brandon was dressed in T-shirt and hiking shorts. The pacing and the tension he was feeling served to tighten his arms and legs into rock-hard bunches of muscles.

Corey tried hard to tear her eyes away from the play of muscle along biceps, thigh and calf since Brandon so clearly needed a sympathetic listener, but his sheer physical beauty took her breath away and made it hard to concentrate.

"The ironic thing is four of the llamas are due within the next three months. If the births go well, especially if there are a high proportion of female babies, I can sell a couple of them in a few more months, keep the others to increase my breeding herd, and I'll be all set for the next year. But right now I'm going under."

Brandon gave a short, angry-sounding laugh. "It's quite a joke, isn't it, to be so close and still be failing? My old man will have a hard time saying he told me so, he'll be laughing so hard."

Brandon crashed back down on the couch next to Corey and smashed a fist into the palm of his other hand. Corey started at the abrupt movement and the loud smack of flesh on flesh. She took a deep breath to regain her composure and then tentatively reached out with one hand to touch his shoulder.

"Brandon," she said hesitantly, "I have some money saved. I could loan it to you until the llamas are old enough to sell."

Brandon leaped up from the couch and shouted so loudly it was almost a roar. Corey had a fleeting impression of a tawny-maned male lion on the attack. For one awful moment she thought he might strike her.

He turned to her, his eyes afire. "I would never, ever, under any circumstances take money from a woman. Don't ever say anything like that again."

He went over to a window and leaned forward with both hands on the sill, staring out at the snow-capped mountain peaks. He seemed to be struggling to regain control.

After a bit he cleared his throat and said in an embarrassed voice, "There is actually something you could do for me, though it's a lot to ask, too much really, and I have no right."

Still miffed at the way Brandon had shouted at her, Corey briefly considered answering in kind, but she knew she had offended what she considered his overly developed masculine pride, so she restrained herself. Besides, she truly did want to help him if she could, so she responded with controlled calm.

"What is it? I'll do anything I can."

He turned to face her. "I've been offered a chance to lead a two-week trek into the River-of-No-Return Wilderness Area. It's a first class operation; the promoters have plenty of money to spend. This time of year can be dangerous in the mountains if you don't know what you're doing—a late snowstorm can come up with hardly any warning, and there's the beginning of the spring runoff. The people organizing the trip want an expert for a guide, so they're willing to pay me top dollar. And they want me to use the llamas, so we can pack in enough food and equipment for gourmet meals. It's a plum job. I'd make enough money to tide me over until I can sell Hot Shot. I won't make much on him because he will have to be gelded since he was with humans so much, but by then, hopefully, I'll have some females to sell."

He paused and frowned, seeming to realize he was off on a tangent. "The problem is I don't want to ask my sister or parents to keep the boys and certainly not their Grandma and Grandpa Thornton. It would disrupt John's schooling, and besides, well, I just don't, so..."

"So you want me to keep them!" Corey finished for him in an excited rush. "Oh, we'll have such fun!" she cried gleefully, already beginning to make plans.

"I'm so glad I live right across from the school," she rushed on. "It will be so convenient for John; he won't have to get up so early. And I can take Robbie with me to Kids' Kloset. He can play with all the toys that come in on consignment. And we can go to the movies—there's a new Disney release playing. And I'll subscribe to the children's cable channel. Since you don't have a TV, it will be a real treat for them to watch all the cartoons. And I'll bake every day. And—"

"Whoa!" Brandon said, holding up one hand to stop the torrent of words. He scowled reprovingly at her, but he couldn't help feeling touched at her enthusiasm and obvious affection for his children.

"Slow down just a minute," he cautioned. "I want you to see that they're safe and their real needs are taken care of—not shower them with all kinds of entertainment and indulgences."

Corey could see so many emotions at war on his face: the wounded pride and embarrassment at having to ask her for help, concern over his children's well being, respect for her and gratitude at her easy willingness to take care of things for him, worry that she would spoil the boys, and a growing excitement over the fact that he would soon be back out in the wilderness he loved.

She would miss that dear, stubborn, proud face. Suddenly, it dawned on Corey that while she might have the boys all to herself while Brandon was gone, she wouldn't have Brandon at all. She leaped up off the couch and threw herself at the startled man, hugging him as hard as she could.

"Oh, Brandon, you'll be gone for two whole weeks; I'll miss you so much," she cried.

Brandon's rugged face softened. He gathered her into his arms and bent over her to stroke her hair. "I know, baby," he murmured, his voice growing thick and husky. "I'll miss you, too. I really don't want to go at all, but I can't think of any other way to make ends meet right now."

Corey knew that wasn't completely true. Brandon loved trekking in the backcountry forests, and part of him was probably delighted at a chance to return there, but she decided
to accept his statement as entirely accurate for the moment.

Besides, all she could really concentrate on right now were the delicious sensations cascading down her body as Brandon's caresses descended from her hair to her shoulders, all along her back to her buttocks. He pressed her tightly to him and groaned. Through the fabric of his walking shorts, Corey could feel him swell against her.

"Oh, Corey, what you do to me," he whispered into her hair, his warm breath flowing over the rim of her ear and brushing it with fire.

He cupped his hands under her bottom and pulled her even closer against him. She molded her body to his hard contours as easily as if she were made of modeling clay, her breasts crushed against the rigid wall of his chest, her pelvis against the hard ridge extending up toward his belly.

She bent her head back as far as it would go so she could look up at his face. His navy eyes had darkened until now they looked like the midnight sky. She lifted her arms to stroke his firm, square jaw and the hard planes of his abrasive cheeks. The coarse, golden, wire-like whiskers tingled against her palms, and her hands began to tremble.

Brandon bent his head, and Corey slid her fingers up higher into the thick blond hair at his temples. Brandon's head swooped even lower so his mouth could capture Corey's. The invading tongue brought her a rush of white-hot pleasure, and she began to moan.

The sound of a ball bouncing upstairs brought Brandon back to reality. With an immense display of self-control, he stepped away from Corey, only gently grasping her upper arms to steady her as he moved back. He knew the look of longing he saw on her face was reflected on his own, and he wished with all his heart he could satisfy it.

"Do you think you could stay tonight until John and Robbie have gone to bed?" he asked in a voice rough with desire.

Corey couldn't even find enough voice to answer, so she mutely nodded yes.

"I, uh, think I'll go check on the llamas," Brandon said and walked outside without a coat, in his shorts and T-shirt, welcoming the cold to ease his body and mind back to an equilibrium.

When he returned to the cabin a half an hour later, feeling enlivened by the crisp air and full of purpose, he found Corey, John and Robbie piled up on the couch with Hot Shot at their feet. Corey was gaily telling the excited boys about all the things they were going to do while they stayed with her.

There, she had impulsively leaped ahead of him, never thinking he might want to tell the boys in his own way and time that he would be gone for two weeks. And she was whipping them up to a frenzy of excitement, telling them about all the special things she had already planned, even though he had told her he would rather she just stuck to the basics. By the time he returned from the trek, they would be completely unmanageable, not to mention a handful while he was preparing for the trip.

"Okay, John, Robbie, go on upstairs and put your toys away before we have supper," he said in what he realized, with a twinge of guilt, was an unnecessarily stern voice.

The boys got up from the couch reluctantly and walked toward the stairs, dragging their feet with every step.

"I'll help," Corey said brightly and hopped up to follow the children.

"No, Corey, it's their job," Brandon called after her, but she was already halfway up to the loft and either didn't hear him or chose not to respond.

Fuming, Brandon waited for a bit before he went up to check on the work. He found Corey sitting on the floor, putting toy trucks and cars in the toy box, while John and Robbie sat on
the bed watching her.

"They're supposed to do that," Brandon said, making an effort to control his voice.

"They did the books; I'm doing the toys. They're just faster than I am," Corey said with an indulgent smile.

Brandon looked at the bookshelf. The books were jammed in haphazardly every which way.

"John, Robbie, remember how I showed you the way the books are supposed to go. Come over here and do it again," Brandon said quietly but firmly.

"Oh, Brandon, they're just little children, surely they don't have to do it perfectly. They did pick up all the books off the floor and put them on the shelves."

"Corey," Brandon said grimly, keeping his voice low since they were talking in front of the boys, "if children don't learn the value of doing a job well when they're young, they grow up thinking something halfway completed is acceptable. I've seen adults lose jobs because they never really do a job right, and they don't even realize what the problem is."

Corey didn't seem convinced, but she didn't say anything, just went back to putting toys away.

Brandon scowled fiercely. A man could never trust anyone to take care of things for him. The boys would be spoiled rotten by the time he returned from the backpacking trip. The old adage "if you want something done right, you have to do it yourself" was right on target. He didn't want to leave his sons with Corey, no matter how generous it was of her to agree to do it.

He had worked hard at turning himself into a parent. He shuddered to think how ignorant he had been when Jane had died. Both of the boys were just toddlers then; Robbie had still been in diapers. He had known absolutely nothing about taking care of them—their likes and dislikes, what they ate, how to dress them. He had been ashamed to admit to himself he really
didn't know anything about them at all.

But he had changed all that. He had tackled child rearing with the same intensity he put into everything he wanted to learn.

When he had stared down at Jane lying in her coffin, he had quaked with terror, but he had promised her he would take good care of her sons. And he had done it, too. Now he felt like a traitor turning them over to some other woman.

Perhaps he should have asked his parents to keep the boys after all. No. They had never approved of a single choice he had made in his entire life. He didn't want the boys exposed to their constant barrage of scolding and criticism. His parents would see the two weeks as a golden opportunity to mold their grandchildren to their own liking, just the way they had tried to shape him.

He wanted his sons to have the self-discipline and value of excellence that would allow them to pursue and succeed at any goal of their choosing. He wanted to instill in them a sense of their own self-worth and teach them to be strong and self-reliant.

He'd had to fight his parents every step of the way to be his own person. They had never understood or respected his love of nature. They had viewed it as some kind of softness that needed to be knocked out of him at all costs.

He would support his sons in their decisions whether they decided to be ballet dancers, doctors or lumberjacks. But first, they needed all the basic life skills and strengths before they developed into the men they were meant to be, sure of themselves and proud. And that included putting things away right, not letting someone else do it.

On a continuum his parents would be at the opposite end of the scale from Corey. Of the two he preferred Corey's liberal ways to his parents' harshness. Plus, he definitely didn't want them to know how short of money he was.

As she prattled with the boys while they straightened the books, Corey looked up and caught his eye. Her lovely soft, full lips turned up in a glorious smile, and he automatically beamed back before he remembered he was annoyed with her and tightened his face back down into a frown.

Corey did so much for him. She cooked meals, listened to him as though his thoughts and plans were of supreme importance, kept his body at a twenty-four-hour fever pitch of desire, and now she was going to take charge of the most important thing in his life—his sons. It was frightening how quickly he had become dependent on her. A woman could take over your whole camp before you even realized she had put up her tent stakes.

He never planned to visit her or invite her to the ranch, but she was like a drug that had gotten into his blood that he couldn't resist. The harder he tried to stay away from her, the more he craved her company. And just like a drug addict eventually became indebted to his supplier, so had he fallen into debt to Corey.

For what did he do in return for all the things she did for him? Absolutely nothing. It wasn't right. The only person in his whole life he had ever owed more to was Jane. It was a miserable feeling. Corey was a generous woman. It was one of the many things he admired about her, but the more she gave him that he had no way of returning, the worse he felt about himself. When he returned from the trek, he needed to cool things down—at least until he found some way to repay part of what Corey had done for him. If he could find a way to repay her.

Nine

In the wee hours of the Sunday dawn, Corey, John and Robbie stood on the cabin doorstep, waving goodbye to Brandon as he drove away. Soft Touch and Plie, the two least-pregnant female llamas, and Jester, the male, were loaded in the back of the covered pickup with the small travel trailer hitched behind the truck. The pickup and trailer would be left at the trailhead when Brandon and his group hiked off into the wild backcountry.

Corey looked down at the two small blond heads on either side of her and restrained a little shiver of fear. She sent a brief prayer heavenward for Brandon's safe return. She swallowed a lump in her throat and gave each of the small hands she was holding a soft squeeze. She was responsible for these little innocents for two whole weeks. She suddenly felt almost dizzy as the enormity of the responsibility swept over her. She had a quick glimmer of insight into the way Brandon must have felt when his wife died.

"Okay, boys, let's check the cabin one more time to make sure we haven't forgotten anything before we drive into Boise for church."

For the children's sake, she resolutely made her voice sound much more confident and grown-up than she was actually feeling at the moment.

John nodded solemnly and led the way to check the windows and doors, lights and water one last time before they left.

Corey studied the boys' faces carefully. Were they frightened at their father's absence? To her relief, Corey could find no evidence of worry. *In fact, they both are looking particularly splendid,* she thought with pride. She had outfitted them both in dress slacks and shirts from Kids' Kloset, over Brandon's protests. John even sported a minute tie.

Corey had been shocked to discover the boys had never been to church. Brandon had not even allowed them to attend their mother's funeral, thinking they were too young to understand what had happened and might be frightened by the burial proceedings.

Corey had attended church and Sunday school ever since she was an infant and was happy to be the one to remedy what she perceived as a deficiency in the boys' upbringing. The first time a child went to church was an important event in his life, and she wanted John and Robbie to be dressed appropriately for such a solemn occasion. Brandon would just have to grumble.

He always complained whenever she brought the boys something from Kids' Kloset, though she couldn't understand why. She only had to pay the consignment amount of the value of the item; it cost her very little out of pocket. He was just one of those people who wasn't very good at graciously accepting a gift, she supposed.

Corey locked up the cabin securely and stowed the keys safely in her purse. She walked over to her little blue sedan and was dismayed to find the boys pushing and shoving each other in a vehement argument over who was going to sit next to her.

Corey felt a moment of panic. *They never acted like this around Brandon. What should I do? How did you settle such a dispute equitably with no hurt feelings?* Finally, she hit upon the solution of drawing straws. Plucking some pine needles from a nearby tree, she offered them to the boys and then reassured John, the crestfallen loser, that he could sit next to her on the way to her house after church.

The boys quickly settled down once they had their seatbelts buckled and Corey started to drive, though the reason they were being so quiet, Corey noted uneasily, was because they were looking at the new picture books she had given them to read in church in case they found it difficult to sit still for such a long period of time. They had both promised they would save the books for church if she let them carry them. She thought she probably ought to say something to them, but instead, she took advantage of the quiet to lapse into her own thoughts.

It had been a whirlwind week, helping Brandon with his preparations for the trip and making her own plans in anticipation of the boys' visit. There had been fun times like when she had observed Brandon loading a lidded bucket with small, odorless pellets.

"Is that what I think it is?" she had asked, appalled.

"Yes," he had replied nonchalantly, not at all abashed to have been discovered packing llama poop to take with him on his travels. "The llamas like to relieve themselves in a spot that's already been established, so I take along a little starter to make a dung heap to help them out."

Brandon hadn't seemed to get what Corey had thought was so funny, but he had chuckled companionably along with her when she had laughed and laughed.

That had been one of the lighter moments, but Corey had noted, with a growing unease, a darker side to Brandon's attitude. He had seemed withdrawn, preoccupied. She had attributed his moodiness to concern over how the boys and the ranch would fare in his absence. Corey had done the best she could to reassure him he was leaving all in capable hands, but the more she tried to prove to him she could take care of everything, the more anxious he'd seemed to become.

The troubled week had culminated last night in their wildly passionate coupling. Brandon had made love to her so fiercely, with such intensity, Corey had almost been frightened. He seemed to be trying to reach the very privacy of her soul with his hands, mouth, body. Corey's body had shuddered with wave after wave of ecstasy under the onslaught. Even now, driving the car, Corey began to tremble, remembering Brandon's passion. He had made love to her like a man who was sharing intimacy with a woman for the last time.

Corey sighed as she pulled into the church's parking lot. She didn't think she would ever understand Brandon.

But now she needed to turn her attention to the task at hand. She ushered the boys into church and settled them into a pew. She wasn't going to sing in the choir this week so she could sit with them. She thought she would burst with pride as she watched their shining faces take in the new surroundings. They were behaving like perfect little angels. She would show Brandon she could take care of his sons. Why, there was nothing to it. It would be the easiest two weeks of her life.

The minister solemnly intoned, "Let us all bow our heads in prayer."

And Robbie called out in a voice that rang clearly from the back choir loft to the front altar, "I hafta go pee-pee!"

~ * ~

Brandon stared moodily into the dying embers of the campfire. He couldn't believe how much he missed Corey. His whole body ached for her. He saw her everywhere. Her warm brown eyes peeked shyly out at him from heaps of pine cones, her soft flowing hair mingled with cascading waterfalls, her glowing face floated before him in the magnificent sunsets.

At night when he lay snug and secure in his mummy sleeping bag, bone tired from a long day of hiking and a sunrise awakening, needing sleep, longing for sleep, he lay wide-eyed for hours, staring at the stars and thinking of Corey's soft, warm, enticing body.

With the toe of his hiking boot he nudged a blackly charred tree limb into the remains of the fire. *Damn the woman!* She wasn't even here, and she was taking over the whole expedition.

It was a good group—not a whiner in the bunch. They enthused over the grandeur of the mountains, admired the elegant, hard-working llamas, enjoyed his cooking and didn't complain about the rigors of the climb. The Big Horn Crags, Salmon River and Ship Island Lake were even more beautiful than he remembered from his last visit.

Under normal conditions it would have been an ideal trek. But nothing had been normal since he had made the mistake of entering Corey Tierney's clothing store.

He felt as though he were stumbling into a trap, just like he had felt trapped by that childish nursery-figure mobile the first time he had walked into Kids' Kloset. And if he wanted to be totally honest with himself, the way he had felt trapped when Jane had told him she was pregnant.

Not that he thought she had gotten pregnant on purpose, and he certainly wasn't fool enough to deny the truth that it took two to make a baby, but deep down in his heart, unfair as it was, he blamed her. And what was even worse, he blamed her even more for dying, for it wasn't until then that he had truly faced up to his responsibilities to the children.

Brandon leaped up from the campfire, finding it impossible to sit still any longer, and reached for the collapsible spade the llamas had packed in. Vigorously, with a much greater expenditure of energy than was necessary, he banked the campfire with dirt. He crouched low to duck into his tent, quickly stripped off his clothes and, naked, climbed into his mummy bag. In spite of the cold, he left all but the mesh portion of the tent flap unzipped so he could see the stars.

The constellations blazed fiercely against the clear, dark mountain sky. The crisp, clean mountain air was fragrant in his nostrils, the tethered llamas dozed in the pines nearby and a lone coyote sang soulfully to the moon. He was exactly where he wanted to be, so why wasn't he happy?

Because he had fallen into another trap, that was why. Corey probably hadn't intended to ensnare him anymore than Jane had. This was a different kind of trap—one of caring too much, of shared decisions, compromises and, ultimately, dependency. The kind of emotions a man couldn't afford to dabble in, not if he wanted to remain strong, self sufficient and independent.

Corey probably didn't realize what she was doing. She didn't know how much he was beginning to care for her and rely on her. She was a warm-hearted and generous woman. She enjoyed his company, only the Lord knew why, and she loved children, so she was spending time with him. She probably thought of him as some kind of charity case.

When that idea occurred to him as he lay in the darkened tent, Brandon scowled so hard his facial muscles hurt. He had to put a stop to this. He couldn't allow Corey to take over his whole life. It would weaken him until he no longer respected himself as a man. And what would happen to him and his sons when she got tired of playing earth mother? They would be devastated, that's what. He had to break it off. It would hurt now, but if he waited any longer, it would be impossible.

There. He had made a decision. It was unlike him to think about anything for so long and with such uncertainty. Usually, he knew exactly what he needed to do, and he did it. But now that the decision had finally been made, he was bound to start feeling better. He moved restlessly within the confines of the sleeping bag. So, why did it seem as though the mountains had crumbled down upon him and were crushing his heart under their weight of stone?

~ * ~

Corey plopped down on the couch in Brandon's cabin for a well-deserved rest. Thank goodness for Mrs. Gordon, her helper at Kids' Kloset. Mrs. Gordon had readily agreed to work afternoons while Corey was keeping John and Robbie. Corey wasn't sure how she would have managed if she had had to put in full hours at the store in addition to taking care of the boys and making the daily trip to feed Brandon's dog, Whiskey, and check on the llamas. Even with the shorter hours at the store, she fell into bed every night completely exhausted, not long after she had put the children down.

But it was definitely worth it. Caring for children full time was just as fascinating as she had always imagined it to be, though admittedly a bit more difficult than in her daydreams. She wondered how Brandon coped with the day-in, day-out rigors of child rearing.

How she admired him! He always seemed to know just what to do with the boys. He'd said he'd had little to do with their care when his wife was alive. He certainly must have been a fast learner when she'd died so suddenly. Thinking of the dozens of times during the past week she had felt uncertain and confused, she wondered again how he had managed.

Plus, he had made many improvements on the property—all with two little boys playing at his feet while he mended fences and built shelters.

Then there was all the time he spent promoting llamas in the community and throughout the state. He and the boys and the llamas marched in parades, visited schools and convalescent centers and attended every kind of fundraiser from the Girl Scouts to the Lions' Club. It was mind-boggling, really—his dedication and unflagging energy.

The thought of Brandon brought on a sharp pang of loneliness. She wrapped her arms around herself. Another whole week before she would see him again. She missed him dreadfully. Her body ached for his touch—both the grand, glorious sexual encounters and the little cuddles and kisses. And there were so many things she wanted to share with him. A dozen times a day she caught herself just before calling out his name when the boys said or did something funny. Plus, there was just something reassuring in his solid, silent strength when he was with her.

Corey sighed. She could hear the boys playing companionably upstairs in the loft, the last light of day warmed the rich golden wood of the cabin's fir logs, and Whiskey was curled contentedly at her feet. It would all be perfect if only Brandon were there to share it with her.

She glanced around the main floor of the cabin. Well, perhaps not quite perfect. The cabin was so... bare. The wood and architecture were beautiful, but everything was so plain. It really needed curtains, throw rugs, decorations—a woman's touch.

Corey sat straight up. She could do it. She was intimately acquainted with every thrift and recycle shop in Boise. A few side tables, old-fashioned lamps, a hooked rug or two, maybe some hunt or Western prints, and she would have a pulled-together look. And she could sew the curtains herself. Didn't she have a bolt of fabric in her back closet—one with a leaf design in muted shades of brown, green, gold and rust? It might do.

She hesitated. Brandon could be a little prickly sometimes when she baked for him or gave the boys presents. *What would he think if she redid the whole cabin?* She squeezed her eyes shut. In her imagination she could already see how beautiful the cabin would look. *Brandon would have to love it. How could he not?*

Overcoming her qualms, she began to think of dozens of other possibilities. Of course, she was already feeling overworked and unusually tired, but it would be such fun to surprise Brandon. She imagined the happy, amazed look on his face when he walked into the cabin upon his return and saw his home transformed by a little creative magic.

The llamas were thriving, the boys were happy and healthy, and Brandon would hardly recognize his newly decorated, picture-perfect cabin. Corey chuckled to herself. She would prove to him what a capable, multi-talented person she really was.

She hopped up from the couch. She knew where Brandon stored his tools. She could use his tape measure to get the window dimensions right now. Then, when she got home, she would cut out the fabric if it was as appropriate as she remembered and if there was enough of it.

Corey scurried to the toolbox. She only had a week to put her plan into action. She mentally rummaged through her basement and garage. Were there any odds and ends stored there she could use in the cabin? She hummed gaily as she measured the window frame.

~ * ~

Brandon is coming home today! What a long two weeks it's been, Corey thought, as she piled cans of dinosaur-shaped pasta in tomato-and-cheese sauce into the shopping cart. She added chicken-alphabet soup to the mountainous load. She wanted the cabin's kitchen pantry to be well stocked with food when Brandon returned. She didn't want him to have to run right out to buy groceries the minute he got back. *Poor dear, he'll probably be exhausted after two weeks of wandering in the wilderness.*

Corey couldn't quite imagine being in the woods for such a long stretch herself, but Brandon seemed to love it. She would massage his aching muscles when he returned tonight.

She paused by the canned fruit. Though, on second thought, perhaps she was the one who needed a massage; she was feeling rather tired herself. She wondered briefly if she might be coming down with something. It was unlike her to feel so fatigued, even with all the work of taking care of the boys and the redecorating. Normally, she was bursting with energy.

But she pushed concern over the puzzling exhaustion out of her mind at the thought of massive bunched muscles beneath her fingertips. She started to blush right there in the very public supermarket as a delightful tingle began to spread from a very private part of her anatomy.

Would he have grown a beard? Would it tickle? Corey beamed in anticipation. Robbie, who was sitting in the little seat at the back of the shopping cart and sucking on a lollypop, gave her a sticky smile in return.

But where was John? He was supposed to be walking right beside the cart. Guiltily, Corey realized she had been so lost in her daydream of Brandon's homecoming that she had completely neglected to keep an eye on John. She felt a quick spurt of panic, thinking of all the stories she had read in magazines and newspapers of children who had disappeared forever when their parents had failed to watch them for only a few minutes.

Corey pushed the unwieldy grocery cart as fast as she could toward the end of the aisle. When she was almost to the end, John popped around the corner, his face lit with the triumphant glow of a warrior returning from the hunt loaded down with prey. His chubby little arms crushed six giant packages of cookies against his chest.

"Look what I found!" he cried.

Corey was flooded with relief. She supposed that was why she added all six packages of cookies to the already overflowing cart, though she knew she really shouldn't.

Now that she had found John, Corey took a place in the checkout line before she was tempted to add anything else to the shopping cart. The machine the clerk used to scan the barcodes made a sound as it read each item. Soon Robbie began imitating the sound.

"Ka-ching, ka-ching, ka-ching." Every single time the machine made the noise, Robbie imitated it.

Bemused at first at Robbie's persistence, Corey began to feel slightly alarmed as the ka-chings seemed to go on forever. When the checker finally told Corey the total, she was astounded. No wonder Brandon had needed to earn extra money. Two little boys could easily eat you out of house and home.

Three hours later the arduous task of marketing was complete. Corey had loaded bag after bag of groceries into her car, made the drive from Boise to Roby Creek, unloaded all the heavy grocery bags from the trunk, lugged them into the cabin and stowed every last can and package in Brandon's pantry and refrigerator. Now everything was ready for Brandon's return, but all Corey wanted to do was sleep for a month or two.

She was feeling a little sick to her stomach, too. *I really must have caught a virus,* she thought. *What a terrible time to be sick!* Brandon would be back any minute now. But perhaps it was only nerves. She chuckled softly to herself, amused at the way her own body seemed to react to Brandon, entirely independent of her will. Her breasts were obviously anxious for his touch as well— they felt tender and swollen, heavy and full. Corey flushed as she thought of how addicted to Brandon and his lovemaking she had become. She wondered what her fellow choir members would think if they knew what went on in Ms. Tierney's head these days.

At the sound of the pickup engine straining to pull the heavy load of llamas and the trailer up the drive, Corey rushed to the door and flung it open. Her heart was beating so fast with nerves and excitement she felt a little faint. John and Robbie raced past her to greet their dad. In a panic she ran after them and grabbed their hands, afraid they were going to dart right in front of the truck.

Brandon saw the trio waiting for him and blinked back moisture that scalded his eyes like steam from a hot-springs geyser. It had been a gloomy drive home as he had rehearsed the words he would use to tell Corey he couldn't see her anymore. She might be a little upset at first, but it wouldn't take her long to get over it. He refused to dwell on how long it would take him to get over her.

She would soon find other children she could lavish with gifts and attention and some other man she could shower with her warm-hearted laughter and loving. At that thought Brandon gripped the steering wheel so hard it felt like he might rip it away from the steering column.

He wished he could find some way to repay her for all she had done for them before they went their separate ways, but he couldn't think of any way to do it. Over the past few months whenever he had been at Corey's home, he had looked for things he might do for her: patch the roof, fix a leak in the plumbing, repair an appliance, work in the yard—but she was so darned self-sufficient and well organized there never seemed anything for him to do.

On the trek he had collected things he thought were beautiful or intriguing to give her: a hummingbird's nest no bigger than a walnut, an ancient fossilized fish skeleton, moonstones and eagle feathers; but just before his return, he had thrown them all away, disgusted with his own naiveté. A city girl like her would probably think it was nothing but a parcel of trash.

No, if he couldn't give her real store-bought gifts like jewelry or clothes—and there was no question that he could not with his finances in their current state—he would just have to accept the fact, no matter how painful and humiliating, that when they separated, he was going to leave greatly in her debt.

He was already burdened with a heavy load of guilt for not having given Jane the emotional support, time and attention she had deserved, but at least he had supported her and their children financially, even if it hadn't been exactly a lifestyle of luxury.

With his mind a whirling jumble of thoughts and emotions, Brandon braked the pickup and turned off the motor. John and Robbie tore away from Corey's grasp and assaulted the truck, leaping off and on the running board, plastering their faces against the window glass and calling out, their voices shrill with excitement, for their father to hurry up and get out.

Brandon climbed down from the cab of the truck and scooped them up in a fierce embrace. He felt overcome with guilt at letting them get attached to someone he had no right to keep in his life. Their mother had disappeared, never to return; how would they react when Corey was gone for good?

He looked over the bright blond heads nestled under his chin and stared at Corey. She looked absolutely radiant. The sun was coming from behind her, creating a halo of light around her hair; she had a wide, beautiful, welcoming smile on her face, and her eyes glowed with... what? He was very much afraid to analyze just what that expression was in her eyes.

He nuzzled his chin in the boys' hair—they were squirming in his arms like a pair of puppies—and then looked at the ground, unable to greet her with honesty. He couldn't bear to change that shining look of welcome to one of hurt. In spite of all his good intentions to tell Corey they couldn't continue on such unequal footing, he felt himself begin to waver.

Surely, they could find a way to keep on seeing one another. Perhaps they could work out some kind of compromise that wouldn't eat away at his sense of honor and self-respect. If only Corey would let him find a way to do things for her for a change instead of her doing all the favors and gift giving. She was an intelligent woman; surely she would understand how she was undermining him as a man and allow him to even up the balance sheet. It was hard for him to express his feelings in words, but she was worth the effort of trying to say it.

He set the boys down and gave her a tentative little smile. Suddenly, he felt like a dam had burst and a floodgate of happiness was released. It only took two giant steps to reach her and enfold her in his arms. She felt so right, so good, snuggled up next to him. *How could I have ever thought I could give her up?* he wondered in a daze.

Corey sighed in utter contentment at being held in his strong arms. "Oh, Brandon, I missed you so much," she whispered.

"I missed you, too," he said gruffly. "I thought about you all the time."

He pulled her even closer to him and lowered his head, seeking her soft lips for a kiss that was so full of tenderness it brought tears to Corey's eyes.

John and Robbie giggled and tugged at Brandon's shirttail. Reluctantly, it seemed, Brandon released her. "I guess we had better get the llamas unloaded," he said, his voice a husky growl of what she hoped was suppressed desire.

Corey's nerves were skittering with impatience. She could hardly wait for Brandon to see the cabin, but she knew the animals had to be taken care of first.

Jester, Soft Touch and Plie seemed to realize they were home, for they scrambled down the ramp from the back of the pickup without any prodding and had what looked like a joyful reunion with the other llamas in the pasture. Brandon carefully inspected every llama, noting that two of them would be delivering new babies soon and exclaiming over how much Hot Shot seemed to have grown in just the two weeks he had been gone.

Hot Shot appeared to feel right at home in the meadow by now. All the other llamas had accepted him, even though they hadn't quite known what to make of him at first when he had still been wearing Brandon's sweater.

"Everything's in tip-top shape, Corey. You did a fine job of taking care of the ranch," Brandon said, his voice warm with respect and admiration.

Just wait, Corey thought, flushing at the praise, *until he sees what I've done to the cabin. He's going to be so surprised!*

Corey and Brandon walked back to the house with their arms around one another's waist, each of them holding one of the boy's hands. All four of them continually interrupted each other as they bubbled over with the news of the past two weeks.

Corey preceded Brandon through the door then whirled around, her heart in her throat, to watch his face as he took in the altered surroundings.

It had all turned out even better than she had hoped. *The cabin really could be featured in Country Living magazine,* she thought, not bothering with any false modesty.

The curtains were perfect—the golden tones of the leaf design picked up the color of the fir logs, and the green and rust provided accent points that were echoed in the pillows tossed on the couch.

She had found numerous used hooked and braided rugs of various sizes to scatter over the bare wood floor. The rugs were old but still serviceable, and Corey thought their colors were even more beautiful now that they had mellowed.

She had discovered an assortment of old tables, none of which matched, but all of them looked great tucked in the nooks and crannies of the living area. There were odd, old-fashioned lamps; a sheepskin hide (legs and head attached) stretched on the wall; the scrubbed pine kitchen table was set with kid-proof green marble enamelware; and one of her best finds, a bent-twig rocker, was pulled up next to the potbellied stove.

And everywhere there were flowers—a riot of flowers—displayed in canning jars and jam pots. She and the boys had spent a good part of yesterday afternoon picking the very first blooms of spring to decorate the cabin. She beamed with pleasure.

There was a stunned look on Brandon's face.

After a long silence, while Corey held her breath, he finally said in a tight voice, "John, Robbie, would you please go get my backpack for me? I left it on the ground by the pickup."

The boys ran outside, and Brandon shut the door after them. He whipped around to face Corey.

"No, no, *NO!*" he shouted, sounding like a locomotive building up a head of steam.

Corey stared at him, her eyes wide with disappointment and hurt. Then she dropped down on the couch and burst into tears.

Brandon stalked to the window. He saw the trees outside through a red mist of anger. He felt like a poleaxed steer. How dare she waltz into his home and change everything around? Okay, he amended, so he had invited her there himself for the supremely important job of taking care of his children. But still, it was exactly the kind of thing he hated about women; they were always rearranging your life.

Corey's sobs tore through him. He felt like a jerk for yelling at her. He couldn't stand to hear her cry.

He would never have believed anyone could have so completely transformed the place in only two weeks. She had changed it from a hermit's shack to a house fit for a king. It was warm, welcoming and, in spite of the flowers, comfortably masculine. It was everything a man could want in a home, but he never could have made it like that if he had worked on it for the rest of his life. He hated himself for hurting her feelings after she had presented him with such a marvelous gift, but now she had added about a million dollars to the debt he already owed her.

He took several long deep breaths to calm down. What to do now? Did he want her to take everything away just because she hadn't had permission to put it there? Did he really want everything his way when her way was better?

He went to her and gathered her into his arms, but she was crying so hard she hardly seemed to notice. Her body felt limp and boneless. She sounded as though her heart were breaking.

"Corey, I'm sorry," he began. "I shouldn't have yelled at you. The place looks great. I can see you went to a lot of trouble."

He looked at her more closely. Feeling alarmed, he noticed her pallor. "You look a little pale. You've probably worked yourself half to death fixing it up, but you shouldn't have done it. In the first place, this is my home, and you shouldn't have changed anything without asking me."

"I... I'm sorry. I never thought... I just wanted to make it nice for you," she sobbed.

"Shh, shh." He soothed her the same as if he were holding Robbie when he was having one of his nightmares, brushing her hair away from her face, pulling out one of his bandannas to wipe away the tears and rocking her in his arms. He wished he could just claim her mouth with his own to stop the crying, but as hard as it was for him to use the right words, he had to try to make her understand.

"And in the second place," he continued resolutely, "you've already done way too much for me. Don't you know how hard it was for me to ask you to keep the boys?"

She shook her head from side to side in a silent "no." She looked so sorrowful it made him ache inside, but at least, he noted with relief, the tears had stopped flowing.

"Well, it was. It seems like every time I turn around you've done something special for me, and I don't do anything for you."

At that, Corey sat up straighter and started to say something, but Brandon put a finger to her lips to gently shush her.

"It's true. And it makes me feel bad inside. I want you to make me a promise. Will you do that?"

"Maybe. It depends on what it is," she said slowly.

Brandon couldn't help but grin. That was more like the listen-to-the-man-then-make-her-own-decision Corey he knew than this sad-eyed, woebegone person he was holding in his arms.

"I want you to promise not to do one more thing for me—no clothes or toys for the boys, no cleaning or baking, and especially no redecorating—until you give me a chance to do some nice things for you. Promise?"

"Well," she hedged, "the boys will miss the desserts."

"Not even one cookie. Promise?"

"Okay. I promise." She smiled a wobbly smile and held up her fingers in the Scouts' honor sign.

He had never been so relieved in his life as when he saw the light come back into her eyes.

"Of course, this kind of sweet doesn't count," he said as he bent his head to steal as many kisses as he could before the boys dragged his backpack to the door.

Ten

Corey woke up feeling groggy and disoriented. She yawned, stretched and then blinked several times in dismay. Four pairs of curious eyes were trained on her.

Brandon sat in his new bent-twig rocker, and John, Robbie and Whiskey were sitting on the floor in a straight line at his feet. All of them were staring at Corey, who was lying on their couch.

"Welcome to the world of the living," Brandon said, sounding amused.

"My goodness, what happened? Why am I here? What time is it, anyway?" Corey asked in confusion.

Brandon made a great show of looking at his watch. "Going on just about noon, I'd say," he drawled lazily.

"Noon!" Corey sat bolt upright and threw back the blanket that was covering her, then snatched it back up to her chest, not feeling overly confident about what she might be wearing under it. But it was okay. She was fully clothed except for her shoes, which she saw were neatly aligned by the firebox next to the stove. She was still dressed in the new light blue top and dark blue slacks she had bought for Brandon's homecoming.

"Why am I still here? Oh! And it's Sunday. I've missed church—and I was supposed to sing a solo for the choir."

"Don't worry," Brandon reassured her. "I'm sure they'll get along without you just this once. You fell asleep right after supper while I was doing the dishes. You looked so worn out I just let you sleep. I couldn't see you driving back to Boise when you were so exhausted. I was right, too. You've been sleeping over fifteen hours straight. You didn't even wake up with all the noise we made cooking breakfast."

"Daddy said we might never get to sit on the couch again," John said.

"I thought you'd gone to heaven," Robbie added. "But Daddy said you couldn't have, 'cause you were snoring."

"Snoring! I don't snore!" Corey gave Brandon a baleful look.

"Sure you do. You were rattling the lids on all the pots in the kitchen."

"Harumph," was the only rejoinder Corey could think of, not being at her most brilliant after fifteen hours of sleep.

"We saved you some breakfast, though I suppose it's brunch by now. How about we serve it to you where you're sitting? Would that count as breakfast in bed? I'm going to have to get really creative at finding ways to pamper you if I'm going to repay you for all the new stuff in the cabin."

"I think I'd be a lot more comfortable at the table, but thanks for saving me something to eat; I'm starving. Just let me wash my face, then I'll be right there."

Corey quickly freshened up, then hurried into the kitchen. She felt like she could eat a bull moose, she was so hungry, but the minute she sat down to the stack of pancakes and ham and eggs Brandon had cooked for her, she was overcome with a wave of nausea. *What a peculiar virus,* Corey thought, *to come and go so unexpectedly.* The food was beautifully prepared and served up on the second-hand green enamelware Corey had found for Brandon. She didn't want to hurt his feelings by not eating, but the huge appetite she had felt just a moment ago had totally disappeared, and her face felt like it was as green as the plate.

Experimentally, she took a tiny sip of the strong, hot coffee to see how it affected her stomach. As her insides roiled, Corey got ready to make a dash for the bathroom.

The telephone rang, and Brandon went to his desk in the living area to answer it. Corey took advantage of his absence to scrape the contents of her plate into the garbage. The boys had gone upstairs to play, so they couldn't tell on her.

When Brandon returned to the kitchen, walking as though he were in a trance, and sank down despondently on one of the chairs, the dazed expression on his face took precedent over even her upset stomach.

"What's wrong?" Corey asked, feeling frightened at his strange behavior.

Brandon looked around to see if John or Robbie was in earshot. "It was Mrs. Thornton, the boys' grandmother," Brandon said, his voice hollow. "She'd hardly said hello before she just flat out stated she and her husband want their grandchildren to come and live with them."

"What!" Corey exclaimed, surprised and shocked. "I don't remember you ever saying anything before about them wanting the children."

"I hadn't. I didn't know anything about it. At the time of the funeral, they never talked about raising the boys. Or at least I don't think they did; it's hard to remember. Of course, I knew it was a terrible tragedy for them, too—Jane was their only child—but everything was so confused. I had so much to do then, to take care of, and I was hurting so bad—I probably wasn't too careful of their feelings or what they wanted."

Corey didn't know what to do or say. Brandon's rugged face was wracked with pain. She quietly slipped over to stand beside him. He reached for her hand like a drowning man and clasped it so tightly she thought her bones would surely be crushed. She squeezed back as hard as she could, trying to silently tell him she was there for him.

"I thought something didn't seem quite right at Christmas when the Thorntons picked up John and Robbie for their visit. They seemed different somehow, and it made me feel uneasy, but then... well, you remember what happened with you and me?"

Brandon looked up into Corey's eyes, and a ghost of a smile flickered in his navy eyes as they both remembered the joy they had shared Christmas Eve under the twinkling lights of the Yuletide tree.

"When Grandma and Grandpa Thornton brought the boys back," Brandon continued, "I was floating sky high. They could have stood on their heads naked, and I probably wouldn't have noticed."

"What did you say to Mrs. Thornton?" Corey asked softly.

"She took me totally by surprise. I didn't know what to say, so I acted like I thought she meant she wanted the boys to come for a visit again. I said they could go see their grandparents this summer as soon as school lets out, but she didn't buy that for a minute. She said they wanted the boys living with them full time, but she would allow her grandchildren to see me on holidays. My own sons! The old biddy," he concluded bitterly.

"Oh, my!" Corey couldn't believe what she was hearing.

"But that's not the worst of it. There's more."

"More?" she said incredulously.

"Yeah. The teeth in her demand," he said, his voice hard. "They knew I wouldn't just hand John and Robbie over to them, so ever since Christmas they've been complaining to Idaho Health and Welfare about my care of the boys. They've told the authorities I'm a neglectful and abusive father."

"No! They couldn't," Corey exclaimed indignantly. "There would be no evidence, no grounds at all. Why, you're the best parent I've ever met."

"Thanks," Brandon said and bent his head to kiss the hand he was clutching so tightly. "That means a lot to me."

"So the social workers will just ignore the Thorntons, won't they?"

"Who knows?" Brandon scrubbed his free hand across his brow. "Mrs. Thornton said that at Christmas time she took pictures of John that showed bruises on his arms and legs. And they know about the time I was late picking him up at school and that I took him out of the regular school district because I had an argument with the teacher. All of that might look bad to a social worker."

"How did John get the bruises?"

"I don't know." Brandon shoved his hand through his hair. "I don't remember any special accident back then. Kids almost always have a bruise somewhere—roughhousing at school, a stumble on the stair steps, climbing on the bunk beds—it could have been almost anything."

Corey gently smoothed his savaged hair back into place. "Well, if the social services people work with children all the time, they must know the difference between little mishaps and real abuse, don't you think?"

"I sure hope so. I don't know anything at all about the way the Health and Welfare Department works. Could be they're not going to check on me at all. They might think the Thorntons sound like a couple of cranks and ignore the whole thing. Mrs. Thornton said they'd been calling the Department since Christmas. It's April already. Wouldn't the social workers have already contacted me, if they were going to?"

"I don't know, either," Corey said slowly, trying to think the situation through. She wanted to reassure Brandon, but she thought he ought to take the threats seriously. She didn't want to give any false encouragement. "Perhaps they're just so overloaded with cases it's taken them all these months to get around to you."

Brandon sighed. "Maybe so. Or it's even possible the Thorntons never complained to the Department at all. They might just be trying to scare me. I don't know what to think, but I know Mrs. Thornton didn't sound like she was playing with a full deck."

"Is there anything I can do to help?"

For the first time since the telephone rang, Brandon grinned, though the smile was so twisted it looked more like a grimace. "This is one time I'd gladly accept your help. I don't know what I'd do if I lost the boys, but it's my battle. I don't think anyone can help me."

He silently pondered the dilemma for a few moments, then added, "Though Mrs. Thornton may have helped me a little herself without realizing it. At least if the Health and Welfare people investigate me, I'll be prepared. I'm not sure what I might have said or done if they had called without any warning. Or worse yet, if they'd just showed up at the ranch. I have a feeling I might have hurt my case by booting them off the place."

He smiled again with that awful twisted grin that showed so clearly the pain he was feeling.

Corey bent to brush her lips against his cheek.

Corey's presence is a comfort, Brandon thought, in spite of the fear he didn't want to admit to that was tearing him up inside. He pushed his chair away from the table to make enough room to pull her down onto his lap. She felt so good cuddled close to him. He nuzzled his face into the soft, delicate skin just under her chin. She giggled as she twisted and squirmed on his lap.

In spite of the seriousness of the situation, he could still make her laugh. He knew his scratchy whiskers tickled her neck. He smiled; it made him feel better to hear her laughter. He kissed her throat, then trailed a path of tiny kisses up over the angle formed by the fine bones of her jaw and continued along her smooth cheek until his mouth found her soft, pliant lips. She was so very lovely—girlish and womanly at the same time—and utterly, enticingly female.

A rush of desire hit him. If the boys hadn't been so near and if she had been willing, he would have liked to claim her right there on the kitchen table.

Brandon squeezed his eyes tightly shut and fought to control his body. Was it wrong to want her so much when he was facing such a difficult problem? Did it make him less of a man to think of a woman when he needed to be resolute and strong to plot a course of action? Was it a sign of weakness to welcome her sympathetic understanding?

On the backcountry trek he had decided to break off with Corey. He had resolved to put an end to this relationship where Corey contributed so much more than he did. He had been thinking mostly about the material, financial side of things, but he was obviously becoming emotionally dependent as well.

The Thorntons' phone call had clamped a leaden weight to his heart. Somehow Corey's presence made it easier to bear up under the burden. He had always thought of Jane—of any woman, really—as someone who had to be taken care of, to be provided for by a man. *Could a man allow a woman to also take care of him and still be a man?*

A man and a woman both giving each other all they had. Could that be what people called love? He knew he loved his children unconditionally; he felt a kind of love that was mostly respect for his parents, but he wasn't sure if he had ever really loved a woman. Could he have fallen in love with Corey?

The idea of love had never crossed his mind. It was such a disturbing thought he surged up out of the chair, almost tumbling Corey onto the floor. Quickly, he grabbed her arm to steady her.

"Whoa there. I'm sorry. I didn't mean to throw you on the floor. I guess I'm still too upset to think straight."

"It's all right. You didn't hurt me—just startled me a bit," she replied a trifle shakily.

Brandon inspected her more closely. "You still look a little pale even after all that sleep. You really have been working too hard. I know I haven't even begun to thank you properly for keeping the boys for me, and now here I go again worrying you with my problems."

"I had a wonderful time taking care of John and Robbie. Truly, Brandon, it was my pleasure."

"Somehow, I have a hard time believing it was all a pleasure. Taking care of kids is a big job. I've learned that the hard way."

He hunched his shoulders and roughly ran his fingers through his hair once again, undoing the smoothing Corey had done. There were so many unsettling thoughts buzzing around in his head, it felt like it might spin off his neck and fly out the cabin. He looked through the window, then turned back to Corey.

"Do you feel up to a little walk? When something's bothering me, I need to get outdoors. Maybe the fresh air would be good for you, too."

Corey brightened. "Yes, let's. Spring is so beautiful here in the mountains. So different than in town. You can't do anything about the boys' grandparents right now anyway. We might as well enjoy the sunshine before I have to drive back to Boise."

Brandon walked to the stairs and called up to the children, "John, Robbie, come here. We're going for a walk."

Their whoops of glee rang down from the loft. Brandon smiled to himself. They shared his interest in nature and loved playing outside. At least that was one thing he had given them.

His smile turned to a frown. He wondered what the Thorntons wanted to give the boys. The furrows across his brow deepened. Did they really think he was a neglectful parent, or were they just using those accusations to achieve their own goal of custody of their grandchildren?

John and Robbie came tumbling down the stairs, and Brandon gratefully allowed the immediate needs of the children to take his mind away from his worries. Corey helped him get the boys into their jackets, and then they all walked together along the path leading to the meadow.

It was a beautiful day. There were only a few patches of snow left in the low-lying areas that were always in shade. The sun was shining brightly. The meadow was tinted in waves of blue and purple from the profusion of early-blooming camas and grass-widows. In the shady wooded area along the fence line, there was a luxuriant growth of wakerobins, the white flowers that would stay fresh for days after being cut. Corey had had plenty of blooms to choose from when she had decorated the cabin.

Brandon knew there could be many more bouts with bitter cold before summer, but right now he felt himself relax and rejoice in the perfect spring day. He was surprised to realize he was glad to be home. Usually when he was on a packing expedition, he wanted to stay in the backcountry forever, but now as he looked at Corey's radiant face and watched his sons, as agile as little squirrels, tearing through the field to climb the trees in the woods, he felt there could be no better place to be in the whole world.

The llamas, all—except Hot Shot—much too dignified to hurry, came ambling toward them through the blue and pinky-purple blossoms. Corey greeted each llama by name as if they were all old friends. It had become her habit to grab a handful of carrots before leaving the cabin for the meadow, so now she had a treat for each of the animals.

Brandon watched her play with Hot Shot, admiring her exuberance and zest for living. He hadn't been ready to allow a woman in his life, but she had taken him by storm with her beauty, warm heart and loving ways. He sent a silent prayer of thanksgiving for his great luck in meeting such a wonderful woman. He had failed with Jane, but now he was being given a second chance. Jane had been a good woman, too, but he had never had the strong feelings for her that he was experiencing now with Corey. He felt his heart swell with pure pleasure as Corey tossed her long, wavy hair over her shoulder and graced him with a glorious smile.

All of the female llamas were in varying stages of pregnancy. Brandon examined them with a speculative look. If all went well with the crias, he might soon be out of his financial difficulties. Then he would be in a position to offer Corey a relationship of more permanence. If she would have him. He felt a tremor of fear at the possibility of her rejection.

He'd thought he wanted her out of his life, but he'd been lying to himself. It was hard for a man to admit to himself that he was frightened, but that's what he was. He'd been overwhelmed with the responsibility of raising his sons alone, consumed with fear that he would fail. Attempting to woo a woman had seemed like just too much to add to what he was already struggling with, no matter how happy that woman made him feel.

He'd tried to find fault with Corey, but it had been hard to do. True, she was generous to a fault, but what kind of nitpicking was he indulging in to complain about too much of a good thing? And she did sometimes question his disciplining of the boys, but if he wanted to be honest with himself, perhaps he was just a mite too sensitive to criticism.

No, she was a very special woman, and he hoped he wasn't fooling himself by thinking he might have a chance to someday make her his wife.

Brandon broke off a tall spike of camas and stripped away the bright blue petals. *What a rotten time for the Thorntons to demand custody of John and Robbie,* he thought, as he ripped the flower apart. He wasn't the kind of man to just sit around hoping a problem would go away; he always met a challenge head on. He would talk to Mr. and Mrs. Thornton face to face. Perhaps he could convince them their grandchildren were in good hands. He would reassure them they could be a part of John and Robbie's life without taking total control. Surely, they knew their charges of abuse were ridiculous. He was a tough disciplinarian and had no intention of ever changing that, but he would never strike his children as a punishment.

Corey gave Hot Shot and Jester one final pat each then came to stand by Brandon. She shyly reached out for his hand. Her soft little palm felt exactly right enveloped by his hard, work-scarred fingers. They strolled along together through the meadow, the boys and the llamas trailing along behind them, forming a jolly little parade. Perhaps, Brandon fervently hoped, if all went well, he would be able to hold that small hand forever.

Eleven

In startled disbelief, Corey shot bolt upright to the edge of the examining table. "I can't be!" she exclaimed in a shocked, shrill voice.

Dr. Gettle snapped off his gloves and dropped them in the waste receptacle. "There's very little chance of error, because you're so far along. I'd stake my thirty-five years of practice on it. Of course, we'll do a blood test just for confirmation, but you're definitely pregnant—about four months I'd say."

He patted Corey's cotton-draped thigh comfortingly. "Get dressed and wait for me in my conference room. We'll discuss your options then."

He bustled busily out of the small room and on to his next patient. Corey remained perched on the end of the examining table for several long minutes before she could gather her wits sufficiently to climb down and collect her clothing. "It's impossible," she muttered half aloud. "It just can't be; I can't get pregnant."

She stared at her reflection in the little mirror hung on the back of the examining room door. Did she look different? But other than her eyes were wide with wonder and her face flushed with excitement, she appeared to be the same old Corey. Suddenly the reality began to sink in.

"I'm going to have a baby," she whispered to the mirror.

She started to get dressed, but she was so sizzling with excitement she couldn't concentrate on such a mundane activity. Hugging her slacks and shirt to her chest, clothed only in her underwear, she began a triumphant dance of joy within the confines of the examining room. "I'm going to have a baby!" she whooped.

Feeling foolish when she realized what she was doing and where she was doing it, she paused to pull on the rest of her clothes. Her fingers trembled so badly she had major difficulties with snaps, zippers and buttons.

She had wondered why her doctor had insisted on a pelvic after she'd described her flu symptoms to him when she'd arrived at his office for her appointment. When he'd asked her how long it had been since her last period, she'd been unable to tell him. It was a conscious decision on her part to not keep track of her cycle. As far as she was concerned, the less she thought about it the better.

When she and Wayne had been trying to conceive, the whole business of charting her periods and her daily resting morning temperature, trying to pinpoint ovulation, had gradually become hateful to her. The saying that menstruation was a desolate uterus shedding tears of blood over the absence of a baby was true for her.

But now! Now her lifelong dream was coming true. She quickly pulled a brush through her hair and double-checked her appearance. She hurried into the doctor's conference room and took one of the comfortable leather-upholstered chairs placed in front of his huge, cluttered desk. She waited for him impatiently. He seemed to take a very long time.

Corey looked around the room, trying to distract herself. Dr. Gettle had a collection of little figurines of doctors at their tasks, displayed in an old-fashioned shadow box hung next to his numerous diplomas. One miniature was of a stork laboring to carry a jolly, red-cheeked doctor who was proudly carrying a tiny, roly-poly, equally rosy-cheeked baby.

Corey put a hand to her own flushed cheek. *Could it really be true?* She hoped she wasn't dreaming. Was the stork finally, after all these years of hoping and praying, going to pay her a visit?

It did make sense, now that she understood what was happening. All the signs had been there all along. Her "flu" symptoms—the bouts with nausea, fatigue, breast tenderness and, the clincher, no periods—had all been shouting pregnancy if she'd only been listening. She had just been so utterly convinced for so long that she was unable to have a child that she had not been able to make the proper connections to recognize her condition. She had certainly searched for those very signs often enough in the past.

Corey grinned as tears of joy began to trickle down her cheeks. She quickly swiped them away. What an old silly she was. She didn't want Dr. Gettle to get the wrong impression. And she wished he'd hurry up, too; she could hardly wait to talk about her baby. *My very own baby,* she thought with a profound sense of wonder and supreme satisfaction.

Finally, the doctor entered the room, sat down behind the desk and cleared his throat. "Before we discuss anything else, I want to clarify one point. You being an unmarried woman and all, is there a possibility you might decide to terminate this pregnancy?"

Corey shrank back in horror into the recesses of the deep chair. "Absolutely not," she said, putting both hands over her abdomen as though to protect the developing baby from being snatched away from her.

"Good," Dr. Gettle beamed, wagging his bushy gray eyebrows at her. "I prefer not to perform any of the procedures after the first trimester."

"Doctor, how could I have possibly gotten pregnant?"

Dr. Gettle allowed himself a little chuckle, his rosy plump cheeks pushing the wrinkles around his eyes into a million crinkles. "Oh, I imagine in the usual way, my dear," he said gently.

Blushing furiously, Corey persisted. "But... I mean... the endometriosis? I thought I couldn't have children."

"Ah, I see. So you didn't take any precautions?"

Corey shook her head in a silent "no."

Dr. Gettle leafed through the thick file on his desk. "But according to the medical records I received from your doctors in Twin Falls, the laser surgery and drug therapy were considered successful."

"That's true. But my husband, I mean my ex-husband, and I tried to have a baby for over a year and nothing happened. We were very... uh... clinical about it. I thought the doctors were wrong."

The doctor observed her for a moment with his wise, old eyes. "Assuming, of course, your husband had also been examined for potency and checked out okay, another possible medical explanation might be you were simply too stressed to conceive. Sometimes the harder you try to have a child, the more difficult it becomes. Stress can be a powerful contraceptive."

Dr. Gettle gave the papers in Corey's file a few quick taps with his pen. "And, frankly, my dear, medical science doesn't always have all the answers. A midwife whose work and opinions I respect once told me a woman doesn't conceive a child until her soul is ready to welcome one. Perhaps your ex-husband just wasn't the right father for your baby."

Brandon. Corey thought of what a wonderful lover he was. She thought of how good he was with John and Robbie. If she had been able to scour the globe for a perfect father for her child, she would have chosen Brandon. She only hoped he would feel the same way.

"Now I'm going to ask you some questions you'll think are none of my business, even if I am your doctor, but let me assure you they do have a bearing on both your and your baby's health and welfare."

Dr. Gettle adjusted his spectacles over the bridge of his nose and peered over the top of the frames at Corey. "Are you planning on getting married?"

Corey sucked in a quick gasp of air. "Well, I'm not really sure," she hedged. "You see, I never imagined I could get pregnant, so we—the baby's father and I—have never actually discussed marriage."

Dr. Gettle could pull out her tongue with hot pinchers before she would admit to him the baby's father had not only never, ever mentioned marriage to her, he had also never told her he loved her. *In fact,* she thought with brutal, painful, humiliating honesty, *there are times—like when I surprised him by decorating the cabin—when I'm not sure if he even likes me.*

"I know modern young women these days think they can take care of a family all by themselves, and they can, too. I've seen a many of them do it. But it takes its toll. It's very, very difficult. If you have a good income and other family or friends to help, it's a little easier, but I'm not ashamed to admit I'm old-fashioned enough to think a child needs both a mother and a father. I want you to just think about that when you make your decisions about your and your baby's future."

Corey nodded in solemn agreement. She knew she would be thinking of little else in the days to come.

Before leaving the clinic, Corey made follow-up appointments with her doctor and filled his prescription for mega-vitamins. She was going to take the very best possible care of her baby. She would even give up coffee and drink milk instead—though she loathed it. And she would manage to fit into her busy schedule a daily walk and be sure to get in eight hours of sleep every night.

Corey remembered during her marriage when she had been so desperately trying to have a baby. Everywhere she had looked it seemed she had seen some kind of advice on how to have a healthy pregnancy. Every magazine she had picked up, every TV show she had turned on, every chance conversation she had overheard—all had been about babies and pregnancy. It had made her miserable then, but now at long last, she would be able to use the information. She was definitely well informed and well prepared.

And when the baby was born, she would give it what children needed most: lots and lots of love. But she wouldn't spoil her child; that was something she had learned from Brandon. She still thought he was a shade too strict sometimes—a little indulging occasionally never hurt anyone—but watching Brandon with John and Robbie had convinced her discipline was important, too.

Feeling much too excited to go back to Kids' Kloset, Corey drove home, called Mrs. Gordon and asked her to stay the rest of the day and close up the store. It seemed Mrs. Gordon was putting in more hours these days than Corey was, but the older woman didn't seem to mind. To Corey's amusement, Mr. Gordon often accompanied his wife to the shop—just to keep her company he said, but Corey knew he helped out if it got busy. *Now there's a wonderful marriage,* Corey thought wistfully. The Gordons had been married for over forty years, yet they still held hands every chance they got and were loving and supportive of one another.

Could Brandon and I ever have a marriage like that? She tried to peer into the future and envision a life together, but to her dismay, she couldn't get the picture to focus. It was a cloudy portrait at best.

Craving some kind of action and feeling something close to panic, she flurried into the kitchen to pour herself a glass of skim milk. She took a tiny sip and made a face worthy of a gargoyle. *Ugh, it tastes awful, but it's worth doing penance if it means strong bones for my baby,* she admonished herself sternly.

She stood looking out the window over the kitchen sink, resolutely sipping at the milk, resisting the urge to dump it down the drain, as she thought about what she should do.

The children would come spilling through the school doors soon, and Brandon would be there to pick up John. She had parked her car in the driveway instead of putting it away in the garage—Brandon would know she was at home and more than likely would come over for a visit and supper, too, if she could convince him to drop his silly idea that she shouldn't cook for them anymore.

How am I going to tell him about the baby? What should I say?

She saw Brandon park his pickup at the curb in front of her house just moments before the loud clanging of the bell announced school's dismissal for the day. She watched as he uncoiled his large frame from the cab of the truck, helped Robbie out, then carried him with long strides across the street and up the sidewalk to the school. As the children burst through the doors like water released from a dam, they flowing around him like a river parted by a huge boulder. With his broad shoulders and long legs, Brandon looked like a giant next to the school children. Even from across the street, Corey could see how the sun turned his hair into a mass of gold. *What a beautiful man he is,* she thought, as she waited for him to come back out with John.

Brandon seemed to be taking an unusually long time. He was probably conferring with Miss Dougherty, John's kindergarten teacher, Corey guessed, and immediately wondered, with a prick of jealousy, just how short the teacher's skirt might be today.

Stop it! she scolded herself, but she couldn't slow the heavy pulse beating at her throat or quiet the little gasp of relief when Brandon emerged from the building. *Pregnant women are often subject to unfounded fears,* she reminded herself, then rushed to the front door when she saw Brandon and the boys pass on by the pickup and start up the walk leading to her house.

"Hi." She welcomed them a bit breathlessly as she opened the door.

"Hi, yourself." Brandon returned her greeting in such an effortlessly sexy voice Corey instantly felt her blood heating.

Brandon looked at Corey's mouth closely, grinned and leaned down to kiss away the tiny white mustache she hadn't realized was there. He smacked his lips mischievously and said, "Milk?" in a questioning tone.

Embarrassed, Corey wiped at her mouth. "I thought maybe I should cut down a little on coffee," she mumbled.

"Why are you home so early today? You're usually still at Kids' Kloset," Brandon asked.

"Oh, well, I... I had some bookkeeping I needed to do," Corey fibbed guiltily.

Corey was glad she hadn't told Brandon she had made a doctor's appointment for today. She hated even the tiniest untruth, but she hadn't decided yet how to tell him about the baby, and she was glad he wouldn't be quizzing her about what the doctor had said. It felt awkward and dishonest to hold on to her secret, but she couldn't very well just blurt out the news in front of John and Robbie. It was a subject that she wanted to approach with extreme delicacy and tact.

She had been absolutely certain she couldn't have children. That was why she had told Brandon with such conviction they didn't need to use birth control. And now she was pregnant. *Will he think I lied to him? Or worse yet, that I deliberately tried to trick him?* Corey felt a cold trickle of sweat slide between her breasts. She was grateful when John broke the increasing tension she felt.

"Can we watch cartoons? Can we?" John begged.

"May we watch cartoons, please," Brandon corrected.

"You want to watch, too, Daddy?" Robbie asked in surprise.

Brandon grimaced and threw up his hands in good-natured mock despair.

Corey laughed. "Yes, you may watch TV. John, you know how to turn the set on now, don't you? I left it on your channel the last time you were here."

The boys scampered away.

"I... I'll just go start a bit of supper," Corey stammered and turned away to head for the kitchen. This was terrible. Now that she was alone with Brandon she felt so uneasy she couldn't even look him in the eye.

Brandon grabbed her hand as she turned and pulled her around to face him. "Wait just a moment there, young lady. Haven't you forgotten something?"

"What?" she asked guiltily.

He shook a reprimanding finger right under her nose. "You're not supposed to fix anything for us, remember?"

"Oh. Well, I forgot. You didn't really mean that, did you?"

"I most certainly did. It just so happens we're having supper courtesy of the Colonel this evening. Of course, his fried chicken isn't nearly as good as yours, but at least I'm the one providing it," he said with satisfaction.

Brandon tugged gently at Corey's hand to pull her over to the couch. He looked toward the small study where Corey kept her TV. The muted roar of cartoon mayhem drifted in to the living room. "But now that the boys are occupied, I think we'll just let the Colonel cool his heels out in the pickup for a while. I need a little appetizer before supper."

Brandon settled in the corner of the couch and pulled Corey down onto his lap. He nibbled delicately at the rim of her ear and her earlobe. His warm, moist breath whispered of exotic pleasures. All of the tiny little hairs on the back of her neck prickled into rigid excitement.

Corey slid her arms around Brandon's neck and tangled her fingers in the thick gold of his hair. He showered her closed eyelids with tiny kisses as gentle as raindrops. Corey gasped with pleasure just as Brandon claimed her mouth. The first kisses were soft, light, almost refreshing like a gentle spring breeze, but as Corey began answering the kisses, Brandon intensified and deepened the contact with his tongue—probing, seeking, searching for all of her. Corey's fingers closed spasmodically, clutching at his neck and hair.

Brandon groaned deep in his throat. His strong, blunt fingers were shaking as he unbuttoned her blouse. Corey's full, heavy breasts were spilling over the lacy cups of the bra that had already become too small for her. Bending low, Brandon rained a torrent of hot, urgent kisses along the curving swell of her lush breasts then began to suckle through the lace at the engorged and swollen tips.

Corey felt as though she were drowning in a rush of sensual pleasure. But it wasn't the right time or place. The boys were just in the other room. They needed to slow down. She said the first thing that popped into her head.

"Have you heard any more from the Thorntons?" she managed to gasp out.

Brandon raised his head abruptly. His eyes were smoky with the heat of passion, but they cleared instantly into dark blue ice. He looked as though someone had dashed cold water in his face. Releasing Corey, he let his head drop back against the corner of the couch and squeezed his eyes shut. He roughly scrubbed his face with both hands. His breathing was ragged and harsh.

Corey pulled her shirt together shakily. Now why had she said that? She'd only meant to slow down their lovemaking, not bring it to a screeching halt. Not only had she ruined a beautiful moment, she had most certainly spoiled Brandon's good mood, and she had wanted him to be relaxed and receptive later in the evening when she told him about the baby.

Perhaps her feelings of being deceitful had intruded. Maybe she couldn't share truly intimate contact with Brandon unless she was also totally open and honest.

He raised his head. Corey could hardly bear to look into his pain-filled eyes.

"Not from the Thorntons. I've been trying to put it out of my mind," he said dully.

Corey felt a rush of guilt. She'd reminded him of the very thing he'd been trying to forget.

"A social worker called me today. She's going to come by the ranch next week to check me out."

Corey put her hand to her mouth. "Oh, no. They really meant it. I'd hoped they were bluffing."

Brandon sighed. "No such luck. I just hope the social worker is half way reasonable—not one of those government people with an ax to grind."

Corey clasped one of his large hands between both of hers. She couldn't think of a word of encouragement. Boy, she had stuffed her foot in her mouth about up to the knee. Brandon had been putting up such a brave front. He had probably started kissing her in a desperate attempt to take his mind off his troubles, and she had practically slapped him in the face with a cruel reminder.

"It's hard for me to believe they might have the power to take my children away from me. I don't know what I'd do without them," he said in a tight voice.

"I can't believe it would really come to that," Corey said.

"You wouldn't think so, would you? But it scares the hell out of me just considering the possibility. I've been trying to decide if I should say anything to the boys about the social worker's visit. You know, so they'd be on their best behavior."

"I don't know," Corey said slowly. "It might just make them nervous, so they wouldn't act natural."

"Yeah. You're probably right. That's what I thought, too."

He sat up straight, thrust his hands through his hair to smooth it and took a deep, lung-filling breath. He looked like a man gathering his resources. He dropped a little passionless kiss on the tip of Corey's nose.

"I guess we'll just have to be our regular irresistible selves and hope for the best," he said, giving Corey a crooked grin. He gently patted her bottom. "Hop up, and I'll get the chicken. It's probably as cold as a frozen dinner by now. Maybe we can microwave it. How about rustling the boys in to the table while I get the food?"

Trying not to be too obvious, Corey observed Brandon closely all through the meal as he passed the big red and white striped bucket of fried chicken, wax-paper-wrapped biscuits and little white containers of mashed potatoes, gravy and Cole slaw.

He was so attentive to the boys: he corrected their manners and saw to it that they ate the messy fried chicken as properly as a five and four-year-old could manage, but he didn't scold Robbie at all when, in spite of his very best efforts, a glass of milk got away from him and spilled all over the table. Brandon calmly went into the kitchen and retrieved the big sponge Corey used to wipe off counter tops. He handed the sponge to Robbie and patiently waited while Robbie cleaned up the mess.

Corey's own hands itched to help, but she forced herself to remain seated, for by now she knew if she tried to interfere and do the clean up herself, Brandon would give her a lecture on teaching children to be responsible for their own actions.

How ironic that Brandon should be accused of being a neglectful parent. Guiltily, she remembered she had once wondered if Brandon did not provide John and Robbie with enough affection. Perhaps

Brandon was right when he said people didn't trust a man alone with small children. Now it was perfectly obvious how much he loved his sons and how well he cared for them.

But what did Brandon feel for her? Did he love her?

Corey gulped down a sigh and stirred the by-now gluey potatoes and gravy around on her plate so it would look like she was eating them.

She had absolutely no doubt Brandon would marry her when she told him about the baby. He had made his thoughts on the subject very clear when he'd told Corey about his wife and why he had married her. Corey knew Brandon hadn't loved Jane, and yet, he had married her without a second thought because of their child. Corey tightened her grip on the fork until she thought she felt it bend between her fingers.

It wasn't enough. She couldn't live in another marriage without love. Wayne hadn't loved her, and she knew she hadn't loved him, either. A marriage with Brandon would be a thousand times worse because she loved him more than anything on earth other than perhaps the baby growing inside her. She couldn't bear to live with him if he didn't love her, too.

One man had divorced her because she couldn't conceive; she couldn't stand the thought of another man marrying her because she had. Wasn't she a person in her own right? Didn't she have some value other than her ability to bear children? Very close to tears, Corey squeezed her eyes shut.

"Corey, is there something wrong?" Brandon asked softly.

Startled, Corey jumped up from the table. She had been so lost in her thoughts, she had almost forgotten where she was. "No!" she said too abruptly. She fought for control of

her voice. "I'm fine. I'll just start clearing away now."

Corey grabbed up her plate and hurried into the kitchen. She had whipped her supper into a disgusting-looking glop. She put the chicken in the garbage, then turned on the water at the sink and scraped the rest of the food on her plate into the garbage disposal. *I'm not going to cry,* she told herself sternly, *at least not until everyone is gone. Pregnant women are often unduly emotional,* she reminded herself.

Carrying the rest of the dishes, Brandon and the boys joined her in the kitchen. The cleaning-up chores were quickly accomplished with all of them working together.

Whenever Brandon thought the boys weren't looking, he stole a kiss from Corey. She returned his kisses somewhat warily. There was no doubt Brandon desired her, but that wasn't the same as love. Just wanting her body wasn't enough; he had to want all of her.

The boys had finished their part of the kitchen detail and wandered back to the TV when Brandon pressed up against Corey's back as she worked at the sink. He lifted her hair to bare the nape of her neck and to kiss every inch of exposed skin. Corey shivered. He felt so good curved against her bottom and back, so strong and solid. She seemed to fit perfectly into the arch of rock-hard thighs, belly and chest as he bent over her. The kisses were meltingly sweet; she loved all the shivery, quivery feelings Brandon so easily aroused in her.

But even as she acknowledged how wonderful Brandon made her feel, Corey made her decision. She wasn't going to tell him about their baby. At least not until he told her he loved her. Brandon had to ask her to marry him because he loved her and wanted her, not because of his sense of duty.

Corey shivered again, but this time it was a quiver of terror. She was taking a terrible chance. What if Brandon didn't love her? He had never said a word or given any sign that he did, other than passionately loving her with his body. Maybe it was only sex to him with no deeper feelings involved. *Could a man really do that? Probably.* She had to find out.

As Corey finished scouring the sink, Brandon stepped away from her. Corey picked up a towel to dry her hands and turned to face him. She studied his face. His smile looked warm and tender, but perhaps it was only a reflexive wooing tactic triggered by the very apparent hard ridge straining at the worn denim fly of Brandon's jeans.

She didn't have much time to find out if his smile signified devotion or a rush of hormones. She would be showing soon. If Brandon wasn't willing to commit to her, she needed to be well away from him before the baby announced its own imminent arrival.

Corey shuddered to think of arguing with Brandon about what they should do about their child. He was so strong and forceful, so opinionated and pigheaded. She wouldn't stand a chance in a confrontation with him. He wouldn't even ask her what she wanted; he would just run right over her as he enforced his own code of honor.

But perhaps his ideas about pregnancy and marriage were right. *Am I being unfair to our baby?* she worried. Could there ever be any justification for denying a child its father? Was she putting her baby's happiness and well being at risk by selfishly trying to insure her own?

She couldn't answer any of those questions. She only knew she couldn't marry Brandon if he didn't love her.

"I suppose we'd better go," Brandon said regretfully. "I need to get the boys to bed."

He noted the intense look on Corey's face and chuckled to himself. She was probably thinking the same thing he was—he would lay odds on it—that they were the ones who really needed to go to bed. He would give up his best mummy bag forever if he could just go lie down for a few hours with Corey on that frilly white mountain of pillows in her bedroom. He'd never wanted a woman so much in his life. He was glad she seemed to feel the same way.

"Do you suppose you'd be able to make time for a visit out our way this weekend? Perhaps you and I could think of something to do to take my mind off the Department of Health and Welfare's little inspection tour." He grinned roguishly at her and cocked one dark blond brow suggestively.

The inspection! She kept forgetting about it. Her own overriding concern with her baby kept pushing aside all other thoughts. The social worker's visit couldn't have come at a worse time. How could she get Brandon to admit he loved her and to ask her to marry him when he was so worried about the boys? Well, bad timing or not, it couldn't be postponed. She was either going to say yes to a proposal of marriage this weekend, or she was never going to see Brandon again.

Twelve

Stretched out flat on her back, Corey sucked in her stomach, held her breath and gave her jeans' zipper one more hard, exasperated yank. But it was no use; the zipper's metal pull-tab, stuck half way up the track, stubbornly refused to budge. Her gently rounding belly had defeated her.

Corey groaned in disgust and sat up. The snap at her waistband—the snap she had so laboriously closed before lying down on the bed—burst open with a loud pop. Corey wailed and flooded her shirt with a sudden torrent of tears. Catching sight of herself in the bureau mirror, she began to giggle just as abruptly. Wasn't she just in fine form for one of the most important days of her life?

She used the tail of the already dampened shirt to mop up her face, then quickly slipped out of both the blouse and the offending jeans. She had lots of other roomier pants she could wear. True, black jeans were especially slimming; and she had wanted to look her best today for Brandon; but if they no longer fit, well, it was for an excellent reason, Corey thought, as she softly patted her rounded tummy.

Rummaging through her closet, Corey found a pair of baggy, drawstring tan trousers. She pulled them on and added an out-of-fashion, oversized, long-sleeved white T-shirt. She tucked in the shirt and checked her appearance in the full-length mirror on the back of the closet door. Not so good. She pulled the shirt out and looked again. Ugh. Even worse; however, it was a perfect disguise for a thickening middle; it made her look as though she didn't have any waist at all. No matter, it would have to do; it was time to go, and she didn't want to be late.

She hated to visit the ranch without taking a treat for the boys; she was sure they would be disappointed when she showed up empty-handed, but today she didn't want to take any chances on irritating Brandon. If all went well, she would have a lifetime of baking cookies for John and Robbie and the new little one. This time a trifle nervously, she once again patted the gentle swell now hidden by the voluminous T-shirt.

It certainly is a gloomy day, Corey thought, as she started her car and backed out of the driveway. She peered through the windshield at the overcast sky. She supposed a few May showers were inevitable, but she wished today could have been bright and sunny. There was nothing like a good strong dose of sunshine to inspire optimism and courage, and she needed all the support she could get on this momentous occasion.

As she ascended the final drive leading to Brandon's home, Corey shivered. Even the cabin, perched halfway up the rugged mountainside and surrounded by towering pine trees, looked slightly forbidding today. *Stop being so silly,* she chided herself. It was a perfectly fine day. *May showers bring spring flowers,* she chanted silently, as she walked toward the entrance of the cabin.

Pasting what she hoped was a reasonable facsimile of a cheery smile on her chill lips, Corey knocked lightly at the door. It swung open immediately, and Corey's forced gaiety turned into the real thing as John and Robbie greeted her boisterously, and Brandon enveloped her in a giant hug.

"Come and see what we did! Come see!" Robbie cried, waving about a large wooden spoon with thick brown sludge oozing down the handle. His face and hands were liberally decorated with the same dark goo.

Small, alarmingly sticky fingers grabbed her hand and tugged her toward the kitchen.

"Daddy said it was our turn to be the cookers. We poured some water into a box and put it in the oven and brownies came out. But we haf to wait for you before we can eat them," John said, as he hurried her into the kitchen area.

Corey could now identify the sweet, chocolaty, slightly burnt smell permeating the air. A bake-in-the-box batch of brownies cooled on a trivet set in the middle of the scrubbed pine table. The edges of the brownies were baked to an ominously charcoal-colored crispness.

"Somehow everything I cook on a wilderness trek turns out better than what I fix here at home," Brandon said ruefully.

"Maybe it's because you're so hungry from all that hiking around, anything would taste good," Corey said, trying unsuccessfully to hide a giggle.

"Laugh at me, will you, you ungrateful wench. We baked these for you, you know," Brandon said with mock ferocity and menaced her with a light tickle along her rib cage.

Corey shrieked and raced around the table. Brandon gave pursuit.

John and Robbie looked at each other wonderingly, surprised at such antics from grown-ups, then came to a quick, wordless, mutual agreement to join in the fun. Robbie dropped his spoon on the table, and both boys bolted after Brandon as he chased Corey into the living area where they all collapsed on the couch in a wild melee of tangled arms and legs.

Alternately laughing and gasping for breath, Corey managed to sit up. The deviltry in Brandon's eyes changed to tender amusement as he carefully wiped away a smudge of chocolate batter from the tip of Corey's nose.

Corey stared into the deep blue depths, trying to read his mind. *Isn't that a loving look?* she wondered hopefully. *He surely loves me, doesn't he? He just has to,* she thought, with a sudden stab of stomach-tightening anxiety.

"Okay, boys, it's almost nap time. Go get washed up, and we'll have some of our world-class brownies and milk before I tuck you in."

Brandon's voice dropped to a huskier register after the boys dashed off to the bathroom, and he spoke to Corey alone. "We can have a nice, private little visit after the boys are asleep."

Yes, they certainly would, Corey thought, her heart starting to pound. But the subject of the discussion would probably be considerably different than anything Brandon had in mind.

When the boys returned, having managed to wash off most of the sticky batter, they all gathered around the kitchen table, and Brandon ceremoniously cut the brownies.

"Coffee?" he offered Corey, after pouring two glasses of milk for John and Robbie.

Corey almost said yes before she remembered just in time. "No, thanks. I'll have milk, please."

Brandon filled another glass with milk for Corey and poured a cup of coffee for himself before he sat down at the table.

Corey forced herself to eat the brownie so as not to hurt the boys' feelings, but it could have been a pile of ashes for all the pleasure she got out of it. Her throat felt so tight she could barely swallow.

"It doesn't taste like Ms. Corey's brownies," John said, smacking his lips with all the seriousness of a connoisseur pronouncing judgment, "but can I have another one?"

Brandon chuckled. "May I have another brownie, please. That's enough for now. We'll have some more for dessert after
supper. Go wash your hands again and scoot on upstairs."

The boys reluctantly shuffled off to the bathroom, then, after lots of loud splashing, climbed up the stairs. Brandon stood and walked over to Corey's chair.

"I won't be long; I'll only read one short naptime story today. Just relax, please, and DON'T do the dishes. I'll be right back." He stooped to tenderly kiss Corey's forehead, then followed the boys up to their bedroom.

Too restless to just sit, Corey cleared the table and started to fill the sink with water before she remembered she didn't want to irritate Brandon. This was one time she would follow his dictatorial orders. She paced about in the living area, nervously straightening odds and ends by a few fractions of an inch. Only one story seemed to be taking an awfully long time.

Her preoccupation with thoughts of love and marriage didn't prevent her from noticing with pleasure that Brandon had refilled a few of the jelly-jar flower vases she had brought to the cabin. She began to rearrange stalks of white-pedaled wakerobins. She remembered that Indians had once used the thick underground rootstalks of the plant during childbirth. Some people still called the flower birthroot. *Maybe the blossoms' presence here today are a good omen.*

Or at the very least, she hoped that the fact that Brandon had followed her example and filled the vases with flowers meant he had forgiven her for decorating the cabin without asking his permission. She didn't want any past mistakes to mar today's conversation. Not that she had a clue as to what she was going to say.

Just how on earth does a woman get a man to declare he loves her, anyway? After all her worrying and wondering, not a single one of the opening-the-conversation phrases she had rehearsed sounded even halfway right. She would just have to wing it and hope for the best. Corey sighed and set the jar of

wakerobins back on the end table.

"You sound as though you're carrying the weight of the world around on those pretty shoulders," Brandon said as he grasped both her arms from behind and kissed the top of one shoulder.

Corey let out a startled squeak and jumped so quickly she almost spilled the flowers. She had been so preoccupied with her thoughts she hadn't even heard Brandon's approach.

"Nervous as a doe in hunting season, too," Brandon observed. "Let's see if we can't find a way to relieve all that nasty tension."

He scooped her up in his arms and easily carried her to the couch. *Will he notice I'm heavier,* Corey wondered, feeling foolish.

Brandon settled them on the couch and began to sensuously massage her neck and shoulders. He kissed her throat and lips. His unique scent filled her nostrils. Oh, no, all the things she wanted to talk about were flying right out of her head. Her senses were reeling; all she could think about were the wonderful sensations engulfing her. But she was determined to follow through with her plan. *It's now or never.*

Corey shifted her position slightly to move away from Brandon. "Br... Brandon, we need to talk," she gasped out.

He drew her back to him and stroked all along her spine in a lazy, luxurious caress. "So," he said between kisses that left her breathless, "talk."

"Well, have you... have you ever considered remarrying?"

This time Brandon was the one to pull away—a sudden, violently reflexive move that wasn't at all encouraging.

"What do you mean?" he asked sharply.

"Well, we've been seeing each other for quite awhile now, and I, well, I..." no, she mustn't tell him how much she loved him unless he said it first, "...do care about you. And then there are the boys." *No! That was all wrong, too.* This didn't have anything to do with the children; it was only how Brandon felt about her that counted.

Brandon exploded up off the couch, practically knocking Corey to the floor, and stormed over to a window. "So that's what this is all about," he ground out through clenched teeth.

"About? About what?" Corey asked in confusion.

He turned back to Corey, his face an angry mask. "My kids. You've never thought I could take care of them by myself, have you? So now this thing with their grandparents has come up, and you've decided you're going to help me out, right?"

"No!"

"Sure, you're going to give me another of your gifts just like you fixed up my home because it wasn't up to your standards." He picked up one of the old lamps Corey had brought to the cabin. It was heavy and unwieldy, but he waved it around angrily as though it were no bigger than a toothpick. He banged it back down on the table. "But this time you're going to fix up my whole life. You think we're a real charity case, don't you?" he asked bitterly.

"I never meant—"

"Sure you did. You've made it clear since the first time I met you that you think you know a whole lot more about raising kids than I do. Now you're even willing to make the ultimate sacrifice. You're going to give me a handy-dandy little wife to convince the social workers my sons are in good hands. Of course, everybody knows kids can't get along without a mother, so you're going to see to it that they have one. You must be some kind of martyr," he said in disgust.

This is terrible, Corey thought, close to panic. It was worse than even her most horrific nightmare. Brandon was completely on the wrong track; he was totally misreading her intentions. She would give up right now in despair except underneath all that terrible anger she thought she heard a cry of pain and hurt. Somehow, she had to make him understand. With trembling lips, she tried again.

"Brandon, I do not think I know more about children than you do, and I did not mention marriage because I wanted to help you in any kind of way."

"Sure sounded like it to me," he growled.

"It was for myself that I asked. I want to know how you feel about me."

Brandon rubbed his forehead wearily. "Corey, I can't figure you out. I still think you're up to something, but if just for the moment I give you the benefit of the doubt, I'd still have to say you have God-awful timing. How could you even think about marriage when I don't have more than a dime in my checking account, and I'm about to be hauled in front of the Department of Health and Welfare for child abuse?"

"Just forget about marriage for now," Corey said desperately. "Just tell me how you feel about me. Do you think our relationship is ever going to mean anything to you?"

"Don't push me, Corey," Brandon warned. "I never promised you anything like that, and I'm not the kind of man you can push into a commitment before I'm ready."

Corey fought back the tears threatening to overwhelm her. "Just tell me if you have any feelings for me."

"Now is not the time," Brandon repeated stubbornly.

Corey squeezed her eyes tightly shut. *You're so wrong,* she thought, *now is the only time.*

She had hoped his initial outburst had stemmed from wounded pride—she knew how important it was to Brandon to make his own way in the world—but she had misread him, probably because she'd been so frantic to find feelings for her where none existed. She was going to have to face the bitter truth, what she had fearfully suspected all along. *Brandon doesn't love me.*

"Brandon, if you can't tell me you care about me—at least a little bit, so I have something to build on—then I can't see you anymore," she said dully. There, she had done it; it was finally out in the open; she had laid it on the line.

"I don't take kindly to ultimatums; you must know that by now."

He sounds as sullen and stubborn as a little boy, Corey thought, suddenly angry. She was trying to make it possible for them to have a future together—to give their child a good start in life. She had swallowed her pride and practically begged him to say he cared about her, and what had she gotten in return? Absolutely nothing but humiliation.

Well, she was through with begging. Corey lifted her chin and swept up off the couch with as much dignity as she could muster. He was going to be the loser. She was a darn fine woman whether he realized it or not.

No, her conscience whispered to her, *our baby is the one who's going to be the loser.* As that thought sank in, the backbone that had just stiffened immediately sagged, and Corey had to grab hold of the back of the couch to support herself.

"I think we should make a clean break of it then, if our relationship isn't going anywhere." Her voice was sharp with pain. "Please, don't call me; I don't think I want to talk to you anymore." Dear God, she was shaking so hard she was afraid she might fall to the floor.

Brandon started toward her. "It doesn't have to be this way, Corey."

She held up one hand like a policeman directing traffic, as though that could stop Brandon, but when she saw how violently her arm was trembling, she let it drop.

"Please, don't," she said raggedly. "Would you try to explain to John and Robbie that I won't be able to see them anymore? I know I should tell them myself, but I don't think I can."

"I don't understand what the big problem is. Why can't we just go on like we have before?" Brandon asked, his voice twisted and rough with hurt. "Why now, Corey? Why does it have to be right now?"

Damn it, he thought, *why is she pushing me?* He loved her; he knew it well by now. He didn't know how it had happened, but it had. He hadn't wanted to let anyone into his life; he had too many worries and responsibilities. He hadn't known where he was going or how he was going to get there; all he had been sure of was he didn't want anyone trying to tell him the way.

But Corey had bustled right into his heart anyway, bringing light and laughter, love and warmth. He hated to think of the lonely, cold time before he had known her. But he couldn't stand to be pushed. He wanted to tell her he loved her at the right time, *his* time. He was the man; it was his place to bring up the subject of marriage. He should be doing the asking, and he wasn't ready yet.

"A woman needs some kind of commitment," she said. "I don't want to waste my time if our relationship isn't going anywhere."

I have to hurt him, she thought, *hurt him badly enough that he will stay away from me. It's the only way.* He didn't love her, but he wanted to continue a casual relationship, sexual but not serious. She needed to wound his pride, insult him in some way, so he wouldn't look her up one day just because he was feeling a little lonely and at loose ends. She had to make sure he stayed away.

"You didn't think I did all this for nothing, did you?" she said, waving her hand airily at the new decor. Her lips felt frozen, numb, yet her heart was pounding so hard she though she might faint. She could feel the blood pulsing through her body. Everything she said sounded to her as though someone else were speaking it; her voice sounded as though it were coming from some far away place. But she had to continue no matter how difficult it was. She had to drive him away forever.

"You looked like prime husband material to me, so I went after you. I thought I would help you with your sons—it was obvious you needed some guidance," she added cruelly, "and in return you would provide me with a marriage certificate."

"Corey, why are you doing this? Why are you saying all these things?" he cried, his voice anguished.

"You suspected all the time, didn't you? You said so earlier. Well, you were right," she said brutally. "I'm not getting anywhere with you, so it's time to quit. There are lots of other men who'd be glad to marry me, and they aren't so much trouble, either. This thing with the Department of Health and Welfare is just about the last straw."

She banged her hand on the back of the couch for emphasis. "I don't want to listen to you cry on my shoulder when they take your sons away if I'm not going to hear some wedding bells in return for the favor."

Corey felt sick to her stomach, and this time it wasn't because of the baby. She had never dreamed she even knew how to say such cruel things. She turned blindly toward the door. She had to get away. She couldn't stand to continue this ugly farce a moment longer.

"Get out!" Brandon roared. "Get out of my house and don't ever come back."

It worked, Corey thought tiredly. *He'll never want to see me again. I can have the baby by myself, and he'll never know. I won't have to worry about him looking me up for a friendly little chat and accidentally finding out my secret.* Now, if she could just drag herself home to try to recover. She wasn't sure she could ever forgive herself for telling him such dreadful lies.

As she stumbled toward the door, she saw John descending the stairs, sleepily rubbing his eyes.

"You were being awful noisy, Daddy," he said disapprovingly. "But I'm glad you woke me up 'cause I was running away from a big, old, mean bear, and I was 'fraid he was going to catch me."

"Oh, John," Corey said, hugging him to her, a sob tearing at her throat. "I'm glad you woke up, too, so I could say goodbye before I go home, but I bet that bear could never catch you anyway; you're such a fast runner."

"Yeah, I am the fastest, aren't I?" he boasted proudly.

Corey brushed the white blond hair away from his eyes. It was getting a little long; she should trim it a bit. *No. I'll never be able to,* she thought, as a new pain squeezed her heart.

"I wanted to say goodbye because I'm not going to be able to see you for a long time. I'm going away."

"Like Mommy?" he asked sadly.

Corey clutched him tighter. "Oh, no, not like your mother. I just... well, I'm just going to be gone for a long time, that's all. Will you tell Robbie goodbye for me?"

John nodded "yes" then hugged her back fiercely, burying his face in her mid-section. It occurred to Corey that he was hugging his baby sister or brother as well. And it was probably going to be the only time in his whole life he would ever get the chance. *Oh, dear Lord, what have I done?*

She kissed John's forehead and gently released him. Somehow, she managed to walk out of the cabin and get into her car. Daggers of rain slashed at her, soaking her through in only a few moments time. The brooding clouds had finally fulfilled their promise.

Somehow, she managed to drive home, though afterwards she never understood how she'd made it over the storm-lashed roads, because her eyes were as wet from tears as the windshield was with rain, and her heart howled more loudly than the wind.

Thirteen

"What a lovely home you have, Mr. Wolfe," Janet Ludlow, the social worker from Idaho Health and Welfare, said admiringly as she looked around the cabin.

What is she really looking for, Brandon wondered as he silently ground his teeth together, then forced a stiff smile in response. "Thanks," he said tersely.

He couldn't think of many things that would be worse than having a complete stranger come into his home and pass judgment on his parenting. He was sorely tempted to tell this woman just what he thought of the whole process, but he didn't dare jeopardize his sons' future by giving into his own hotheadedness. No, he would smile and dance to the system's tune and continue the charade to the bitter end no matter how much he hated it.

Ms. Ludlow walked over to the couch and picked up one of the small pillows lying there. "The color scheme shows quite a remarkable eye for color. Most men don't pay much attention to such things. Did someone help you, or are you the one interested in interior design?" she asked conversationally.

Corey! Brandon thought with a burst of pain. So she was helping him with the social worker's inspection tour whether she was ever going to get any payoff for it or not. She had made the cabin look warm and comfortable enough to impress even a prying government official. And to think Corey had gone to all that work to try to catch a husband.

Though why she had set out to snare such unpromising marriage material as himself was a riddle he couldn't solve. He'd thought of little else since she'd revealed her true intentions last Sunday. He should have spent the time since then planning what he should say and do today to convince the Health and Welfare Department the boys were being well taken care of, but all he could think of was Corey.

That pillow Ms. Ludlow was admiring was just one of many ciphers in Corey's cold-hearted calculations to trap a husband. The thought made him want to rip it out of the social worker's hands and throw it, along with the oh-so-well-coordinated curtains and rugs, into the potbellied stove and reduce them all to ashes—the same kind of ashes Corey had made of his heart.

But the social worker had asked him a question. He wrenched his thoughts back to the present. It was time to forget about Corey's treachery and concentrate on the business at hand before he lost his children. "A friend helped," he said, trying hard to sound pleasant.

"A woman friend?" Ms. Ludlow queried, a smile flitting across her round face.

Is that a trick question? Brandon wondered in alarm. Surely it wasn't considered a bad influence on the children for a man to have a women friend, a woman close enough to help out with fixing up their home.

He had to quit this. He would go mad if he had to second-guess every single thing the woman said. His instincts told him Ms. Ludlow wasn't out to get him. She seemed a pleasant enough woman: attractive, middle aged, well dressed, slightly plump, with only a few sprinkles of gray in her dark hair. Surely he could relax and just be himself. He was doing the very best he knew how with John and Robbie. Wouldn't Ms. Ludlow realize that after they woke up from their nap and she visited with them?

But then, look how wrong he had been about Corey. He had fallen in love with her, and he had thought she had grown to respect and love him, too. But she had been nothing but a conniving female out to trap him from the very beginning. He had better keep his guard up with Ms. Ludlow, even if on the surface she seemed to be a perfectly fair and levelheaded woman who truly cared about children.

"Yes. A woman," he answered shortly.

"It must have been very difficult for you when your wife died, having to raise two little boys all alone," Ms. Ludlow said sympathetically.

"Yes, it was."

No one would ever know just how difficult it had been. He'd been afraid to ask anyone for advise or help for fear he would expose just how terrified he was of failure.

Wait. Was that really what had been going on all along? He had always told himself he didn't want to take suggestions from anyone because he knew what was right for his sons. Had he actually only been trying to hide his uncertainties from his demanding family and, most especially, from himself?

Ms. Ludlow carefully repositioned the pillow with the others on the couch. "I'm glad to hear you have someone to help you out occasionally. I hope she's as good at listening as she is at decorating. Single parents, well, really all parents, need a lot of moral support. Raising children is just about the hardest job there is in the world. If you don't have someone with whom to share your feelings, a good sounding board, you can go a little crazy."

Brandon thought back to all the times Corey had heard him out when he had expounded on his child care theories—even when it had been clear to him she didn't entirely agree. She had been a wonderful listener.

Though she hadn't been quite as good at following directions.

In spite of his bitter feelings, he remembered, with something close to amusement, all the times she had gone right ahead and given the boys some kind of treat when he had told her not to do it. He had thought she was spoiling them. Perhaps he had been unwilling to admit he might be wrong about a few things—like letting them enjoy a cookie now and then—for fear it would be an admission that he could be wrong about everything. And, as much as he hated to think about it, there had even been a few times he had felt jealous of all the attention she had showered on the children. He had suspected she might be more interested in them than in him.

The truth was they had all benefited from her care and concern. She had a wonderful knack for turning the most ordinary event into a special occasion. She had brought so much grace and warmth, so much joy, into all of their lives. *Were those really the actions of a cold-blooded, calculating woman? It didn't make sense.*

Brandon tensed. He heard the distinctive sounds, coming from the direction of the loft overhead, that indicated John and Robbie were waking up. He steeled himself for the interview to come. So much depended on the impression the boys made on Ms. Ludlow.

Suddenly he realized he wished Corey were there with him to face the social worker. He had spent two long years denying he needed help of any kind, and now he would give almost anything just to have one special woman's soft little hand to hold.

He would probably never know what Corey's true intentions had been, but she had accomplished one thing whether she had meant to or not. She had achieved what Brandon had always sworn would never happen—he had become dependent upon someone. He yearned for the love and support of a woman, and that woman was Corey.

The boys clattered halfway down the stairs at breakneck speed, then paused when they noticed they had a visitor. *Are the stairs too steep? Will Ms. Ludlow think they're unsafe?* He had never even considered the pitch of the stairs as a safety factor before now. At least there was a good sturdy railing next to the stairs and all along the edge of the loft. She couldn't find fault with that.

"John, Robbie, come on down. I want you to meet Ms. Ludlow."

They descended the last few steps slowly, hesitating a few moments on each step before going down to the next one.

Brandon noticed Robbie was sucking his thumb again. *Damn!* He thought Robbie had given that up, but then, both boys had been acting a little insecure since he and Corey had the big blowup. They hadn't seen her for almost a week. If there were already changes in their behavior after only a few days without her, what could he expect as the lonely months to come dragged by?

"I heard a lady's voice, so I thought it was Ms. Corey," John said in a hostile tone.

Robbie moved behind Brandon and clung to his leg.

Brandon wanted to reprimand John for his rudeness, but perhaps the social worker wouldn't notice if he didn't make an issue of it. "No, Corey isn't here today. This is Ms. Ludlow. She's going to visit us this afternoon."

"Don't want Ms. Ludlow. I want Ms. Corey," John said in a whiny voice.

Social worker or not, no kid of his was ever going to get away with a smart mouth like that.

"That's enough, John," Brandon said sharply. "Mind your manners and say hello."

"No," John said, looking sullenly defiant and little-boy scared at the same time.

Brandon took one step toward him, then watched in shocked dismay as John threw himself on the floor, kicked the back of the couch as hard as he could and pounded on the floor with his small fists. "I want Ms. Corey," he screamed. "I want Corey."

Brandon's heart plummeted to the tips of his boots. He couldn't believe what was happening. This was a full-fledged, no-holds-barred tantrum. Never had he ever seen John or Robbie act this way before today. Would Ms. Ludlow think this was normal behavior in his household? And how did a child protection agent expect a good parent to deal with a tantrum?

He had no idea. Brandon scooped up the flailing, distraught child, holding him carefully so he didn't hurt himself, and carried him over to the rocking chair, no small feat even for someone of Brandon's size and strength. He sat down with his son on his lap and tucked John's legs between his knees, exerting just enough pressure to prevent the child from kicking. He hugged John from behind, effectively pinioning the small arms.

Brandon no longer cared what Ms. Ludlow thought. His son was in pain, and Brandon's heart ached for him. His children needed him. Brandon was going to do what he thought was right and damn the consequences.

He held the tense little body still until it slumped in defeat. The only sound in the room was John's sobbing. Brandon shifted John so he was sitting on one side of his lap and held out a hand to a wide-eyed, obviously frightened Robbie. Robbie scrambled over to the chair and climbed up onto Brandon's lap, too.

Brandon began to rock the two little boys slowly back and forth in the old bentwood rocker. "All right," he said gently, "it's time for us to have a nice long talk."

~ * ~

Corey dumped the contents of the last of the big plastic bags full of clothes onto the long table she used for sorting consignment items at Kids' Kloset. She straightened and tried to massage the kinks out of her lower back. It was really time for a break; she had been working at this for hours, but she did want to finish before stopping for lunch. She had always enjoyed going through all the darling children's clothing people brought in to sell, but now there was an extra incentive to complete the sorting, since she was looking for a layette for her very own baby.

Corey turned the numbered dials on her label maker until they matched the number written in her account book next to the name of the young mother, Helen Stone, who had brought in this particular bag of clothes. Now, as she determined the value of each item of clothing, she could stamp Helen's account number next to the price on the sales tag to keep track of her consignment monies.

In spite of her youthful appearance, Mrs. Stone had several children in a surprising range of ages. She was a regular customer, both buying and selling apparel at Kids' Kloset, so Corey already knew she took very good care of her children's things, and the clothes she brought in were likely to be in good repair. Corey also knew Helen had an infant only a few months old, so she was anxious to see if there were any baby things in this latest batch of resale items she could use herself.

Just as she had hoped, there was an adorable yellow sleeper decorated with fuzzy ducks. It was in perfect condition. She added it to a pile of infant wear she was storing in a cradle a couple had brought in for resale last week. *The impressive stack of clothing and the cradle, too, are all for the very special little person developing inside of me,* Corey thought with glee.

She was careful to assign a slightly higher value to the items she was keeping for herself than she would have asked for them if she had put them out on the floor. She wanted to be scrupulously fair to her customers who sold their children's things through her store.

The next two items she picked up were too badly stained to be resold. She put them in a pile that would be donated to charity.

Then she picked up a little shirt that looked like it would be just right for Robbie. Corey started to put it aside for him but then remembered, with a sudden sharp stab of pain, she wouldn't be seeing him anymore. Her hands spasmodically squeezed into fists as she clutched the shirt to her chest. Tears began to trickle down her cheeks.

It kept happening over and over again. She would feel on top of the world with the joy of her pregnancy, then she would be plunged into despair as she thought about Brandon and John and Robbie. *Such a terrible roller coaster of emotions can't be good for the baby,* she thought, as she wrapped her arms protectively around her abdomen.

But how could she help it? She loved Brandon so much she didn't see how she could possibly live without him. But since he didn't love her, she couldn't possibly live with him, either.

Corey heard the door open in the front of the store and felt a breath of fresh spring air stir through the stuffy back room. She dropped the small shirt, now crushed into a wad of wrinkles, back onto the sorting table and eagerly went to wait on the customer who had just entered, grateful for any distraction that would take her mind off Brandon.

Oh, no, Corey thought, when she saw who had come into the store. It was her closest friend, Kim Jones. Normally, she would be happy to see her friend and confidant, but Kim was the only person, other than the Gordons and her parents, who knew she had been seeing Brandon. She definitely didn't feel up to a discussion with Kim today.

"Hi. How's it going?" Kim said breezily when she saw Corey emerge from the back room.

Feeling self-conscious about her thickening midsection, Corey stayed behind the counter to greet Kim. "Just fine, though I do have a lot of work I have to finish today. How are you?"

"Tip top, as always," Kim said airily. "It's gorgeous out, and my boss's gone from the office for the day, so I thought I'd take advantage of a golden opportunity for a two-hour lunch and a chance to catch up on the love life of my elusive best buddy. Just how long has it been since we've talked, anyway?"

"It sounds nice, Kim, but I can't go out today. I don't have anyone to watch the store. Besides, I have all this work to do."

Kim narrowed her eyes. "So who said anything about going out? Sounds like a poor attempt at a brush off to me, but it isn't going to work. I'll go get take-out, and we'll share it here."

"No, really, Kim, I can't today. I brought a sack lunch, and I've a mountain of clothes to sort, and I'm way behind in my bookkeeping."

"Now, look here, Corey Tierney," Kim admonished, shaking her finger as she walked around the counter, looking like she was thinking of giving Corey a good thump on the head, "just because you've taken up with a gorgeous new boyfriend doesn't mean you can neglect your old girlfriends. After a man is long gone, you can still rely on your women friends to..."

As she rounded the counter, she stopped stock still in mid-sentence when she got her first glimpse of the lower half of Corey's body. There was a long moment of silence.

Corey flushed bright pink. "I was going to tell you, Kim. I just wasn't quite ready yet."

"After we celebrate, I'll give you a tongue lashing for holding out on me. A baby is just what you've always wanted, isn't it? Well, I say glory-be and hallelujah!"

Kim rushed over to Corey and gave her a congratulatory hug. Corey beamed with pleasure; it made her feel wonderful that her friend could be so happy for her.

Kim released Corey and stepped back, grinning from ear to ear. "So when's the wedding?"

Corey's rising spirits crashed to the ground. Everything about her pregnancy was like that: peaks of joy followed by rushes of despondency.

"There... there isn't going to be any wedding," Corey stammered, twisting a ring on her finger. If only it were an engagement ring presented with love.

Kim puffed up like a banty hen. "What! Why that no good so and so. He ran out on you when he found out you were pregnant! Why, I ought to hog-tie him and drag him to the altar by the scruff of his neck."

Corey could almost smile at the image of curvaceous but tiny Kim trying to drag Brandon anywhere. "No, it isn't like that. I didn't tell him about the baby. I broke up with him. We're not seeing each other anymore."

Kim shook her head in disgust. "Well, you're the crazy one then." She paused, obviously struggling to figure it all out. "He does already have the two little boys. I suppose it would be a lot to take on— raising somebody else's kids, I mean—but I still think it would be a lot harder to raise even one all by yourself."

"It doesn't have anything to do with John and Robbie," Corey protested. "They're wonderful children; I wish I could take care of them. It's hard to explain. You see, Brandon doesn't really love me."

Kim looked at her incredulously. "Love!" she sputtered. "What does love have to do with anything when you're pregnant? What about responsibility? He must not hate you, or you wouldn't have gotten in this condition in the first place. Have you told your family yet?"

Corey sighed. "Yes. I think they feel pretty much the same way as you do about it. They want to be happy for me, but they still think I ought to get married. Mother got that pinched look around her mouth just like she always does when she doesn't approve of something but doesn't want to say anything. She'd probably like to brag to all her friends about her youngest daughter finally having a baby, but it's pretty hard to boast about an illegitimate grandchild."

Corey paused, squeezing her hands together. She felt terrible about hurting her family, but she was glad she could now talk it over with Kim. "And my father blustered on for a while about how he had thought he didn't have to worry about unwed mothers ever since his daughters had grown out of their teen years. But he hugged me anyway." She smiled as she remembered. "They're good parents. They'll try to be supportive even if they don't understand."

"I'll support you, too," Kim reassured her, "but I still think you're nuts. I'll bet you'll find most people around here don't approve of having babies without getting married even if it is the twenty-first Century. Especially everybody at church. You'll probably get some hints pretty soon from the reverend that perhaps you might not be setting the best of all possible examples for your Sunday school class. Maybe you should go away until after the baby comes—stay with some of your family in Twin Falls. Mrs. Gordon could take care of the store, couldn't she?"

Corey dropped her head to stare miserably at the floor. Always practical at heart in spite of her surface frivolity, Kim had raised issues Corey hadn't considered until now.

All she had been able to think about was Brandon. She had been worried Brandon might show up at Kids' Kloset and discover her pregnancy. She had debated with herself before about going away to have the baby so he wouldn't find out, but she hadn't given any thought to her standing in the church and the community. Which just went to show how distracted with unhappiness she had been, because she should have known people were going to gossip about her, at the very least. In fact, they probably already were. Look at how quickly Kim had recognized the fact that she was pregnant.

Should I go away? She looked around at the store she was so proud of owning. She thought of all the special projects she had taken on for the community and her church. *Should I run away to hide the most blessed event of my life? And what if I did—what about when I returned with my newborn in tow. What then?*

Oh, fudge! Corey straightened her shoulders and raised her head. She wasn't going to be chased away from her home and business by anyone. Let them all think whatever they wanted. And as for Brandon, she was no longer the shy, young bride who had considered her husband's every word a command. She was a mature woman now who knew her own mind and could stand up for her decisions. Brandon couldn't make her do anything she didn't want to do, no matter how bullheaded he was.

If he did see her, perhaps she would tell him the baby was some other man's child. After all, he had never asked her about her social life. She could have had a dozen boyfriends for all he knew. After they had started seeing one another, he had just seemed to take it for granted she would always be available. He had never discussed any kind of commitment or exclusive dating agreement with her.

No, she valued truth far too much to lie about anything as important as the father of her baby. Perhaps she would just tell him to go take a fast flying leap off one of those mountain crags he was so fond of if he tried to tell her they had to get married because of their baby. Yes, she could do that if she had to stand up to him.

Corey looked resolutely into Kim's eyes, her back straight, her head erect, her voice firm. "No, Kim, I plan on staying right here. But I think a celebration is definitely a good idea. I'll throw my sandwich away. You can go get us the most decadent take-out food in town; we'll have a feast. And don't forget the skim milk."

Fourteen

Brandon leaned against the meadow fence and watched the stock truck rumble down the mountain, carrying Starshine's daughter to her new home. It was hard for him to believe how rapidly his finances had improved over the last few months. Four healthy female llamas had all been born within a few weeks of one another in May and June. The odds were heavily against having all females, but it had happened.

He had sold Hot Shot for a higher price than he'd expected and had also received a fair amount for Lacey's baby, but the real blockbuster had been Starshine's cria. She had turned out to be a spectacular-looking woolly llama, even more beautiful than her mother. Breeders had practically broken down the barn door as they had tried to outbid each other for the little weanling. She'd really sold herself at a price that would comfortably support his family for the next two years even if he didn't make another dime. It was phenomenal.

Now he wouldn't have to sell Guinevere and Tulip's crias; he could keep them to build his own breeding herd. Plus, Plie would deliver any day now, and Soft Touch was expecting again with a due date in early December.

Since the word had gotten out within the fairly small community of llama breeders about how Jester was such a terrific stud, Brandon had received numerous calls requesting Jester's services. He could collect a goodly fee for that as well—it would be pure gravy on top of all the other money from the sales.

Jester seemed to know Brandon was thinking about him. He watched Brandon closely from one of the small, pie-shaped pens where he had to be isolated to prevent inbreeding now that two of his daughters were running with the herd. Jester hummed loudly in a dissatisfied, accusatory tone.

Brandon let out a gusty sigh. He knew just how Jester felt. None of his newfound riches meant a damn thing without Corey.

He looked out across the sun-dappled pasture at his growing herd. John and Robbie were playing there in the meadow with the two little llamas Brandon planned to keep. They were all frolicking together in the green grass, having a wonderful time just the way healthy, happy young creatures were supposed to act. The boys' behavior had improved markedly since that awful day the social worker had come to visit.

On that day Brandon had talked at length about the meaning of relationships and separations. About how even if you couldn't see someone who was important to you, they were still there in your thoughts and your heart. He thought he'd done a pretty damn good job of explaining some very difficult concepts in small-fry language.

Apparently, Ms. Ludlow had thought so, too. She'd made a mess of her crisply starched and ironed handkerchief by the time he had finished. And she'd promised to close out the file on him. She had said she would report he was a first-rate father.

He had felt full of pride and relief. Until he discovered John and Robbie thought he meant Corey would be coming back to them soon. In spite of his best efforts, he had somehow given them the impression there was going to be a happy reunion any day now. They talked about her all the time as though she were going to walk in the door any minute. They were so sure of it, some days they just about convinced him they were right.

Brandon hunched his shoulders guiltily. *If only it were true.*

He ought to be on top of the world now. He had been found innocent of the abuse charges—his sons were safe from being snatched away from their home—and he had earned a certain measure of financial security, proving to his overly critical parents llama breeding was more than a pipe dream. He was engaged in a legitimate, moneymaking endeavor worthy of an adult's time and interest.

He should be happy now, content and proud, but all he could think about was how he wanted to share his success with Corey. Why, he even had enough money in the bank to support a wife.

Brandon snorted, feeling disgusted with himself. How ironic! Now that he had money it no longer seemed to be what was most important.

Corey knew that all along. It had been just a little over a year since he'd first met her. He had spent the last few long, lonely months remembering every moment he had spent with her. She had given unstintingly to him and to his sons, never stopping to measure what she was receiving in return.

When she had broken off with him, he'd been furious at first. He had thought she had been devious all along, that she had been using him, manipulating him to her own ends. But the more he thought about it, the more convinced he became the only time she had ever been dishonest was on that last day. He didn't know why she had told him untruths then, but he was absolutely sure that was what had happened.

It had become clear to him as he thought about all he knew of Corey. How she loved to do things for people, how she delighted in bringing pleasure to those around her. She knew love wasn't a balance sheet, that you couldn't keep score, tallying up points on each side. No. People in love didn't try to figure out who was giving the most or count the cost. They just gave all they had. It was never enough, and yet it was everything. And that was what he should have given Corey, just as she had always given it to him.

As Brandon crossed the fence and walked across the pasture to collect the boys for bath and bed, he hoped this hard-won knowledge hadn't come too late.

Tomorrow was the beginning of the school year—the very first day of kindergarten for Robbie and first grade for John. After he deposited the boys at school, he planned on dropping in on Corey at Kids' Kloset.

He hoped she wouldn't kick him out before he had a chance to talk to her. No, he wasn't going there to talk; he needed to keep very clear in his mind what he had to do. He was going to apologize. It wasn't a word he very often included in his vocabulary, but that was what he was going to do—apologize.

It was a hard word for a man to work his teeth and tongue around easily. Maybe he needed to say it out loud a few times to get used to it.

"I apologize," he shouted to the mountaintops.

Nine sets of banana-shaped llama ears, two sets of little boy ears and one set of floppy dog ears all swung in his direction. Brandon winked at them, and they went back to playing, John and Robbie with a "Daddy's being silly" look on their faces.

Yes, that's the word, he thought, not at all chagrined by his impromptu exhibition of feelings. Corey had needed him that terrible day she had walked out of his life. He didn't know why, but she had needed his reassurance for some reason. Just as he needed her, without even realizing it, on many other occasions. She had always come through for him, but the one time she had ever asked him for anything, he had failed her.

And now he was suffering for it. But one good thing had come of his failure—he knew now how much he loved and needed Corey. Perhaps he should be grateful for the lonely months apart. Not one to often analyze his feelings, he'd had a chance to think about what was important to him. He now knew, without any doubts, Corey was what mattered most to him. If only she felt the same way.

Brandon plucked a blade of grass from the field, stuck it in his mouth and worried it anxiously between his teeth. All summer he had avoided Boise as much as possible, only going into town for absolutely essential groceries and supplies. Last week when he'd taken the boys to the school for pre-registration, he had been overcome with memories at the sight of Corey's neat little white house.

While Brandon, wedged in one of the ludicrously tiny chairs provided for parents, filled out endless forms, Robbie stared relentlessly out the windows at Corey's house across the street, hoping to get a glimpse of her. He'd taken at least ten years off Brandon's life by suddenly screaming, in a fire-siren shriek, that he saw her. Brandon had been unable to prevent himself from leaping up, sending the silly little chair clattering to the floor. By the time he got to the window, there was nothing to be seen. Robbie claimed Corey had been in the garden, and she looked fat, like Mrs. Santa Claus.

Brandon chuckled to himself, imagining Corey's slender, graceful form padded with a few extra pounds. It wasn't impossible, he supposed. He knew women sometimes turned to food for comfort whenever they were under stress. Men were more apt to turn to a bottle for their solace.

Maybe, if Corey had actually gained some weight, it meant she was just as lonely and unhappy as he was. That would be a good sign as far as he was concerned. If she missed him even half as much as he missed her, he would be content. And he would be more than happy if there were a little bit more of Corey to hug if she would only hug him back.

If. That's the operative word. What if she doesn't want me anymore? His phone hadn't exactly been ringing off the hook. *What if all this time apart has made her decide she likes it better that way?*

The mere thought made him break out into a cold sweat on this still-hot September afternoon. Well, he'd find out tomorrow. If he didn't have a nervous breakdown before then. Waiting made him as itchy as a bear on an anthill.

~ * ~

Brandon smoothed his hair and tucked his new white shirt more neatly into his best pair of dark slacks. His heart was hammering as hard as if he had just climbed Borah Peak. Standing on the sidewalk in front of Kids' Kloset, peering over an elaborately stacked pyramid of used toys in the display window, he could see Corey sitting behind the cash register at the counter.

She was sitting well under the counter with her head propped on her hands, elbows on the counter, staring dreamily off into space. He was in luck, there was no one else in the store. It was perfect timing for his mission.

Brandon rolled his shoulders trying to relax the tension in his neck and back. He was too tight. A man needed to be loose for the lightning quick reflexes necessary for major undertakings like scaling a mountain or shooting the rapids of the Big Salmon—or proposing to a woman.

Resolutely, with confidence more feigned than real, he pushed open the door, remembering just in time to duck under the Little Red Riding Hood mobile, and strode toward Corey.

When the door opened, Corey looked up and saw Brandon bearing down on her. She was as startled as if she had been shocked by a live wire, and her heart began to beat so hard it felt like it might leap out of her chest.

"Sorry, little baby," she murmured as she patted her enormous belly.

How dare he storm in here when I'm in my ninth month and finally have begun to believe I just might have made a clean getaway? She didn't need any harassment at this late stage in the game. *And I certainly don't need to be reminded of the daily regrets and uncertainties that have plagued me,* she thought as she stared at the towering spectacle of the glorious, golden giant before her.

She hunkered even further under the chest-high counter to hide her tummy but lifted her chin to face him.

Brandon drank in the sight of Corey with the thirsty look of a man long deprived of water. She was even lovelier than he remembered, with a special glow to her face that seemed different, somehow. Her skin looked as smooth and soft as the petals of a flower. He longed to reach out and touch her, but he could see he needed to go slowly so as not to scare her. She was already hiding under the counter as though she needed some kind of shield between them; one false move on his part and she might bolt like a startled deer.

Robbie had been wrong about Corey getting fat; he must have seen someone else in the garden. She still looked, at least what he could see of her, as slim as ever. Her neck rose swanlike from some kind of loose-fitting, sleeveless green top—not a double chin in sight—and her arms were almost too slender. They were only spared from being sticklike by the subtle rounding of feminine muscle.

Brandon let his gaze slide a little lower. He swallowed hard. Corey was breathing far too fast for someone who was doing nothing but sitting, but the nervous, rapid breaths caused her bosom to rise and

fall in a most enticing way. The tent-shaped blouse was cut so that the buttons began at a fetching point, showing a bit of cleavage. Brandon's mouth suddenly went very dry. Perhaps that's where Corey had gained weight; her breasts looked considerably fuller than he remembered. Not
that he was complaining.

She was, without a doubt, the most beautiful woman in the world. What would he do if she turned him down? He hated to think of how lonely and empty his life would be without her. He was a man who never allowed fear to prevent him from plunging into the unknown, but now he hesitated. He cleared his throat, preparing to force himself to speak, but Corey broke the long silence first.

"What are you doing here?" she said imperiously.

Brandon was some what taken back by her tone; it was so unlike the usually soft-spoken Corey, but he was going to have his say no matter what. Besides, the look in her soft brown eyes was more wary than authoritative. He suspected she was attacking out of desperation rather than aggression.

"I've come to tell you I'm sorry about the way I acted the last time I saw you."

"All right. Apology accepted. Now, since we don't have anything else to talk about and I have a lot of work to do, I would appreciate it if you would just—"

Brandon broke in on her. "Please, Corey, give me a chance. We have a lot more to talk about. Don't you even want to know what happened with the Department of Health and Welfare? About John and Robbie?"

Corey swallowed a lump in her throat. If he only knew how many times she had wondered and worried about them. She had prayed every night for their well being.

"Yes," she admitted, in spite of the urgent need to get Brandon out of the store. "What happened? How are they?" She had to know.

Brandon broke into a broad grin. "They're terrific. You helped me out, you know. With the child protection agent. She thought the cabin was a 'nurturing environment for the tactile and visual developmental needs of young children.' She actually wrote that in her report. Can you believe it?"

Corey gave him a feeble little smile in return and shook her head. She wondered wistfully if the boys ever thought about her.

"Well, the boys acted up something fierce while she was there." He hoped Corey never found out why they had behaved so badly. "I thought we were goners, but after I quieted them down, Ms. Ludlow, that was the social worker's name, said that was the norm in good homes."

Brandon paused to gage Corey's reaction. She was looking down at the counter, but she seemed to still be listening. He nervously plunged ahead with his account. "It seems when parents are nervous, regular kids, kids who aren't scared to death of their parents, pick up on it and often misbehave. And she said normal parents are always nervous and fearful for their children when the child protection people get involved. It's the way the parent deals with the inappropriate behavior that counts. And she said I did a good job of 'setting limits on the boys' conduct without resorting to punitive discipline,'" Brandon concluded proudly. Then he wondered if he was bragging too much.

He examined Corey's face carefully. She had looked up from the counter and was closely following what he said as though she was really interested. She didn't seem to be put off by what he considered justifiable pride in the outcome of what could have been a tragedy.

"What about the Thorntons?" she asked.

Brandon frowned. He hoped there would be a day when he could forgive them, but it hadn't come yet.

"I went to see them, and we had a long talk. They tried, especially Mrs. Thornton, to bluster on for a while about how what they did was in the best interests of the boys, that they had been concerned about them, but after a bit of that, they broke down and more or less admitted they're just lonely. And a little vindictive, too, I'd say, but of course they didn't."

He scowled as he recalled the conversation, struggling to be fair. He ran his hands through his hair, then remembered how carefully he had combed it before he came to see Corey, trying to look his best. He shoved his hands in his pockets, to keep them from doing any more damage, before he continued. "It's clear they haven't recovered from Jane's death yet—maybe they never will. I tried hard to be understanding, but I'm afraid I was still too mad to be very good at it. I don't want the boys to go alone to visit them for a while; I guess I'm afraid their grandparents might run off with them, but I did say the Thorntons could come to the ranch to visit whenever they wanted. They came several times this summer."

"I feel sorry for them," Corey said softly.

"I don't," Brandon said in a hard voice. "Not after what they put me through. I think I'm being pretty damn generous to let them visit the boys at all."

Then he brightened. "Wait until you see the new baby llamas. They're beautiful. We had four females in the spring. I sold Starshine's cria for an astronomical amount and..." He paused. *No, no!* He was going about this all wrong. That wasn't what was important; he was off on a wrong track. It wasn't what he had come to say.

How I wish I could see the new babies, Corey thought, remembering all the happy times at the ranch, but she never would be able to now. "I'm happy for you, Brandon," she managed to say.

But she doesn't sound happy, Brandon thought. She sounded sad, downright gloomy, in fact. Her hands were lying on the counter, tightly clasped together as though she were holding onto something for dear life. Brandon reached out to take her hand, but she quickly pulled them away, leaving his hand dangling foolishly in midair. It didn't seem possible, but this was even harder than he had thought it would be. He jammed both hands back in his pockets and began again.

"Corey, I made a mistake when I said it wasn't the right time for a commitment. You had every right to want to know where our relationship was heading. I'm a man, and I'm old-fashioned, and, well, I guess I'm kind of stubborn and—"

"Kind of!" Corey broke in. "That's like saying the Sahara Desert is kind of dry."

Blamed female doesn't have to rub a man's nose in it when he's trying his damnedest to say he was wrong, Brandon thought, a shade resentfully. But at least she looked a little livelier now, not like some kind of wooden statue.

"—and," he picked up with what he thought was admirable smoothness, "I wanted to be the one to choose the time and place to ask you to marry me, but it just didn't work out that way."

Marry? Did he actually say he wanted to be the one to ask her to marry him? Corey shook her head, thinking she must not be hearing right.

Thinking the movement meant "no," Brandon's heart plummeted. He tried to think of how he could ask her more persuasively. She couldn't turn him down, at least not without hearing him out; she just couldn't.

"I know I'm not an easy man to get along with, and it's hard for me to say this, but I'm ready to try to compromise. I promise I won't automatically reject all your suggestions about the boys and the house and, well, everything. I want us to make all our important life decisions together." Brandon looked at the floor. He needed to marshal all his best ammunition.

The blood was pounding in Corey's ears so loudly she could barely concentrate on the wonderful things Brandon was saying. She hoped she wasn't making this all up. Maybe she ought to pinch herself.

"What I'm trying to say is, I've been a jackass..." Brandon stole a quick peek at Corey's face to make sure she wasn't agreeing too enthusiastically with that particular point. Actually, she looked stunned. Her mouth was hanging open, and her eyes were wide and staring,. He hoped that was a good sign. "... at least on a few occasions, but I'm going to try to do better. The fact is I love you so much I don't think I can live without you, so I'm willing to do just about anything to get you to marry me."

Brandon loves me! Corey exalted. *He said it like he means it. He really and truly loves me. I could die right now, and I'd go to heaven happy.*

Brandon shuffled his feet restlessly. She still hadn't said a word, though she did have a mighty peculiar look on her face. He had one card left to play. He had thought it up as he was driving to Boise, and it was a trump. He might as well go ahead and throw his ace on the table.

"I'm awful sorry we can't just go right ahead and start a family of our own as soon as we get married. I know how much you've always wanted children. Of course, there's John and Robbie, and I know you care a lot about them, but I thought maybe, if you wanted, we could adopt a child together. A little girl sure would be nice."

Damnation if he would ever be able to figure out women. Now she looked as guilty as a hen sitting on goose eggs.

"I'm afraid I have a confession to make, too, Brandon. You see, I... I was mistaken about something," Corey began haltingly. She was ready to tell him about their baby, but she felt a little giddy with apprehension and with the sheer joy of Brandon's proposal. All nerves, she began to giggle.

Brandon looked at her in amazement. Here he was, practically on his knees, begging her to marry him, and she had the gall to laugh at him. Well, he'd put a stop to that. He was sick of skulking around in front of this stupid counter, anyway. He was going to go around there and grab her and kiss her senseless. They'd just see if she could still laugh after that.

Brandon stalked around the end of the counter. Corey hopped down from the stool she'd been sitting on, to face him. At least, she hopped as best she could, nine months into her pregnancy.

Brandon froze and stared in stunned disbelief at Corey's distended middle.

"She... she's a girl; I had an ultrasound. I... I didn't tell you about it, because you said you weren't ready for marriage. I didn't think you loved me, and I love you so much."

Shocked silence.

"I'm sorry, Brandon. I shouldn't have kept our baby a secret. You had a right to know. I just felt so bad when I thought you didn't care about me."

He was still frozen in exactly the same position as when he had first seen she was pregnant. *Have I made a horrible blunder? Have I misjudged him all along? I thought he would insist on marriage if he knew I was pregnant. Is he so angry with me for keeping the baby a secret that he's going to abandon me now that he knows I'm carrying his child?*

Corey raised her hand to her mouth to stifle a cry of anguish. A huge tear slid down her cheek.

Brandon blinked as though he had just awakened from a trance and rushed to Corey. He took her carefully in his arms as though he was handling the most priceless treasure imaginable and tenderly kissed the tears away.

Enfolded in Brandon's strong arms, Corey felt as though her world had suddenly come right. She felt safe and warm and cherished. Now the tears began to flow in earnest, but they were tears of relief.

Despite her added girth, Brandon picked Corey up easily and set her on the tall stool as gently as if she were made of fragile porcelain. He knelt down on one bent knee and lifted the edge of her green maternity blouse so he could kiss her smooth, round belly. He rubbed his hot cheek against her satiny cool skin.

"Hello, Little One," he whispered.

A sharp jab smacked against his jaw.

Brandon grinned and stood up, meticulously pulling the shirttail back into place. He took Corey's hand and kissed the knuckles.

"She takes after her mother—socks you with a roundhouse punch when you least expect it," Brandon said, his face suffused with delight and pride. "You should have told me about the baby, though I know I'm mostly the one to blame. I was kicking up a pretty good ruckus when you tried to let me know. But all that matters now is you love me and I love you."

He carefully splayed one of his big hands across her abdomen. "I'm sorry I wasn't able to share the pregnancy with you; it appears to be just about over, but if you'll let me, nothing would make me happier than to be there with you when our daughter is born."

"Oh, yes, Brandon, I would like that so much," Corey said, her eyes shining.

Brandon pulled a velvet jeweler's box from his trouser pocket and opened the small container to reveal a wide gold band set with three diamonds. He slipped it on Corey's finger. Corey felt so happy she thought she might burst.

"But first," Brandon said urgently, "I think we'd better go round up a preacher. It looks to me like we don't have a minute to spare."

Meet

Linda Wallace

I was born in Marshall, Missouri, and lived the first few years of my life with my mother and father and grandparents in a big, old farmhouse. It was mysterious and spooky with front stairs and back stairs, antiques and ghosts. I still have dreams about that house. It apparently penetrated deep into my psyche.

A few months before my sister, Barbara, was born, my mother, father and I moved a short way down the road from my grandparents' house into a clapboarded log cabin with only three rooms. Baths were taken in tin tubs in the kitchen with water heated on the stove, though we did have an indoor toilet in a small, converted pantry. The smaller round tub had been soldered, so you had to be very careful how you sat in it to avoid a rude poke. When Barbara and I were old enough for clamp-on roller skates, we were allowed to practice in the kitchen, but you couldn't go very far before you had to turn around.

My father was a farmer and probably would have preferred to have had sons, though I don't ever remember him complaining about his two daughters. I don't think he had very high expectations for us, but that proved to be a benefit, as he and our mother always seemed surprised and delighted at everything my sister and I achieved.

Perhaps the deep love and support I felt all through childhood and on into my adult years formed the interest I have in writing about families and relationships. Whether I was living in a coffee shack in Hawaii where the rent was paid by picking up macadamia nuts or in an attic in the Bronx, my family was always there for me. I wish my father had lived long enough to see my first book published. He would have been amazed.